W9-BKV-786

DISCARDED

WAYNE PUBLIC LIBRARY

SEP 0 2 2009

The
Battle for
Duncragglin

Andrew H. Vanderwal

TUNDRA BOOKS

Copyright © 2009 by Andrew H. Vanderwal

Published in Canada by Tundra Books,
75 Sherbourne Street, Toronto, Ontario M5A 2P9

Published in the United States by Tundra Books of Northern New York,
P.O. Box 1030, Plattsburgh, New York 12901

Library of Congress Control Number: 2008903008

All rights reserved. The use of any part of this publication reproduced,
transmitted in any form or by any means, electronic, mechanical,
photocopying, recording, or otherwise, or stored in a retrieval system,
without the prior written consent of the publisher – or, in case of
photocopying or other reprographic copying, a licence from the Canadian
Copyright Licensing Agency – is an infringement of the copyright law.

Library and Archives Canada Cataloguing in Publication

Vanderwal, Andrew H.
The battle for Duncragglin / Andrew H. Vanderwal.

ISBN 978-0-88776-886-6

1. Wallace, William, d. 1305 – Juvenile fiction. 2. Scotland – History –
Wallace's Rising, 1297-1304 – Juvenile fiction. I. Title.

PS8643.A69B38 2009   C813'.6   C2008-902058-8

We acknowledge the financial support of the Government of Canada
through the Book Publishing Industry Development Program (BPIDP)
and that of the Government of Ontario through the Ontario Media
Development Corporation's Ontario Book Initiative. We further
acknowledge the support of the Canada Council for the Arts and the
Ontario Arts Council for our publishing program.

ONTARIO ARTS COUNCIL
CONSEIL DES ARTS DE L'ONTARIO

Design: Kelly Hill
Typeset in: Goudy

Printed and bound in Canada

1 2 3 4 5 6   14 13 12 11 10 09

For Jan, Eric, Graham, and Mame

And special thanks to the citizens of the town of Dunbar, who (acting admittedly under the authority vested in them by no one in particular) bestowed upon me the status of "Honorary Scot" with the presentation of a humorous certificate that I display proudly. A greater honor is hard to imagine!

CONTENTS

PART III: A CHANGE IN DUNCRAGGLIN

PROLOGUE

"There it is, Dad! That's where they left it."

The man glanced up the cliff to where a board was wedged in the rocks. He shook his head. "If even *they* didnae want it, Grant, it cannae be worth anything."

Undeterred, the boy ran across the sand at the water's edge, leaping clusters of seaweed stranded by the tide. Shells crunched under his boots as he climbed the rocks at the base of the cliff. Reaching the board, he yanked it loose and turned it over. *Yes, this is it!*

Here they were, those strange animal engravings that had so intrigued him earlier that day, when he saw that foreign boy holding the board. He examined the engravings closely: the sharp-tusked boar that stood so ridiculously erect on its hind legs; the ant that looked like it was brandishing a weapon; the bird with the long pointy beak and the piercing eye that seemed to stare all-knowingly out from the board.

But the carvings were faint; the wood rotted, green, and slimy. The boy grimaced. His dad was right: this was not the kind of thing that would sell in their Scottish artifacts and antiques store. Moreover, being waterlogged, it was heavy, and he didn't feel like hauling it back to the car. The only reason he was interested in it at all was because of that foreign boy.

Although he did not want it badly enough to carry it, he did not want to leave it either. That foreign boy might come back for it. So he lifted the board by one end and, with a grunt, gave it his best Scottish caber-toss. The board arced and plonked end-first to disappear underwater. Seconds later, it rolled back up to the surface, where it nodded gently in the drift and tug of the swells coursing over submerged rocks. But instead of drifting away, it was slowly being pushed back to shore by the waves. *The tide must be coming in,* the boy thought. Annoyed, he watched as the board disappeared behind some rocks. He climbed to the water's edge to see where it went. To his surprise, it was gone.

Kneeling low to the water, the boy saw an opening beneath an overhang. Intrigued, he hung his head down further and peered into the darkness. The hollow extended far under the rocks. Wherever it led, it was big enough to suck in a board and make it disappear without a trace.

This was important, and he knew it. This just might be what he and his father were looking for – the way into the underground caverns that legend had it were sealed off ages ago, caverns that his father suspected might contain all kinds of valuable ancient relics, or better yet, treasures . . . huge chests filled with gold coins, guarded only by helpless grinning skeletons clutching rusted swords studded with priceless, gleaming gems. *Ha!* They would sell it all, the swords too. The boy didn't believe those tales of ghosts and demons; tales of how people who went in never came out. And *so what* if some people had found a way in and had gotten lost? His father was smarter than that. He wouldn't get lost. They would find things never found before. They would be rich! His father would have what he always wanted. And then he would be content, and then he wouldn't be in the pub all the time, and he wouldn't hit him and his mother anymore, and everyone would be happy. . . .

The boy scampered back up the rocks. Waving urgently, he persuaded his reluctant father to climb around the outcropping.

His father leaned over and shone his torch into the opening. The light traveled a long way down a narrow, water-filled tunnel. The incoming tide was almost to its ceiling. Waves slapped the sides, rose up to fill it completely, and receded as the seawater came gurgling out.

The man let out a low whistle. He straightened. "Yes," he said softly. "You just might have found it. And if you have, this is the start of something big . . . something very big."

PART I

A CHANGE IN PLACE

Travel to Scotland

Alex knew he had been to this airport before, back in those early, awful days when his parents went missing. He took in the tall arch of glass, the web of steel girders, and the dizzying array of signs, but nothing looked familiar.

His uncle Larry stayed close beside him, muttering the whole time about how he had to be sure Alex got on that plane. Together they waited their turn at the counter, where a conveyor belt whisked away Alex's battered brown suitcase and his ticket was exchanged for a boarding pass. Together they waited their turn at the security check, below a sign that read PASSENGERS ONLY BEYOND THIS POINT.

"But I need to accompany the boy to the gate," his uncle argued, fretfully running his hand over the top of his balding head. "He's only twelve, and I *have* to make sure he gets on that plane!"

The security agent held up her hand. "We'll have an airline agent accompany him the rest of the way, sir," she said, with a quick glance at Alex's boarding pass. She beckoned impatiently for Alex's bag. Dismayed, Alex watched as she dropped it onto a moving conveyor belt that fed into a big machine.

Alex didn't want his comic books damaged – they were the only things of his father's that he had left. He'd found them years ago in a damp and mildewy box, pressed into the furthest recesses under the basement stairs of his uncle's house.

"Yeah, sure, I don't care. Just keep them in your room," his uncle had said.

They were classics: old, illustrated versions of famous books. Among Alex's favorites were *Journey to the Center of the Earth*, *A Connecticut Yankee in King Arthur's Court*, and *The Time Machine*; but there were many more, so many great adventures in such faraway places and such distant times.

The only reason the comics had survived all these years was because Alex's father had wrapped each one in a plastic envelope. Even so, many of the pages were weak and disintegrating.

A guard beckoned for Alex to pass through a metal detector.

"Bye, Uncle Larry," Alex said quietly.

"Be sure you get on that plane!"

The guard glanced at an instrument panel and waved him on. Alex squeezed past the other passengers at the far end of the X-ray machine and snatched up his bag of comics before their carry-on bags could bunch up around it.

Ahead were several long crowded corridors. Alex checked his boarding pass. The ticket agent had circled gate number 5B, but that was not much help. He dreaded the thought of missing his flight, especially the part where he saw his uncle again.

He took a deep breath. *Well, first things first.* He knelt to tie up his laces.

"Alex Macpherson?"

A uniformed woman was standing over him. "Come," she said. "I'll take you to your gate."

Far from missing his flight, Alex was the first to board. The announcement had said families with children could board first, and Alex figured that meant him – even though he had no family.

Happy to discover that he had a window seat, Alex pulled a comic from his bag and settled in to reread the battle conquests of Sir William Wallace in *The Scottish Chiefs.* His favorite part was where Wallace takes a castle by surprise.

But he was distracted, and his mind wandered.

"You're going to stay with your aunt Fiona for the summer," his uncle had announced, only a few days before. Alex had heard his uncle on the phone, working out the details. "I'll pay for the flight, but I see no reason to pay for his room and board. He's your nephew too. I don't see why you can't share more of the burden."

Alex didn't care to know the details of what they ultimately worked out. From what he'd heard, he was to stay with his dreaded aunt Fiona in Scotland for the summer. He had met Aunt "Finicky" the year before, when she was over for a visit. She had paid him little attention, other than to ask him to fetch this or that. Her husband had been a merchant seaman who'd spent most of his time in pubs. "He drank himself to death," Aunt Fiona had told Uncle Larry. "It served him right."

A leather bag dropped onto the seat next to him. A plump, middle-aged man with neatly parted hair hoisted a small suitcase into the overhead bin. Snapping the bin shut, he moved the leather bag to the floor and plopped himself down.

"Hello, traveling alone?" he said, with a friendly smile.

"My aunt is meeting me at the airport," Alex replied hesitantly, over the top of his comic book.

"How nice. What's that you're reading?" The man tipped up his glasses. "Remarkable! You know, I'm studying that very period of Scottish history. I'm a professor of archaeology at the University of Edinburgh. Thomas Macintyre's my name." He extended his hand. "Yours?"

Oh, no. Not one of these talkative types. Alex stifled a sigh. He mumbled his name and reluctantly held out his hand.

"Macpherson, you say." Professor Macintyre gave Alex's hand a rapid little shake. "Now that's a fine name – goes way back in Scottish history, back to even before the time depicted in that comic book you're reading."

Alex raised the comic and made like he was going to read.

"Did you know that many of your ancestors fought in the Battle of Dunbar in 1296? That was a terrible day for the Scots; thousands were slaughtered. It's not that the Scots were poor fighters; the English simply had better weapons, tighter discipline, and superior strategy. But that was before William Wallace came along – oh, yes, that very same William Wallace you're reading about. He changed everything. Oh, how he knew strategy – he outmaneuvered the English at almost every turn."

"So what happened to these Macphersons?" Alex asked, becoming interested despite himself.

"Sad to say, most were killed. But you had one very unusual ancestor who fought with William Wallace, you know. . . ."

"What did he do?"

"Eh? Oh. Well, when he was about your age, he helped Wallace achieve a decisive victory. It was in the battle for Duncragglin, a strategically positioned castle on the east coast, up a ways from the Firth of Forth."

"How did he do that?"

"The records are sketchy. It was a long, long time ago and not much was written back then." The professor hesitated. "But somehow – no one knows how – he helped Wallace and his men get past the enemy defenses. For years afterwards, people thought he had special powers."

"What kind of powers?"

"Well, for starters, he just showed up out of nowhere one day. He had a strange manner of speech and spoke of other worlds and strange things . . . but that's all we really know about him."

"Is the castle still there?"

"Not really. You can see where the keep used to be and the outline of the harbor, but it's pretty much gone. All the entrances to the underground chambers were sealed off hundreds of years ago. Apparently, every now and then, someone would disappear, and folk thought they were getting lost in caves deep under the castle. Others thought the ruins were haunted, which is to be expected – that's what usually happens when a person goes missing anywhere near an old ruin. So they blew up some more of its innards long ago and sealed it up."

"Do they charge admission?"

"Admission! *Och*, no. It's completely abandoned. Scotland has so many ruined castles. There's not enough left of this one to interest tourists."

No tourists, long-abandoned underground chambers . . . maybe there's a way to get inside. Alex shivered with delight. Perhaps he would find dungeons with rusty iron bars, or even bits of old weapons and armor!

"I think, though, that there is something even more interesting there than the castle." The professor lowered his voice. "Quite by accident, I found reference to an extensive underground labyrinth in some Roman writings. The Romans found this labyrinth to be quite mysterious. Now, no one has yet made the connection between the labyrinth the Romans wrote about and the caves beneath the Duncragglin ruins, but I think they could be one and the same."

"What was the labyrinth used for?"

"Who knows? It could have been a form of defense. It would be hard for invaders to defeat people holed up in a spiderweb of caves deep under the cliffs. I have a theory, though, that there was much more to it – something very frightening. . . ."

"What was frightening? Professor?"

"Well, that's what I've been trying to find out. From what the Romans wrote, the labyrinth might hold one of the world's great mysteries. But how a people who lived so long ago could have been so advanced, that's hard to understand. . . ."

"So it's very old?"

"Yes. It was there long before the castle, dating back to prehistoric times. I believe it might have been built about the same time as many of the standing stone circles we see in Scotland. There might even have been a relationship between all these things – they might have worked together for some religious or magical purpose – but that's only a theory of mine."

"I was born in a place called Strath Mern . . . or something like that," Alex said. "Are the castle ruins anywhere near there?"

"Straith Meirn?" The professor pronounced it with rolling *r*'s, which Alex had no hope of imitating. "Oh, yes, very near – the town's only a few miles south of the ruins."

Alex was listening to Professor Macintyre so intently that he was only dimly aware that the airplane had been taxiing. The engines swelled to a deep roar, and Alex felt himself being pressed back into his seat. The runway markers flashed by faster and faster. The plane tipped up and the ground fell away.

———————

Night fell, and the lights were dimmed. People reclined their seats, adjusted pillows, and pulled blankets up over their shoulders. Everyone seemed ready for sleep – everyone, that is, except Alex. Next to him, the professor sat with his seat-back reclined, eyes closed, making annoying little snorting noises. Alex debated whether to prod him to make him stop.

The professor's chin waggled down to his chest and the snoring ceased. Alex breathed a sigh of relief and tried to get comfortable, leaning back and tucking the airplane blanket under his chin.

Suddenly the professor gave out a deep gasp that left his jaw hanging open. Then he snorted louder than ever. To make matters worse, his head slowly lolled toward Alex – despite all of Alex's telepathic efforts to will it back the other way.

Irritated, Alex twisted to face the window. He raised the blanket up over his head and tried hard to ignore the gasping and gurgling behind him. He imagined himself preparing for battle back in the time of William Wallace. He was covering hand-dug trenches with branches and heather to lay a trap for the enemy. Indeed, he'd come up with the very idea and was commended for it by none other than William Wallace himself, who clapped Alex warmly on the shoulder and said, "Well done, son. Wherever did ye learn such clever battle strategy?"

———————

Morning came quickly – too quickly. A flight attendant pushed a cart down the aisle, but it didn't feel like breakfast time.

Groggily, Alex lifted the blind. The horizon had turned into a band of brilliant red that pushed back the black of night. It was becoming altogether too bright for this hour. Alex snapped the blind back down.

2

THE MCRAES

"Let me take those bags – I've got a cart – how have you been – it's *so* good to see you – how was your flight?" The babble of voices swirled around Alex as he stood by himself, waiting and watching passengers reunite with family and friends.

The arrivals hall was emptying. Alex had no idea what to do next. His aunt Fiona's telephone number was with him, but he had no money to make a call. He was tired and wondered miserably if there was a bench somewhere to take a nap.

"Alex Macpherson – would ye be Alex Macpherson?"

A short, squat man with a round nose and a blotchy complexion was staring intently at him, cap in hand. Beside him, a boy about Alex's age (or about his size, anyway) was eyeing him curiously.

"I'm Alastair McRae." The man extended a big callused hand. "This is my son Willie."

Alex was uncomfortable with all this hand-shaking. Back-slapping and high-fiving, yes . . . hand-shaking, no. When Willie extended his hand (prompted by his father),

Alex slapped it and held his hand out for Willie to return the slap. He did.

"Y'r aunt Fiona isnae feelin' well, so she's arranged fir ye to bide wi' us fir a week or two."

Alex blinked. "She's not well?"

"It isnae serious – just a head cold. Ye can gi'e 'er a call once we git to the farm. Until she's better, ye'll be staying with me and my three bairns: wild Willie here; my dochter, Annie, who's a wee bit older'n ye lads; and the wee rascal Craig, who's the youngest."

Alex looked around for the others.

"They're back on the farm gettin' the place ready fir ye. Here, I'll take y'r bag."

Mr. McRae looked down in surprise at the bag of comics Alex handed him. Willie stifled a snicker. Alex flushed, suddenly realizing that Mr. McRae must have meant his suitcase. They crossed the car park, Alex struggling with his suitcase and Mr. McRae lightly swinging the bag of comics.

Soon they came to a large boxy van with bold letters that read FRESH ORGANIC PRODUCE. Mr. McRae opened the back door and Alex gratefully slid in his suitcase.

"It's no locked – hop in."

Not until Alex had swung open a door did he notice that the steering wheel was on his side. Willie was snickering again. Embarrassed, Alex slid across the bench seat to the middle.

Willie climbed in the passenger side and bounced impatiently. "C'm on, Dad. Let's get this truck in gear."

Mr. McRae heaved himself up behind the wheel. He leaned forward to look past Alex to Willie. "Now you just hold on. Alex has had a long trip and no much sleep. You can show him about the farm and the loch if he feels like it, but remember, you boys are no to be running about the coast; ye know full well how I feel about that."

Mr. McRae turned the key and stomped on the gas pedal until the engine sputtered to life. A blue cloud mushroomed out the back of the van and drifted away.

It felt strange to Alex that the front wheels were under their seat. When they turned, the front of the van swung out precariously. Ahead was nothing but the windshield and the road.

For a while, Alex imagined himself driving, veering crazily around cars coming at him on the "wrong" side of the road. But, before long, lack of sleep caught up with him. He slumped in a daze as the misty Scottish hills rolled by. The drive took them across the high Forth Road Bridge and along narrow, winding country roads.

Eventually, the truck bumped down a dirt road lined on one side by a low stone wall. They wound around a small, irregular-shaped loch nestled in the surrounding hills and came to a farmhouse with a steep tiled roof. Farther back were ramshackle sheds and a barn. Several cows stopped to stare.

"The wailing rocks are over that way." Willie gestured past the loch. "Down by the sea."

"If I've told ye once, I've told ye a hundred times – ye'll no be going to the sea." Mr. McRae stopped the van and pulled up the parking brake. He waved a threatening finger at Willie. "And don't ye start up about wailin' rocks, ghoulies, and those other tales ye like to tell. I don't want ye frightening our guest."

Hauling his suitcase up the path, Alex saw curtains moving in a window. He caught a glimpse of the top of a head and eyes peering over the windowsill. The eyes caught him looking back and disappeared, the curtain filling the spot where they had been.

A slender girl stood leaning against the door frame, arms folded and head tilted quizzically. Her long brown hair was parted in the middle. She looked to be fourteen or fifteen.

Alex wondered what she was thinking as she watched him trudge up the walkway – the foreign boy struggling with the battered brown suitcase, Fiona's overseas nephew. Had she been told that his parents disappeared years ago, that he was sent to Canada to live with his uncle? Did she feel sorry for him, or was she wondering if he would be a bother?

"Yon's Annie," Mr. McRae said. "Craig's about the place, somewhere."

"Hello," Alex said.

The girl stepped aside and held the door open. She smiled shyly.

"Craig, where are ye? Come and say hello," Mr. McRae bellowed. There was no answer. Mr. McRae gave a tight smile. "That's Craig for ye."

Alex followed Mr. McRae up a creaky wooden staircase to an attic room with a sloped ceiling. A dormer window overlooked the loch. There were two beds up against low walls on either side. At the foot of each bed was a wooden chest, and over each chest hung a bulletin board cluttered with prize ribbons, pictures, and pinned notes.

"Ye'll be sharing this room with Willie and Craig. That's your bed." Mr. McRae gestured to a neatly made-up mattress opposite the window. "There's an empty drawer for y'r things."

Alex studied a poster of a fierce, battle-ax-wielding warrior in a dark medieval dungeon. Ghoulish creatures peered from behind corners. Across the bottom, big Gothic letters intertwined with snakes and scorpions to spell "Annihilation."

"Do you have that game? It's cool. Want to go down and play?" Willie was already halfway out of the room. "Come."

"Leave him be, Willie. Alex will be needing his sleep." Mr. McRae shooed Willie out of the room before him. He turned back, one hand on the doorknob. "I'll leave ye a towel and facecloth in the washing-up room. Call me or Annie if ye need anything."

Left to himself, Alex spent a moment looking over the contents of a tall bookshelf. On the top level, he saw Harry Potter books and what looked to be the entire Redwall series. Several shelves down were football trophies and a team picture. Alex looked closely at the faces, but could not find Willie's.

A piggybank caught his attention. Alex picked it up and carefully tugged on a small lever. An iron fisherman abruptly snapped backward with his rod, pulling a fish up and over. A coin slot in the fish's mouth clanged against a larger slot on the top of a barrel. Alex cautiously shook the piggybank back and forth. It rattled. He pulled the fish back to reset the spring.

"Daaaad! He's trying to steal my money."

In his haste to put the piggybank back down, Alex fumbled. The half-sprung fish snapped against his finger.

Bellowing from downstairs was Mr. McRae. "Craig, get away from there – leave him alone!"

There was a shuffling noise outside the door. Alex heard the boy's voice again, farther away this time. "Why does he have to stay here? I don't want him in my room. It's no fair!"

Mr. McRae said *weesht*, and the voices trailed away.

Alex was beat. He felt unsteady on his feet and heard a faint ringing in his ears. Before getting into his pajamas, he stuffed the end of his sock into the keyhole. Then he closed the curtains to block out as much daylight as possible and gratefully crawled under the cool covers. He felt like he was in the hold of a ship that was gently lolling in an ocean swell. Wave after wave of darkness reached up until one rolled right over him.

The next thing he knew, a voice was calling, "Alex, Alex – time to get up."

Blinking, Alex looked around the dim room. The door was ajar, and Annie was peering around the corner.

"Sorry to wake you, but my dad says you won't get back to sleep tonight if you sleep more now. Come, we're about to have a bite of lunch."

It was hard to get up. Splashing cold water over his face made Alex feel only slightly better. He shut off the tap and watched the water settle in the basin. His pale shimmering reflection stared back hollow-eyed, as if from far away. Alex hoped he didn't look *that* bad. He pulled the plug.

Stumbling down the stairs, Alex followed the sound of voices to a dining room.

"Have a seat, Alex." Mr. McRae thumped the empty chair next to him. "Annie, pass the bread, please."

Annie ripped off a hunk and passed him the loaf. Alex gripped it with both hands and tore off a piece. He'd eaten only sliced bread before and wondered what to do with it. He watched Willie slather butter over his bread, then load it with ham and cheese. Alex did the same and gave the bread a nibble. The inside was soft and chewy, but the crust was another matter. Still, the others were crunching their way through it, so Alex did too.

"That's enough now, Craig," Mr. McRae said sternly. "It's time to come out and get up to the table."

A muffled "no!" came from behind a couch in the adjoining room.

"NOW!" Mr. McRae's shout was met by silence. "Five . . . four . . ."

"Oh, fine!" A young boy's legs, then the rest of him, wriggled backwards from behind the couch. He was a few years younger than Alex, perhaps nine or ten. He plopped himself in a chair between Annie and Willie, arms folded and jaw jutting defiantly.

"Look, Craig." Annie pointed to an aquarium that bubbled in the corner of the room. "Your wormy fish is coming out."

A small eel-like fish had emerged from under the driftwood. It squiggled in the gravel and wound about the plants.

"Don't care," Craig said, but he couldn't help but look.

Willie cleared his throat to catch Alex's attention. "There are nine cows in a field," he said expectantly. "Which one's closest to Africa?"

Alex stared at him blankly.

"Coo eight. Get it? Coo-eight? Say it quickly."

Alex didn't get it. A burst of laughter erupted around the table, and he felt his face turn red.

"Nae more of that," Mr. McRae cut in. "It's time to get the jobs done. But first, Alex, call y'r aunt and ask how she's doing. Willie, once he's done that, take him out to the barn and get twenty bales of hay and ten bales of straw ready for the coos. Craig, off to the henhouse wi' ye to collect the eggs."

—————◦✦◦—————

Alex galumphed down the muddy laneway with Willie, cheerful even though the rubber boots he was given were two sizes too big. He had never been in a barn before and was eager to see the cows.

Thick, low-lying clouds emitted sheens of drizzle. The sun poked through now and then, but it was still chilly. Alex was thankful he had Willie's old jersey. He didn't mind its holes and too-long sleeves: Willie looked equally dorky.

"Why's your dad so much harder to understand than everyone else?" Alex asked.

"It's because he grew up in Aberdeen," Willie replied. "Most Scots don't understand him either."

"And what about your mum – is she away somewhere?" Alex was curious why no one had mentioned her.

Willie looked away. "She's gone."

"Gone where?"

"Don't know. One day, she took our dog Tigger and left; we haven't heard from her since. That was over a year ago."

"Took your dog and left?" Alex was stunned. He thought about his own missing parents. For years he kept thinking they might suddenly show up again, that everything would go back to how it was . . . but it never happened.

Alex recalled all too well the confusion and chaos, the initial reassurances of "don't worry" and "I'm sure they will be found" becoming less frequent, until they stopped altogether. Finally came the chilling and terrifying realization that they could be gone for good.

———◆◆◆———

The boys walked up an earthen ramp to a tall barn door. Willie lifted the wooden latch and pulled. The heavy door creaked open enough for them to slip through, then closed behind them with its own weight.

Alex strained to see in the huge dim cavern. Thin shafts of sunlight angled through gaps high up in the barn boards.

"Watch your step." Willie kicked aside clusters of loose straw. "See these floorboards? Some of them are loose. Those big holes over there are where we throw down the bales."

Snorting noises were coming from under the floor. Shuffling cautiously through the straw, Alex approached a large dark hole. He knelt and peered over the edge. Down in the darkness below were swaying backs of cows that plodded about in a thick slush. The stench was overpowering.

"How do they get out?"

"Through the sliding door on the far side. We leave it open. They can go in and out whenever they want."

Alex wondered why the cows, given half a chance, would not get out and never come back. Then he remembered the exterior pen was not much better.

"You get the straw," Willie said. "I'll get the hay. Don't mix them up."

"What's the difference?"

"Hay is greener. It's what they eat. Straw is for their stalls. Here, use one of these." Willie passed Alex a metal bar. It had a handgrip at one end, a hook at the other. "And don't pull too many bales out from the bottom, or the top will come down on you."

Alex watched in admiration as Willie climbed, using his hook for support. High up on a timber, Willie hooked a bale, pulled it out from the others, and dropped it over the edge of the pile. It landed with a thud, blasting up clouds of dust that sparkled in the shafts of light.

Alex looked dubiously up the wall of straw that loomed over him. Heights made him nervous. He stabbed his hook into a nearby bale, catching the baling twine that held it together. Several hard yanks and it pulled free. The bale next to it didn't look so secure anymore, so he hooked it and pulled it out too. Encouraged, he pulled out a few more.

A rustling noise came from above. Too late, he saw the overhanging bales start to tumble. He leapt, but a falling bale knocked him flat. He covered the back of his head with his hands. Bales thudded down all over him and then it was quiet.

Holding the sleeve of his jersey over his nose and mouth, Alex sputtered and coughed. He cautiously wriggled his pinned leg out from under a bale and felt about in the darkness. The way forward was blocked. Finding the space he was in too small to turn around in, he squirmed backward. He didn't notice that he was wriggling onto a loose board until the front tipped up, the back fell, and Alex dropped like a sack of grain into the depths below.

"Noooooooo!" Alex was all too aware of the sea of sloshy manure that awaited him. He landed with a heavy thud. Tentatively looking up, he saw he had landed on a cow's back, facing the cow's behind.

The cow's head shot up. "*Mooaaooow.*" It leapt into the air and kicked. Alex hung on for dear life. It took to stampeding through the slosh, barn beams and other cows flashing by. Startled moos came from all around.

Suddenly, it was brighter. Bucking and twisting, the cow had left the barn. Alex felt his grip slip and, for the second time, he was airborne. Arms and legs flailing, he landed facedown on the hard ground. It hurt, but it was better than landing in cow plop.

Terrified that the maddened cow's hooves would come crashing down on him any second, he curled into a ball and covered his head with his arms. Hearing nothing, he shifted and peered between his elbows. The cows were all heading away in a rapid little trot, udders swaying to and fro under their backsides. The puny electrical fence there to keep them back didn't even slow them down.

Now I've really done it. Alex picked himself up, brushing straw off his jersey and shaking it out of his hair.

The cows were completely out of sight. Alex didn't know what to do, so he trudged back to the barn, dragging his feet the whole way. Inside, a muffled voice was calling, "Alex, Alex, can you hear me?"

A bale wiggled high up the pile. It flipped end-over-end down the slope. Alex clambered up the bales to the crater where the bale had come from. Down in the darkness, he saw Willie struggling to pull out yet another bale.

"I'm over here," Alex said.

Willie turned and stared, mouth agape. "How . . . how did you get there?"

"I fell down a loose floorboard."

"*Phew!*" Willie wiped his sweaty, dust-streaked brow with the back of his hand. "Dad would've killed me if you were dead."

"You sure moved a lot of bales." Alex felt badly.

"No kidding." Willie chuckled. "I think we've got more ready for the cows than my dad expected."

"I don't think he'll be too happy that the cows escaped."

"What?!"

Willie dashed out of the barn and ran across the field, Alex close behind. Rounding a bend, they almost ran headlong into frightened cows that were being herded back toward the barn by Mr. McRae, Annie, and Craig. Seeing the boys, the cows hesitated, looking about for a different direction to run.

"Quick, this way!" Willie yelled. The two boys sprinted to block an escape route.

"Willie, turn the power off the line." Mr. McRae waved his stick. "The rest of ye, spread out and make sure the coos don't get past. Alex, if they start coming at ye, shout 'coo-boss.' Stand your ground. Jump up and down, if need be."

Willie emerged from the barn. "Power's off," he shouted.

Mr. McRae picked up a length of fallen electrical wire. "Okay, everybody, get it back on the posts."

Checking first to see that the others could touch the wire without getting a shock, Alex cautiously lifted a section and straightened the flimsy insulator posts. Mr. McRae came round to inspect.

"Okay, Willie, turn 'er back on."

Mr. McRae stabbed the air toward the cows with one finger while silently moving his lips. He counted from left to right and back again. His lips tightened. "One's missing. Willie, go check if she's in the barn."

Willie disappeared, only to emerge moments later shaking his head.

Mr. McRae stamped his foot. "It's Vanessa that's missing. Willie, Craig, and ye, too, Alex, spread out and look for her. She cannae be far. When ye find her, bring her in the side gate and close her up in the big stall. She's due to be calving soon, and I hope all this excitement doesnae make her pop. Annie! Help me with the milking. I'm far behind schedule."

3

The Wailing Rocks

Alex squinted against a sun that hung low over the rugged hilly landscape, wondering what a thousand pounds of frightened cow would take to doing. Would she run until she dropped, or find a place to hide? Then again, she didn't look very bright. Perhaps she would forget why she was running and stop to chew on some grass.

Willie tapped his arm. "She won't be that way. The others were brought back from there. She's probably gone off in the direction of the sea."

"She'll be miles from here after the way Alex scared her," Craig said, with a smug little smile.

"Don't blame Alex," Willie snapped. "You're the one who made the bales fall."

Craig protested, his voice rising, "No, I didn't."

"Did too! I saw you up on those bales where Alex was working."

"It was an accident!"

"I'll bet! You never wanted Alex here."

"IT WAS AN ACCIDENT! I was trying to help."

"What? Without telling anybody? Help by sneaking around?"

"BOYS!" The roar came from Mr. McRae, who had emerged from the barn. "Quit your yapping, git out there, and start looking for Vanessa!"

Willie turned and stomped away. He waved for Alex to follow.

Enraged, Craig picked up a stick and swung it hard against a post. It snapped with a loud crack. He threw the broken half at Willie. It missed, spinning over Willie's shoulder to land on the lane ahead. Willie ignored it, continuing on at the same pace. Alex ran to catch up.

They cut through several fields, crossed the coastal road, and came all the way to the cliffs without any sign of the cow. Alex peered over the edge. Down below, waves crashed onto a long stretch of sandy beach. He was relieved to see it was empty. At least the cow was not stupid enough to run straight off the cliff.

The coast curved outwards in both directions to form a bay. Rising above the cliffs at the far end were ruins.

"Duncragglin?" Alex asked.

Willie nodded absently, his eyes sweeping back and forth over the terrain. "Runaways don't usually go this far," he muttered irritably. "At this point, she could have gone either way."

They split up, Alex taking a path north along the top of the cliffs, while Willie headed south. An onshore wind was picking up, moaning as it blew.

Something moved in the shadows near the base of the cliffs. Alex descended along a steep and crumbly path, taking care not to get close to the edge. Halfway down, he heard someone calling.

High up on the cliffs, Willie was waving his arms. "Come baaaaack. We're not allowed down there – too dangerous."

Alex cupped his hands around his mouth. "But, I've found Vanessa – she's up ahead."

"Noooooo – come back. Craig found Vanessa down the rooooad."

Alex was confused. Then what had he seen?

The low moaning grew louder. It sounded as if it was calling him, pulling at him, drawing him nearer. Alex felt a chill. He turned and ran back up the path. The moaning gradually diminished. By the time he reached Willie, it had died out altogether.

"What did you see down there?" Willie asked.

"I couldn't tell," Alex gasped, still panting from his climb. "Something was moving in the shadows. . . . Is something wrong?"

Inexplicably, it had suddenly become very dark.

"Let's go!" Willie yelled. He started sprinting, Alex right behind him. They slowed only when they were finally in the open laneway.

"*Nah, nah*, you missed me." Willie laughed and whooped. He shot a defiant fist up in the air. As if in response, the wind picked up and the light from the moon completely disappeared.

Willie squealed. The boys sprinted again. This time they didn't stop until they had run all the way to the farmhouse.

———— ‣ ◆ ‣ ————

Alex and Willie washed and put away the dinner dishes while Mr. McRae enjoyed a pint of beer at the kitchen table with the newspaper. Annie and Craig were at the table having a game of crazy eights.

"When I was looking for Vanessa, I heard this strange moaning over by the cliffs," Alex said, giving the counter a fast wipe. "Anyone know what it's from?"

Annie and Craig looked up from their game. A small crooked smile appeared on Willie's face.

Mr. McRae lowered his paper. He gave a small dismissive wave. "*Och*, the rock formations catch the wind and make that sound sometimes. Everybody around here calls 'm the wailing rocks."

"What about the castle ghouls?" Willie cocked his head and waited for his father's reaction. He did not have to wait long.

Mr. McRae thumped the table and raised a threatening finger. "How many times do I have to tell ye? There's nothing to them tales of castle ghouls. And I dinnae want any more talk of it!" He glowered, then, catching himself, slowly lowered his finger and sat back. His eyes softened. "Alright, I'll tell ye what, lads 'n' lassie. I'll take the whole lot of ye over to the ruins in the morn, after I'm done milking the coos. You'll see for yourselves that there's nothing to all this but your imaginations."

"The Duncragglin castle ruins?" Alex exchanged an excited glance with Willie.

"Oh, aye," Mr. McRae answered. "The very one your ancestors lived in, so many years ago. The very one that was blasted to bits by the English general, Oliver Cromwell, back in the mid-1600s. Yon old castles weren't built to withstand cannonballs."

"Have you ever been in the caves under the castle?" Alex asked eagerly.

"Caves? Wherever did ye hear of that? There are no caves." Mr. McRae frowned and took up his paper. "Now that's enough of this. Everybody get ready for bed. It's going to be busy in the morn."

Willie, Craig, and Alex crowded the room, each toothbrushing furiously, white toothpaste foam on their lips.

"Quit hogging," Craig mumbled, drooling toothpaste that was about to drip from his chin. He wriggled to get to the sink.

Willie gave Craig a hip check to get him out of the way. Craig flicked his toothbrush bristles out from behind his front teeth and sprayed foam over Willie's face. Enraged, Willie banged his cup on the countertop, splashing Alex's pajamas.

"It's not funny!" Willie shouted, but that only made Craig laugh harder.

Hurriedly putting their toothbrushes away, Willie and Craig rubbed their faces with a facecloth, then promptly tried to throw their cloth into the other's face. Willie ducked, and Craig's cloth hit Alex on the side of the head. Willie's cloth missed and landed half in the toilet. Craig laughed harder than ever. Willie snatched the cloth from Alex and chased Craig from the bathroom.

Alex dried his face and rubbed a towel over his wet pajamas. He gingerly lifted the facecloth from the toilet rim and deposited it in the bathtub, wondering if it was a blessing not to have brothers.

Cautiously looking around the bedroom, wary of an ambush, Alex saw Willie lying on his stomach, reading a book on fishing. Craig was kneeling on the floor, sorting his card collection.

Alex pushed aside the bedroom curtains. The full moon was now bright enough for him to see the horizon. He watched the glow of far-off headlights as a car wound its way along the coastal road. Several shadows passed down a distant hill.

"Do you keep sheep or cattle out there?" he asked.

Willie got up and peered out the window. "Where?"

"It's gone now, but something was moving across that hill there."

Willie groaned. "You're not seeing things again, are you?"

Craig dove under the covers. "Are they back?" he squeaked.

"There's nothing out there." Willie sighed. "It probably was just a shadow from a wee cloud passing in front of the moon."

Alex looked up. There were no clouds. The blackness surrounding the moon was broken only by speckles of stars. "Have you seen anything out there before?" he asked.

Craig's frightened little face popped out from under the bundle of blankets and bobbed up and down vigorously.

"*Och*, ye cannae be sure of what ye've seen," Willie said.

Willie and Alex knelt on the floor to keep a lookout. There were many shadows. Every now and then, they thought one of them moved, but neither ever saw the same movement at the same time.

"I guess there's nothing," Alex said finally.

Craig emerged and squeezed in between them, resting his chin on his folded arms. "There was once a big battle out there," he said quietly.

"Aye, but that was hundreds of years ago," Willie said.

"Who was fighting?" Alex asked.

"The English attacked us Scots," Willie replied.

"Who won?"

"The English. It was the battle where they took over Duncragglin. Granny says it was a very dark day. Lots of our ancestors died."

Alex pictured a battle raging below: swords and shields clashing, horses charging, men slashing and stabbing. The rugged countryside would have looked much the same back then. The hills would have had their same contours, the sea would have been pounding on the same shore. Only the trees would be different, and the buildings.

Craig yawned, which started Alex yawning too. He suddenly felt tired, very tired. Willie turned off the light and the boys went to bed.

———— ◆ ◆ ◆ ————

Hours later, Alex awoke with a spasm from a frightening dream, a tight-fisted grip on his covers. Heart pounding, he wondered if he was truly awake. His dream was so real that the fear was still in him. He'd seen unspeakable monsters from the past. Wailing eerily, they'd clambered up from the base of the cliffs, rising from under the rocks, climbing hand and foot over the hills, all with a single objective – they were coming to take him away.

4

A PLAN

Alex lay wide-eyed in his bed, sweat beading on his forehead, certain that the monsters of his dream were somewhere in the room. It was still dark. Alex wanted nothing more than to stay hidden under his covers, but he *had* to go to the toilet. There were no two ways about it. *And there is no such thing as monsters,* he repeated to himself as he reluctantly got up and tiptoed out to the hall.

The toilet door was shut. Dismayed, he twisted the handle, but it was locked. He rapped softly.

"I'll be right out," called Annie.

Alex danced in a little circle. The door opened and out she stepped.

"Hi, Annie – gotta go." Alex shot past and swung the door shut behind him, not taking the time to lock it. When he emerged, Annie was sitting at the top of the stairs, her arms wrapped about her knees. She was facing away, her head down.

"Hey, what's up?" he asked.

"Can't sleep." Her voice was muffled by the sleeve of her housecoat.

"Why not?"

"Been thinking about my mother."

Alex sat next to her and waited for her to say more. "Sometimes I think about my parents too," he said.

Annie lifted her head. Her eyes were red. "Your parents disappeared from around here too, didn't they?" she asked.

Alex nodded.

"Do you know what I think happened to them, and to my mother too?"

Alex stared, his heart pounding faster.

"The castle. It's haunted . . . or something." Annie brushed strands of hair off her cheek. "Everyone around here knows that. She wouldn't have just left us – she couldn't have. . . ." She looked about to cry.

Alex wondered miserably if he should put his arm around her shoulder.

"Do you know why I don't believe she just left us? Because she took Tig – our dog," Annie said. "She didn't even like him! He wasn't allowed to lie against the furniture – or anything!"

Alex wondered how people could disappear in a "haunted" castle. "Maybe they got lost in the caves," he suggested.

"The what?" Annie looked at him blankly.

"The caves. There's a whole labyrinth of caves under the castle, somewhere – really! A professor on the plane told me about them. Maybe we could find a way in!"

"Okay, let's say there are caves – and let's say we can find a way to get into them. What do you think we'd find?"

"Who knows? But if we find *anything* that suggests that your mother, or my parents, went into them, we could get someone to do a proper search. And then we might find out what happened to them!"

"But there are a few problems," said Annie. "First, we don't know where these caves are, and second, even if we find them, what's to keep *us* from getting lost?"

"I'm sure we'll figure something out." Alex was getting excited. "We'll sneak off when your dad's working. We'll bring flashlights and maybe some chalk to mark the way we came."

"But, that still leaves us with the biggest problem of all."

"What's that?"

"The place is haunted!"

They sat silently. Alex wondered what manner of ghost or being might be in the castle or those caves, and how it might prey on people who entered. It dawned on him that he and Annie might disappear, just like others had disappeared before them. He shuddered.

"Dad said he was going to take us to the ruins tomorrow," Annie said. "Let's see if we find anything that even remotely looks like it might be a way into those caves. If we find nothing, that's the end of that."

"Should we tell Willie?"

"Yes, but not Craig. He might tell Dad – particularly if he gets mad at us over one thing or another. As you might have noticed, that happens a lot!"

They said good night and went back to their beds, both feeling excited and nervous.

———◆◆◆———

By the time the boys came down for breakfast, Annie was watching TV in the front room and Mr. McRae was in from the barn, removing his overalls by the side door.

"What was he doing out so early?" Alex asked.

"Milking cows, of course." Willie punched the power button of a computer at a workstation in the corner of the front room. He slipped in his Annihilation disc and watched the computer flash through its start-up. "They need to be milked twice a day – every single lousy day."

"Do you ever milk them?"

Willie snorted. "Not if I can help it. I sure don't want to get too good at it."

Alex watched as Willie had a warrior, decked out with various armaments, go on a quest to fight underground monsters. Every swing of the warrior's sword sprayed a swath of monster blood. After each battle, the warrior stood, chest heaving, awaiting Willie's next mouse-click commands. Willie directed him to pick up coins and weapons that lay scattered about and to use a special potion to regain his strength.

Alex wished they could have a warrior like that to take with them into the caves.

Annie's show ended and she clicked off the TV. "Time for breakfast," she announced. "What'll it be, French toast or eggs for dipping?"

"Eggs for dipping!" Craig and Willie cried out in unison. They looked at each other, startled.

Willie blurted: "Personal jinx, Craig, Craig, Craig."

Craig yelled: "Personal jinx, Willie, Willie, Willie."

But Willie shouted triumphantly: "I'm first – you can't talk now!"

Lips sealed, Craig made gagged *mmm, mmm* noises and signaled with his hands for Willie to release him from the jinx.

"Are you going to help make breakfast this time?" Willie asked.

"Mmm, mmm."

"Let's get going, Willie," Annie said impatiently.

"But, it's Craig's turn to help . . . oh, darn."

"Thanks." Craig laughed, released from his jinx by Willie saying his name.

"Do ye like your eggs soft-boiled?" Annie asked Alex cheerily. "We can cook yours a bit more if you like."

"No, that's fine," Alex said dubiously.

Alex followed the others' lead as they dipped toast fingers into their eggs, pulling them back up dripping orange and taking a bite. He had never tasted an egg like this before.

"Free-range," Annie said proudly. "Our hens get to move around. It makes their eggs taste better."

Alex wasn't so sure.

"After breakfast, there'll be no more computer and TV," Mr. McRae announced. "If we're to go to the ruins today, we've got to get *all* the jobs done early."

"But we stacked extra straw –" Willie began.

"Aye, there's enough strewn about the barn to last a fortnight," Mr. McRae noted wryly. "But that doesnae count. There are eggs to collect and hens to feed. Craig, that'll be your job. Annie, take Alex and show him how we feed the calves. I've left some milk for them in the buckets. Willie, grind up some more cow feed. Oh, and boys – have ye brushed y'r teeth yet?"

Oh, no. . . . Alex put his hand to his forehead.

The calves pressed eagerly against the bars of their small pens at the back of the barn. They were not nearly as nervous as their mothers. One stuck its nose through the bars and licked Alex's shirt.

Annie held up a plastic bottle. A calf sucked on it with all its might, slurping the milk down in seconds. Alex held a bottle up for another, laughing as the calf tugged at it, trying to pull it into its pen. The calves were all fed in minutes and were looking at Alex and Annie for more.

Alex stroked one on the forehead. "Why are they kept separate?" he asked. "Wouldn't it be nicer for them to be with their mothers?"

"It's for their safety." Annie collected the empty bottles, tucking as many as she could under her arm. "Otherwise, they'd get trampled by the cows."

"But why not put the calf and its mother together in a separate pen? Then there would be no need for us to feed them."

"Can't you see there are not enough pens for that? And if Dad kept them together, he couldn't milk the mother cow."

Alex didn't understand – the calves end up drinking the milk anyway – but he decided not to press her on it.

Jobs done, they left the barn, the door slamming behind them. They heard the grinder shut down. Moments later, Willie came out a side door, his face, hair, and shoulders powdery white. He slapped his clothes, raising clouds of dust.

"Have you told Willie about our plans?" Alex asked Annie.

"Aye!" Willie said. "And I think you two are right nutters to come up with such a daft idea! Imagine, running off to explore a haunted castle. Who in their right minds would do such a thing? So . . . ," Willie rubbed his hands, "when do we go?"

Alex gave him a shove.

"We've got to get some things ready first," Annie said briskly. "And we have to figure out how to get into the caves. There's no point in us sneaking off and then just wandering about aimlessly."

Willie flung a stone over the plowed fields. Alex tried to match his distance, skipping to build up speed. The stone went to one side of Willie's and pinged off a crate.

"Hey!" The shout came from across the field, where a tall thin man with long hair was shaking his fist at them.

Willie shook his fist back. "Go boil your head."

"Willie! Be nice!" Annie pulled his arm down. "We should be lending him a hand with all those crates, not throwing stones at him. Come on, let's go help him load." Annie started out across the field. Willie followed, grumbling.

"Who is he?" Alex asked.

Willie kicked a clod of dirt. "He's a bum."

"Willie! There's no reason to be so angry with him. You know Dad asked him to keep an eye on us. Dad can't be everywhere, you know, and he worries about us now that Mum's gone –"

"Yeah, but he didnae have to tell Dad about the rifle."

"Duncan grows organic vegetables because he's a vegetarian. It upset him to see you shooting at birds – and besides, you're not allowed to touch that rifle. You could have killed someone!"

"Instead, it was Dad who killed me!"

"That's not Duncan's fault."

Willie jammed his hands into his pockets. "You go help him. I've got better things to do."

"Fine! Whatever!" Annie tossed her head and continued marching across the field.

Alex hesitated, but decided to stay with Annie. Willie did not look like good company right now. He was stomping off towards the farmhouse, where he'd probably do nothing but stare at the computer screen and have his warrior kill troll after troll. That was more fun to do than to watch.

Duncan swung another crate onto a flatbed trailer. He stopped to wipe the sweat from his brow. The field beyond was littered with crates packed full of vegetables.

"Hello, Annie," he said, as she came up. "Have we got a new worker on the farm?"

"This is Alex, Mrs. Murray's nephew," Annie replied. "He's come to stay with us seeing how she's not well."

Duncan looked startled. "Fiona's nephew? George and Marian Macpherson's son?"

"You knew my parents?" Alex asked, equally surprised.

"Aye, that I did. . . . Your parents got me going in this here organic vegetable business . . . that they did. They were always ready to help people out, very fine folk. . . ."

"So what happened to them then? Where did they go?"

Duncan shifted uncomfortably. "No one knows that, I'm sorry to say."

Alex turned away and threw himself into helping. It was always the same: no one ever knew; no one ever had any suggestions as to what might have happened. He struggled furiously with a crate that was heavier than expected. He got it clear of the ground and banged it against the side of the trailer. Duncan raised a hand to help, but held back. Alex staggered and dropped it onto the flatbed with a clatter.

Annie tapped him on the shoulder. "Can you help me with the next one?" she asked. "I can't manage it on my own."

Alex scowled, but he bent to pick up an end of a crate with her. She counted, "One . . . two . . . heave." The crate swung easily onto the trailer.

Annie slid the crate tight up against the others. "Duncan," she asked sweetly, "would you perhaps know how to get into the caves?"

Duncan paused. "Caves?"

"Yes, caves. I'm sure you know about them. There's a whole lot of them under the castle."

"They've been filled in and bricked up long ago." Duncan pulled himself onto the tractor. The spring-cushioned seat creaked under his weight. He turned back to Annie. "And that was done for a reason – it's a very bad place. It's important that you stay away from there."

"So there *are* caves there, then?"

"I didn't say that." Duncan glared.

"Are they haunted?" Annie gave him a disarming, mischievous smile.

Duncan sighed. He pulled his long hair back with both hands, clutched it behind his neck, and let it fall down his back. "I'm not sure 'haunted' is the right word, but there's something strange about the place – which is all the more reason to stay away!"

"For sure! No way *we'd* want to go there," Annie said.

Duncan eyed her suspiciously, but said nothing more. He revved the tractor, ground the gearshift into reverse, and backed the trailer for them to load another crate.

5

Picnic at the Ruins

"Alright, alright." Mr. McRae put down his reading glasses. "A promise is a promise. But let me finish up my paperwork, then we can have lunch and head on out to the ruins."

"Hooray!" Willie whooped. He and Annie threw together some ham and cheese rolls, grabbed a few apples, and persuaded Mr. McRae to let them pack them up and make it a picnic.

"Fine, fine." He laughed. "Such enthusiasm! What's with the lot of ye?"

Since Duncan had taken the van, they all had to squeeze into Mr. McRae's little car: Annie up front, with the picnic basket on her lap, and Alex squeezed awkwardly between Willie and Craig in the back, each insisting on having a window seat. The car looked so old that Alex doubted it would start, but it sputtered, coughed, and revved up.

They rounded a bend and saw the battered outline of the castle rising up above the cliffs. Even in the midday sun, the ruins looked bleak and desolate.

Mr. McRae turned onto a grassy plateau and parked over-looking the sea. There was no paved car park, ticket booth, or guided tour. In fact, there was no one there at all – only hundreds of seagulls wheeling about and screeching from nooks in the crumbled walls.

All that remained of the castle were mounds of earth and stone, basic outlines of foundations, and eroded rem-nants of towers. Everything was so overgrown, it was hard to tell where natural rock formations ended and ancient walls began.

Centrally perched on the edge of the cliffs was a large mound that Alex guessed would have been the castle keep. The upper floors appeared to have collapsed into the lower, filling them in. Grass had grown over the top, and seagulls had taken to building nests in the remnants of the walls.

Alex regarded it dubiously. There seemed little prospect of finding a way in. Perhaps it would offer a good view. "Is there a way up top?" he asked.

"Around the other side there's a wee sloped bit," Mr. McRae replied. "Seeing how it isn't a windy day, we can have our picnic up there."

The top provided a spectacular panorama of surrounding cliffs, with waves crashing far below. Alex leaned against an iron rail and shaded his eyes from the ocean glare. Ahead, a crumbling, overgrown arch connected with more ruins on outcropping rocks. Under it was a water passage to a small natural harbor that would once have been surrounded by castle and walls.

Alex sighed. Such a magnificent castle, so little left.

The midday sun beat down on them. Even on their

perch high above the sea, there was only the slightest warm breeze to ruffle their hair. Mr. McRae spread a tartan blanket and placed the picnic basket in the middle. Willie picked a stem of tall grass and stuck it in his mouth. The end wiggled as he chewed.

"Ah, what a braw day." Mr. McRae stretched out on the tartan blanket, his hands behind his head. "We don't have nearly enough days like this in this country."

Willie reached into the basket and pulled out a roll.

"Hey – that's mine!"

"No, it's not." Willie held the roll out of Craig's reach. "Do you see your name on it?"

"Is too, I called it! Let me have it!" Craig lunged and grabbed Willie's arm.

"Boys . . . boys . . . BOYS!" Mr. McRae waded in and pulled them apart. "Enough of this! Willie, put the roll down. I'll hand them out myself."

Even with all the rolls spread over a napkin, Craig and Willie still wanted the same one, so Mr. McRae evened out the amount of ham and cheese on each roll by using some from his own.

Annie watched with wry amusement. "Pretty silly, aren't they?" She sounded a little embarrassed. She steered Alex away, and they strolled up to the rail. "So far, I haven't seen any way to get inside," she said, "but let's keep looking. We might have more luck after lunch, when we head down below."

Alex scanned the coastline. "It looks different than last night, when I went looking for Vanessa," he said. "I don't remember a beach down there."

Annie laughed. "That's because the tide was in, silly!"

Alex looked away, annoyed. How was he to know? It's not like he grew up next to an ocean.

———◆◆———

After lunch, they all hiked down steep, overgrown steps to explore the harbor. Alex imagined moored boats and a wharf crowded with fishermen hauling out their catch, kids darting between piles of nets and buckets of fish, carts clattering over stones. . . . And now there was nothing, only the steady sound of crashing waves clawing away at what was left. *But is there really nothing?* Alex thought back to the eerie moaning noise, the movements, the monsters from his dream. He shivered and hurried after the others.

They crossed into a shadow, and a blaze of blue sky silhouetted the ruins above them. Alex stopped to study the walls. He could make out the outline of rows of vertical slits for firing arrows, but they all appeared to be filled in.

"Alex, over here." Mr. McRae waved for him to come. They headed down to the sandy stretch at the base of the cliffs.

Out on the wet sand, Alex was careful to step around the brown sea kelp, having spotted numerous jellyfish in its strands. Crunching wet kelp underfoot was one thing, squishing slithery jellyfish was quite another.

The tide had receded further. Slimy green boulders dotted the wet beach. Mr. McRae stopped at a pool left by the retreating tide to point out colorful sea anemones rooted to the rocks. Using a hooked stick, he probed underneath and pulled out a crab. It waved its claws angrily.

"Strange things, these hermit crabs," Mr. McRae said.

"They take up empty shells for a home. When they outgrow one shell, they abandon it and take over another." He looked back to the castle. "And speaking of things that take over dwellings, has anyone seen a castle ghoulie today?"

Everyone dutifully shook their heads.

"Well then, let's no go on so much about ghoulies or ghosts or whatnot – alright?"

Everyone dutifully nodded.

Mr. McRae harrumphed. He wasn't fooled: he knew it would take more than a sunny midday walk around the castle to dispel all the fears and myths that had grown over the years.

Alex stumbled over a board that protruded from the sand. Mildly curious, he wriggled it loose and balanced it on end. Down one side were mud-filled grooves that were not part of the wood grain. Intrigued, he dropped the board into a puddle and kneeled to rinse it off. The faint outline of a bird emerged, its pointy beak stuck into the ground as if after a worm.

"Hey, check this out!" Alex called.

Mr. McRae gave it barely more than a glance. "Just a worthless old plank off a boat," he said. The others quickly lost interest.

Regardless, Alex wanted to keep it as a memento. He tucked an end under his arm and dragged the other end behind him. It left a deep rut in the sand. He soon wished it was not quite so big and heavy.

Shadows from the cliffs were reaching out across the sand. Alex stopped, sure he saw something moving. "Look, there! At the base of those rocks! Do you see it?"

Everyone shielded their eyes. There in the shadows were two figures, one large and the other small.

"Oh, no, not them," Mr. McRae muttered.

"Not who, Dad?"

"If I'm no mistaken, that would be Kenneth Farquhar and his son, Grant."

"Oh, them." Annie frowned.

"Who are they?" Alex asked.

"The Straith Meirn antique dealer and his son," Annie replied. "He's been selling away our heritage to tourists piece by piece. Last year, he even managed to sell the five-hundred-year-old Kintail Bridge. The American who bought it took it away, stone by stone, to rebuild it on his property in Vermont. Can you imagine? Our bridge – a bridge built and traveled by Scots for over five hundred years – sitting in someone's garden in Vermont. That bridge belonged to Scotland – it was not his to sell!"

"Why was he allowed to do that?"

"When he bought rights to the land, it didn't even occur to anyone that he would sell the bridge. We tried to stop it, but he sits on the town council. They pretty much do what he wants."

Willie removed a well-chewed stalk from his mouth. He regarded the mangled end and flicked the stalk away. "I go to school with Grant," he said, turning his head to spit out a leftover piece. "He's a right nutter."

The Farquhars stopped to watch their approach.

"Well, well, if it isn't the McRae clan," said Kenneth Farquhar, a tight lopsided grin on his face. His son's smile looked more openly like a sneer.

"What brings you here, Kenneth?" Mr. McRae said evenly. "Planning to sell Duncragglin Castle?"

"I would if I could." Kenneth Farquhar smiled, not rising to the bait. "It's a shame to see such a splendid castle simply fall into the sea, isn't it? Far better for someone to preserve it – even if that were in a place far away. But alas, even I cannae find a buyer for the rubble that remains."

Mr. McRae snorted. "Better for the rubble of our ancient past to be trodden by the Scots," he said, "than for it to be taken and preserved in some pickling jar."

Kenneth Farquhar gave a short condescending laugh. "Such a quaint, myopic point of view. My sales have raised tax revenues that have benefited this whole community, not to mention the jobs I've created for the townsfolk."

"Aye," Mr. McRae said bitterly. "Ye pay them well to plunder the land."

"Plunder?" Kenneth Farquhar's eyes flashed. "Be careful of the kettle calling the pot black, Alastair. What of the poisoning of our lands from your farming?"

"That's no true and ye know it!" Mr. McRae retorted.

"Do I, now?" The oily smile returned. "I'm no so sure the inspectors would agree with you."

"I'm no afraid of your inspectors, Farquhar."

"My inspectors? What on earth do you mean? Ye know full well that the inspectors are in the employ of the township. Well, it has been a pleasure to speak with ye as always, Alastair, but I have better things to do. Come, Grant."

Grant eyed Alex's board curiously and nudged his father. "Don't artifacts found on the beach belong to the town, Father?"

Kenneth Farquhar's eye swept disdainfully over the worn driftwood plank under Alex's arm. "Let us be charitable, son. Perhaps they need it for firewood."

"See you later, Dilly-Willie," Grant called over his shoulder.

———◆———

Willie stood silently, red-faced, glaring after them.

"What were they doing here, Dad?" Annie asked.

"Kenneth Farquhar wouldnae be out here just to enjoy a walk with his son." Mr. McRae ground the end of his walking stick into the sand. "Let us speak no more of them. They've darkened my mood enough already."

They walked along the shore in the opposite direction taken by the Farquhars. Alex traced the Farquhars' footsteps in the damp sand, but lost track of them as they approached the castle harbor.

Alex heard a shout. Willie was gesturing for them to join him a short way up the side of the cliff. Alex scrambled up, the others not far behind.

Willie pointed proudly to what he'd found: a small bricked-up archway recessed deep in the rocks. He thumped it hard with the side of his fist and grimaced.

"That was stupid." Craig laughed.

"What do you think this is, Dad?" Annie asked.

"It's obvious, is it no?" Mr. McRae was puffing from the climb. "See how it's near sea level and just down from the castle? Think about it. What would it be?"

To Alex, Annie, and Willie, it was obviously a way into

the caves – but it was equally obvious that this was not the answer Mr. McRae was seeking.

"A sewer outlet!" Mr. McRae slapped his leg. "What else? Castles had sinks, baths, and toilets too, you know."

Annie and Alex glanced at each other doubtfully. Whatever it was, it was no help to them. And it would take a stick of dynamite to get past.

They all continued down the beach until it narrowed to nothing and the shoreline became impassable. Alex tugged on Annie's sleeve as the others started to climb a path that wound its way up the cliff-side.

"Look." He nudged Annie quietly. "Those waves over there . . . they look like they go right under that rock."

Staring at the shadows, they watched waves smack up against the rock with a spray. At the low point, it looked as if the water was being sucked in under the rock, only to come gurgling back out a few seconds later.

Annie shrugged. "It's probably just a hollow."

"True. But look at how close it is to that blocked-off archway farther up the cliff. Maybe the water has eroded the rock under there far enough back to connect with a cave."

Annie bent to take a closer look. It was impossible to see how far it went. "It would have to be the lowest of low tides before we could get in there," she said. "And then we might find it leads nowhere."

"When will that be?" Alex persisted.

"Let's see. . . ." Annie counted on her fingers. "The tide's getting lower by the day . . . I think it will be at its lowest point in about a week –"

"What is it?" Alex asked.

"Well," she began, "if I'm not mistaken, the tide will be at its lowest point in the middle of the night."

"That's not a problem – in fact, it's perfect," Alex said, sounding braver than he felt. "Your dad won't even know we're gone."

Annie frowned. "Do you want us to come out here in the middle of the night?"

"Look," Alex reasoned, "once we get in the caves, it will be dark no matter what time of day it is, right?"

Annie didn't reply. Her brow furrowed, she stared at where the waves were being sucked under the rocks.

The board didn't seem important anymore. Alex wedged it between some rocks to mark where they were, and they hurried to catch up with the others.

6

MIDNIGHT EXCURSION

The morning sun projected a window outline onto the opposite wall of the bedroom. Annie sat on Willie's bed, her pen poised over a notepad. "We need to be prepared," she said. "This is going to be a very difficult excursion. Now, what should we bring?"

Willie's hand shot up. "My rock-climbing gear – in case we need to climb some walls."

"Not so loud!" Annie said with a quick hand flutter. "Craig might hear you."

"*Nah*, don't worry. He's watching TV." Willie leapt up to rummage through his closet.

Annie scribbled on her notepad. "We'll also need to bring torches and extra batteries – and our headlamps."

"Headlamps?" Alex asked.

Willie tossed his rock-climbing harness onto the carpet and strapped a circular light to his head. "Got it. What's next?"

"We'll need chalk to mark the way we came." Annie scribbled some more. "And some baler's twine to unroll behind us."

Willie groaned. "Unrolling twine will take too long. And we won't need it if we have chalk."

"It's non-negotiable," Annie said crisply, putting her pad down. "What we're about to do is dangerous, Willie. People *die* doing things like this. We need to take every precaution."

"We need to take every precaution," Willie mimicked, but Annie refused to take the bait. Willie finally agreed to the baler's twine as well as a water bottle and some emergency rations, but only after Annie's suggestion of taking biscuits was augmented with chocolates. He put his foot down, though, when she suggested that they each bring a blanket.

"We're not going for a sleepover," he said. "We'll all be carrying heavy packs as it is. Blankets are too bulky. If we get cold, we'll just build a fire."

"There probably won't be any firewood," Annie retorted, "and even if there is, we can't light a fire as it might use up all the air."

Air? Alex and Willie looked at each other in surprise. They settled on bringing the set of silver emergency blankets that were sealed in a little packet and stored in the back of Mr. McRae's car.

"Shall we take along a hairbrush and a change of clothes?" Willie tossed his head back and thrust out a hip. "Always need to look our best, you know."

Annie picked up a pillow to smack him. She paused. "Actually, that might not be such a bad idea. What if we get wet?"

"No way, no way," Willie howled. "Me and my big mouth."

In the end, they agreed to pack a change of clothes, wear layers, and bring jackets in case it got *really* cold. All that was left was to convince themselves they would need everything that they'd planned to bring.

Willie slapped his knee. "My music! I almost forgot! I need to bring my music."

Alex and Annie stared.

"I cannae go without ma tunes." Willie sat up straight and put his hands in his lap. "It's non-negotiable."

Annie's pillow hit him squarely on the side of the head.

———◆———

In the days that followed, Annie, Willie, and Alex gathered everything they needed, keeping it hidden in Annie's room. "Craig won't find it there," she said, "and Dad never goes into my room since, unlike you guys, I keep it tidy."

Following the calf-feeding and feed-grinding, they had gone into the equipment shed and wound a great long length of baling twine onto a stick. There was such a huge spool in the baling machine that Mr. McRae would never notice some was missing.

They wondered how they would get the emergency blankets from the boot of the car. Mr. McRae usually kept the car keys in his pocket, and the interior boot latch was broken. The problem was solved during the weekly grocery run into Straith Meirn. While hefting grocery bags, Annie managed to slip the set of emergency blankets into the bread bag without Mr. McRae noticing.

For rucksacks, they used school packs that had been stowed away for the summer on the top shelf of the hall closet. Annie emptied the assorted feathers, stones, paper scraps, and outright junk from Craig's pack into a plastic bag, which she left behind on the shelf, and gave the pack to Alex. Craig wouldn't miss it – not until school started. By then, they would be long back.

They checked the weather channel for the precise day and time that the tide fluctuations would reach their lowest point. It was less than a week away. Much to Annie's dismay, her prediction that low tide would be at midnight was confirmed.

They counted down the days, praying low tide would come before Alex's aunt Fiona got better and sent for him. Craig seemed to be getting used to having Alex around and no longer sought ways to challenge him, annoy him, or complain about what he did. Alex suspected Craig was secretly happy to have him help out with many of his regular jobs, especially the nasty chore of shoveling out the henhouse.

Finally the night of the lowest tide arrived, and Alex, Annie, and Willie found it hard not to let on that something was up. They exchanged knowing glances and whispered snatches of furtive instructions at every opportunity.

Annie caught Alex in the hall, away from prying eyes. "I'll bring the rucksacks down and place them outside the back door around ten-thirty," she said. "Pass it on to Willie."

"How will you know when your dad is asleep?"

"He snores. Big, snorting, hungry-pig kind of snores. I can hear them right through my bedroom wall. As soon as I'm sure he's out, I'll go and shine a torch up at your window. Make sure you don't wake Craig."

The bathroom door opened and out stepped Craig. "What are you two whispering about?" he demanded.

"Nothing." Annie casually carried on down the hall.

"Well, you *better* not wake me!" Craig called after her.

Alex encountered Annie again in the kitchen. "What do you think he heard?" he asked nervously.

Annie rummaged through the drawer for a can opener. "Don't worry. If he heard more than the last sentence, he would have let us know by now."

During the evening meal, there were long stretches where the only sounds were the clinking of cutlery against plates and the deliberate smacking noises Craig made while chewing his food.

"Well." Mr. McRae wiped his lips with his serviette. "Everyone must have got a lot of fresh air today."

Willie pushed back his plate. "Not feeling well," he mumbled, keeping his eyes cast down on the table.

Mr. McRae felt Willie's forehead. "Do you think you might be sick?"

Willie nodded. He got up shakily and Mr. McRae helped him up the stairs.

Alex didn't feel well either. His stomach felt like a clenched fist. It seemed that, like Willie, he was suffering from a case of nerves.

———◦•◦———

Later, when Alex and Craig went up to the bedroom, Willie was facing the wall, a bucket next to his bed. He did not stir.

Alex got into bed, his heart beating so loudly that he thought the others could hear. It was hard to lie waiting for Craig to fall asleep, waiting for Annie's signal, waiting for it all to begin.

Finally Alex heard Craig's steady breathing turn into light gasps. Alex propped up his head with one hand and kept an eye out for Annie's signal. It took so long, he wondered whether he should see if she'd fallen asleep. If he met Mr. McRae, he could pretend he was going to the bathroom – unless, of course, Mr. McRae caught him tiptoeing into Annie's room. At that point, he would have a *lot* of explaining to do.

Just when he could stand it no longer, a flash illuminated a sliver of the ceiling. Quiet as a ghost, Alex slipped out of bed and closed the curtains – the prearranged signal for Annie to know he was up. It also made the room darker. Alex bunched up his bedcovers to make them appear as if he were still in bed. He picked up his carefully arranged bundle of clothes, crept over to Willie's bed, and gave him a shake.

Willie groggily raised his arm. "What? What?"

"*Shh!* Come on, let's go!"

Willie dropped his arm over his face. "You go ahead," he mumbled. "I'll be right there."

Alex tiptoed down the stairs to the front room to get dressed. He hid his pajamas under the couch and slipped out the side door. He shivered in the night air as he laced up his shoes.

Annie came around the corner lugging three rucksacks. "Where's Willie?"

"He's coming. I had to wake him."

"He fell asleep?!" Annie stamped her foot. "I don't believe it. You can't count on him for anything."

They sat on the steps, Annie impatiently drumming her fingers on her pack. She jumped up and strode angrily around the house to flash the light at the window again. She returned more annoyed than ever.

"I'll go get him," she said, climbing the steps to the house.

As she reached for the handle, the door suddenly swung open.

"Craig! What are you doing up?"

Craig stepped out and closed the door behind him. "I'm coming too," he said.

"No, you're not." Annie raised her hand to her mouth. "I mean, we're not going anywhere . . . now get back up to bed. Why are you dressed?"

"Because I'm coming with you," he said doggedly. "I want to find out about Mum as much as you do, you know."

Annie stared in dismay. She knew there would be no way to stop him – he was just too stubborn. Either he came with them, or no one went. "Let's get Willie," she said at last.

"Oh, I wouldn't do that." Craig gave a short laugh. "He was hanging over his bucket a moment ago – it wasn't pretty."

Annie sighed. "Okay, let's go. Craig, you take Willie's pack."

They strapped on their headlamps and trudged in single file, Annie in the lead, Craig in the middle, Alex right behind. Alex told himself that, in all likelihood, they would find that the hollow led nowhere, that there was no way into the caves, and they would all be back safe and sound in their beds within an hour or so. In the morning, they would report to Willie that he had not missed anything at all: there were no caves, no anything. Repeating this helped calm his nerves.

It was the darkest night Alex could remember. Not a single star could be seen anywhere across the vast blackness. They could see only what fell in the beam of their lights. The terrain changed from shrub to rock, and eventually they found the edge of the cliffs. A heavy stillness filled the air. It felt like it would rain.

They followed a path that wound down the front of the cliffs. The sea was quiet but for a light slapping and gurgling of swells trickling about the rocks.

Soon they reached the water's edge, but there was no sign of the board. Alex became convinced they had gone the wrong way. He stooped to squeeze through a narrow gap in the rocks, taking care not to get his feet wet. Shining his light into the blackness ahead, he stopped short, suddenly realizing it led straight into the cliff.

"This might be it!" he called.

Annie crowded in behind him. "Can you see how far it goes?"

"Not yet."

Stooping, they entered a long narrow cave. Craig wormed his way ahead of Annie. A narrow stream trickled beside them. Something blue flashed in the water and Alex reached down to fish it out. It was a rope. He pulled it up and found it led deep into the cave.

"What's that doing here?" Craig asked.

"It seems we're not the first ones to go this way." Alex trained his light on the rope and examined it closely. "It's not slimy, so it can't have been here very long."

They had to be going the right way. *This must lead somewhere – why else would there be a rope? And where else could it lead but into the caves?* Hearts pounding, they followed it deeper underground. The cave became smaller, and they walked hunched over to keep from hitting their heads.

The stream ended, and the cave became no more than a fissure. Alex squirmed out of his pack and crawled into the fissure, pulling his pack behind him. His knees were immediately soaked from crawling over wet seaweed and twigs. The confined space made him nervous. If there was an earth tremor and the rock was to shift, even just a bit. . . . Alex shook his head to dispel the thought and continued crawling ever deeper into the darkness ahead.

The rock sloped slightly upward, and Alex wriggled into a cave not much bigger than the space under a dining-room table. Dead end. He felt relieved. That meant they would be turning back. He had had enough of squirming about through tiny cracks under tonnes of rock.

"Budge over," Craig said. He and Annie squeezed in beside Alex.

Alex kneeled on a plank, thankful to get his knees off the rock. It had worn engravings carved into its side. Alex examined it closely and saw it was the very same board he had found during their picnic at the ruins – the one he had wedged between some rocks.

"How'd that get here?" Craig asked.

Alex shrugged. "Pushed in by the tide, I guess." He picked up a short stick, but it was so slimy, he quickly tossed it away and wiped his hand on his trousers.

"What was that?" Annie retrieved it and gingerly lifted it with two fingers. She wrinkled her nose. "It looks like the leg bone of a small animal."

"Like what, a sheep?" Craig asked.

"Maybe."

"How about a dog?"

Annie gave out a tiny squeal and dropped it. *Could it be . . . ? No.* She persuaded herself that it couldn't be Tig's, that it was just some old bone that had floated in with the tide.

Craig flashed his beam about the ceiling. He spotted a narrow shaft at one end. "Look," he called out excitedly, "we could fit through there."

Alex squirmed over to peer up the shaft. It led straight up, farther than his light could reach. "No way!"

"It'll be easy," Craig said, pushing his pack out of the way. "Watch me."

Alex looked doubtfully over to Annie. She shrugged. "You should see him where we practice rock-climbing," she said. "He climbs farther and faster than Willie."

"And higher too. Give me a boost, will you?"

"Wait a second." Annie unzipped the top of Willie's pack. "Not without Willie's harness and gear."

"But it's an easy climb –"

"No, it isn't, and you know it. Besides, we need to use the gear to help Alex up – he's never done this before."

Annie helped Craig into the harness, adjusting his waist and leg straps until they were snug. She took great care to attach the rope to his harness with a proper double figure-eight knot.

"And don't forget to hammer in a piton every few yards," Annie said.

"Yeah, yeah, yeah." Craig stretched his arms. "I'm ready. Help me up."

Alex interlocked his fingers, his hands wobbling as they took on Craig's weight. Craig stepped onto his shoulder and, one painful thrust later, his weight was gone, replaced by a shower of dirt and pebbles.

Annie put her headlamp down on end so that its beam shot up the shaft. She fed out the rope, keeping a tight grip should Craig fall.

Alex ventured a quick look. "How's it going, Craig?" he called.

"Okay so far" drifted down from above.

Bits of dirt and stone clattered around the headlamp. Alex was thinking he should move it when a large stone suddenly fell from the shaft and shattered its lens.

"One down," he said glumly.

"It's okay." Annie calmly brushed aside the broken glass. "We still have three torches and two headlamps."

Alex unscrewed the back of the broken headlamp to save the batteries. He crawled back to grab a pack and felt his knees splash into a pool of water. "What the heck?" He twisted to shine his torch back the way they had come. "Annie . . . look! The tide's coming in. We have to get out of here. Fast!"

Annie looked in horror at the rising water. She quickly turned to call up the shaft. "Craig, come down *now!* CRAIG!"

Instead of a reply, the empty harness dropped from the shaft.

"He can't hear me!" Annie cried. "What should we do? We can't just leave him up there."

The water was now only inches below the ceiling of the lower cave. They could still get out, but they would have to swim on their backs with their noses up for air.

"You go. I'll stay with Craig." Alex pulled the harness from Annie's hands. "We'll get out when the tide goes back down."

Alex struggled into the harness while Annie hastily explained how he was to climb. "When you pass a piton, clip the rope below it to your harness. That way you can't fall any farther than the distance you have climbed since the last time you clipped the rope."

Alex was confused, but there was no time for questions. Annie gave him a boost. He clambered and found a toehold. The shaft was wide enough for him to press his back against one side and push his feet against the other. He inched up, pushing with his hands while his feet slowly walked up the other side. He pulled down on the rope coming through the pitons. Up a few more feet, he found a piton that Craig had hammered into a crack. *What had Annie said to do?* He clipped the rope to his harness and hoped for the best.

It was not easy to find new toeholds, especially in the uneven light. Although he tested each hold before putting his weight on it, he constantly feared one would give way and plunge him back down the shaft. He tried not to rely on any one so he would have a chance of catching himself if he slipped.

Alex was not convinced that Craig's pitons would hold if his weight snapped against them. He tried to reassure himself by thinking that if Craig's top piton did not hold, there was always the next and then the next. Surely one of them would hold.

Alex could not be sure how far he was climbing, but it seemed like a long way. From far above, Craig's torch shone down on him, helping him find grips. Dimly, he heard Craig's shouts of encouragement. A few times, he thought he might slip, but each time, he managed to stabilize his hold and shift to a more secure position.

At long last, the top came into view. Alex wriggled over the edge, feeling Craig pull on his harness.

Arms and hands still trembling from exertion, Alex rolled onto his back. A great sense of relief flooded through him. He'd made it! Now all they had to do was wait for the tide to go out . . . and everything would be alright.

7

TRAPPED

Flat on his back, gasping from his climb, Alex vaguely heard Craig calling for him to take off his harness. "Annie needs it – hurry!"

Alex waved him away. "Annie's gone back out to let people know where we are," he said. "The tide is coming in."

"If she's gone, what's that light then?"

"Light? What light?" Alex rolled onto his stomach and peered over the edge. Something was flashing at them from below.

Alex squirmed out of the harness and lowered it with the rope. Soon the rope started gliding in fits and stops through the pitons. *Could it really be Annie climbing up the shaft?* She was going to leave the cave the moment he had started climbing. But if it wasn't Annie climbing, who or what was it?

Alex cautiously looked down the shaft. The top of the dark form coming up from below had brown hair. If it was a nasty creature from the deep, it sure was doing a good job of disguising itself as Annie.

Suddenly Annie's head and shoulders appeared. She

hoisted herself up and plunked down on the edge. She was soaked.

"I tried to get out," Annie said, picking miserably at the knot on her harness, "but the water's too high."

Craig started to take off his sweatshirt. "Here, have this."

"No need." Annie pulled up the rope, lifting three packs from the shaft. She zipped one open and raked around. "Good thing I listened to Willie about bringing extra clothes."

She started unbuttoning her shirt. "Okay, you two, turn around. I need to get changed here."

Alex obligingly turned his back, using the time to have a look around. Remarkably, the wall near them was straight and the ceiling above them flat. It looked more like they were in the ruins of a man-made chamber than a natural cave.

He shone his light into the far reaches. They were so full of fallen rock, it was hard to see where they went. Spotting something blue, he trained his light on it. There, in a neat coil, was more of that rope they had seen earlier. Alex went to investigate. To his surprise, he found, partially hidden in a hollow next to the rope, several cylinders with gauges and straps.

"Hey, guys. I found scuba tanks."

The others quickly joined him, Annie still buttoning her shirt. There appeared to be a full set of gear for two divers.

Alex cupped his hands to his mouth. "Hello," he called loudly.

"Hello, hello, hello . . ." came echoing back.

"Anyone here?"

"Anyone here, here, here . . ." The echo slowly died away.

They listened breathlessly, but there was no answering call. If one or two people *were* here, they were far away – either that, or they were keeping very quiet.

Alex tried to shake off his feeling of dread. He shone his light on the rock basin containing the tanks. "This looks like it could have been a bathtub," he said. "Do you think this chamber was once a bathroom?"

Craig trained his light back to the opening of the shaft. "I hope not," he said, "because if it was, do you know what we climbed up?"

"The toilet?" Alex offered.

"Yes!" Craig hooted. "Move your backside, please – we're coming through!"

Alex chuckled. "Dodge any missiles on your way up?"

Annie put her hands to her head. "I can't believe it," she moaned. "Here we are, stuck in the worst of predicaments, and all you guys do is mess about. . . ." She flung herself down and wrapped her arms about her knees. "Oh, what was I thinking, coming here with you two!"

Alex shuffled his feet uneasily. "But, Annie," he began. "No one said it would be easy. We can't just fall apart at the slightest bit of trouble."

Annie jerked her head up. "What? Here we are, trapped deep underground, with no way out except at the next low tide – and you think we're in just the *slightest* bit of trouble?"

"But, everything is going according to plan." Alex spread his arms. "We *actually* found a way underground. We've got to explore now, not leave. If we find any sign that your mother or my parents have been here, we can go back and get a search party."

"I did not *plan* to get *trapped*." Tears trickled down Annie's face. "Everyone's going to blame me for this because I'm the oldest. I'm always the person who should have known better."

"Well, maybe there's another way out," Alex said, hoping to calm her down. He shone his light toward the far end of the chamber. "Come; let's have a look over this way. Maybe it leads to the outer edge of the cliffs."

Annie was hesitant, but at least it was something to do. She pulled out her compass and confirmed that the direction Alex indicated was east. Unrolling twine behind them, they climbed over the rubble. Around a corner, they found an entrance to a small cave. They became more and more convinced that the caves were not natural formations.

Each cave led to another until they came to a dead end. They searched the walls for an exit out to the cliffs.

Annie gasped. "Oh, my God . . . blood!"

Her wavering torch was lighting a rectangular rock recessed in an alcove. "HEL" was scrawled across it in burgundy-brown letters.

Alex bent to examine the letters closely. "Oh, it's nothing," he said, struggling to keep calm. "Someone was just going to write 'HELL,' but didn't finish – sort of like graffiti."

"Graffiti, down here?" Annie shook her head. "No, I think it says 'HELP.'" She traced her fingers over faint scratches on the rock. "It looks like someone tried very hard to get out past this rock, but didn't succeed."

Horrified, Alex spotted a fingernail – a *complete* fingernail, ripped in its entirety from a finger. Someone would have wanted to get out very badly to be clawing at the rock with bare hands. *But what is there to be so afraid of? And where is that person now?*

A shiver ran down Alex's spine. It felt as if the temperature had dropped. He stepped on the fingernail, not wanting the others to see it.

Craig tugged Annie's sleeve. "Let's go back," he said quietly.

They retraced their steps, carefully winding the twine back onto its spool. Alex was very tired. All he wanted to do was lie down and curl up with a nice soft pillow. A protective alcove suddenly looked terribly inviting. He stopped.

"Do you know what, Annie? I think we should clear a bit of the floor in there and get some sleep. We'll feel a lot better if we do."

"Good idea." Annie dropped her pack. "When we wake up, the tide will be on its way out. Also, we won't need our lights when we're sleeping, and we *do* need to save the batteries."

The prospect of having no light was not a nice thought. They extinguished all but one torch as they prepared their beds. Alex lay on his extra jersey and did his best to fluff up the end of his rucksack for a pillow. It was better than nothing – but not by much. He pulled his thin silver emergency blanket up to his chin, thankful that the cave wasn't cold.

Craig squirmed to settle in.

"Ready?" Annie asked.

"Uh-huh," Alex murmured.

Craig pretended to snore.

Annie clicked off the torch and they were plunged into utter darkness. Alex wiggled his fingers before his eyes, but could see nothing.

The silence was broken by Craig. "I tooted," he said, giggling.

"Craig!" Annie exclaimed.

"Cannae help it." They heard a rustle and felt a draft.

Annie gave Craig a whack. "Stop fanning!" she ordered.

Eventually the giggling died down. They mumbled good night, followed by complete silence. Sleep did not come easy; but, tired as they were, sleep they did.

Alex awoke and pushed a button on the side of his wrist-watch. It was 6:45 A.M. He had slept all of five and a half hours. They had another four hours before the next low tide – four hours to explore.

Alex found his torch and clicked it on, careful to shine it away from Annie and Craig. He got up, stretched, and followed the twine back to the shaft and the scuba tanks. Nothing had been moved, and the tanks' owners had not returned – yet.

He set off in a new direction, one that led deeper inland. The chamber ended in a steep slope of fallen rock. Scrambling up the slope, he came to a stone arch that looked like it once might have been the top of a doorway. There was a tiny gap under the arch. Grunting, he wriggled a few rocks to widen the gap.

"Alex . . . Alex . . . where are you?" called a voice from far behind.

"Over here." He shone his light back the way he had come.

Alex saw flashes from Annie's and Craig's lights as they approached. They climbed up the slope to join him. Together, they shone their lights through the opening Alex had made. Beyond was a long tunnel.

"Let's pack up and check it out," Alex suggested.

Returning to where they had slept, they had a small breakfast of biscuits, chocolate, and water, carefully rationed by Annie. "I don't want to be the only one left with food and water once you two have run out," she said, pointedly resealing her chocolate in plastic and putting it back into her pack. "We're not here to have a pig-out."

"*Aw.*" Craig reluctantly put his chocolate away, having eaten only two squares.

Eager to get going, they folded the clothes they used for bedding and roughly stuffed them back into their packs. Annie pulled out the baler's twine to unwind behind them.

The first section of the tunnel was so filled with rubble that they had to crawl over painfully rough rocks. It was a relief when the tunnel became higher and they could walk without fear of hitting their heads.

Their lights cast dark shadows past outcroppings. Alex often thought he spotted an opening, but each time, it turned out to be no more than a minor recess in the wall.

The tunnel ended at a rockfall. At first, it seemed like they had come to a dead end, but again they found they were able to clamber over the rocks and continue by squirming on their stomachs. At the peak of the rockfall, they saw that ahead the tunnel opened up into a large cave.

Overlapping each other's beam to make a stronger light, they saw they were entering a huge, semicircular cavern, with tall pillars that formed gnarly, branchlike arches across its ceiling. The semicircular wall across from them was intricately carved with thousands of animals, depicted in a tangled, junglelike background of vines, limbs, and leaves. In its center was the massive head of a fanged, snake-haired monster, its bottom fangs protruding up like gateposts.

"It's so beautiful," Annie breathed.

Craig tilted his head and eyed the monster-head critically. "Actually, I think it's rather ugly."

"Why would anyone build something like this so far underground?" Alex asked.

"Aliens," said Craig. "It has to have been aliens."

"Maybe this was made by a long-lost civilization of prehistoric people – or maybe by some prehuman advanced civilization," Annie suggested.

"Aliens," Craig said firmly. "And I'll bet they're what've been haunting the castle too. . . ."

Hushed, they climbed down the rockfall and explored the cavern. Annie examined a cluster of carvings, gently wiping rock dust from the bumpy ridges.

"What are these things?" she asked.

Alex looked closely. "One-foot-tall insects that stand on two legs . . . and carry spears?" he offered.

"Aliens," Craig said firmly.

Alex was beginning to think that Craig's alien theory was the only one that made any sense. He shone his torch higher up the wall and traced over a series of bird carvings. Some of the birds were in flight; others were hopping on the ground.

He came to a bird with a long thin beak standing poised over what appeared to be a wormhole. It took him a moment to realize where he had seen it before – it was the same bird that was carved on the board he had found on the beach.

"Hey, guys! Look at me!"

Alex shone his light in the direction of Craig's voice and spotted his spidery form clinging to the wall. Craig was carefully maneuvering his foot into the head of an ant and reaching for a higher grip on a huge eyelid.

"Craig! Quit messing about," Annie said. "It's time we head back."

"But this is a great climbing wall!"

Alex wanted to give it a try. He set his torch on end and slipped off his pack. Gripping the wall as high up as he could, he put his toe into a groove and raised himself up to press flat against the cold stone.

"You have to be careful," Craig called down. "Some of the pieces are loose."

Alex stepped on a carving and felt it shift. "I see what you mean." He tried another. It was solid.

Carefully testing each grip, Alex climbed to the bird with the thin beak. He was convinced it was the same as the one on the board, except it was holding its head up higher. Alex tugged on the top of its head and the bird's whole body swiveled until its thin beak inserted into the wormhole. *There, now it looks just like it does on the board.*

A low rumbling started faintly, with a deep vibration. It grew louder and louder until it shook the cavern walls.

Sure the cave was collapsing, Alex tried to scamper down the wall, but slipped and fell. He could not see the ground to prepare for impact and hit hard. He quickly rolled onto his stomach and covered the back of his head with his hands.

Slowly, the rumbling diminished.

"Alex . . . look!" Annie called.

Alex dragged himself up. Dumbfounded, he saw that the huge snake-haired monster-head had lowered into the ground, its top a sloping ramp leading into a dark interior.

"Wow!" Craig exclaimed. "What happened?"

"Maybe we triggered it to move when we twisted the carvings," Alex said. "It could be that they work like a key – or a secret combination."

Annie shivered and peered into the darkness, her arms wrapped tightly about herself. "What's in there?"

"Treasure?" Craig suggested eagerly.

"Craig, don't." Annie reached for him, but missed. Craig had scampered up the ramp.

Alex held his breath, but the ramp remained motionless. He let out a sigh. "Wait here, I'll get him."

Gingerly Alex stepped onto the top of the head. He jiggled his weight, cautiously at first, then harder. The head did not budge. Slowly Alex climbed up the slope into the black depths. The space above him became smaller. By the time he reached Craig, the ceiling was so low he had to crawl.

Craig was carefully checking crevices. "There has to be treasure in here somewhere," he said.

Alex held up his hand for silence. A low rumbling had started up again. Suddenly, the floor dropped. Annie screamed.

Alex threw a terrified glance back at Annie and saw that the entrance behind them was closing fast. The ramp was tipping like a seesaw, with the end behind Alex and Craig rising up to close off the way they came. With a thundering boom, it came to a halt tipped the opposite way from where it started. Before them was a new opening.

Terrified, Alex scrambled off the ramp, stopping just in time to keep from falling off an edge. Panting hard, he clutched his shaking flashlight with two hands. Taking deep breaths, he forced his breathing to slow. *It's alright*, he told himself. He wasn't squished under falling rock; Craig was next to him, also unhurt. Things could be worse.

He took stock of their surroundings. Below was nothing but blackness as far as his beam could reach. Above, a dim watery reflection of his light shone back at them, as if from far away. They were trapped, perched on a ledge high up the side of a large circular shaft.

"This must be where the aliens launch their spaceships," Craig said quietly.

Alex had to admit, it did look as if they were inside the barrel of a cannon big enough to blast a spaceship into outer space.

Climbing back up the ramp, they found it came to a dead end above what they knew was the head. They jumped up and down and stomped on it, but could not get it to go back down.

"Annie!" Alex shouted into a narrow crack where the block met the rock wall. "Annie, can you hear me?" He listened carefully, shouting her name again and again, but there was no reply.

"I hope she's okay." Craig's voice quavered.

"I'm sure she is." Alex was about to add that it was him and Craig who were not okay, but he bit his tongue. "She can't hear us – that's all. The rock is too thick."

"How will we get out of here?" Craig sounded close to tears.

Alex did not know. He tried to stay calm, but his heart was thumping and there was a ringing in his ears. He knew that if the ramp did not lower back down, they were in a bad situation. Their packs were on the other side with Annie, and they could last only so long without food and water.

A thought struck him. "The ramp started moving after we shifted some of the carvings on the wall," he said. "Let's try that on this side."

To their dismay, they found that the wall of the shaft had no carvings. Craig attempted to climb it, but its surface was too smooth.

Alex shone his light along the ledge. At one end was an abrupt drop-off. At the other, it narrowed until it was no more than a ridge on the side of the shaft.

They were stuck.

Dismayed, Alex pressed his head against the wall. All the climbing gear was with Annie. It was impossible to scale the wall without it. One slip and they would plunge into the blackness below, falling, falling for who knows how long before . . . Alex did not want to think about it. This could be where so many missing people met their end. Down below might be his parents' bones. Would he become a grinning skeleton, perched here on the ledge, or be reunited with his parents in a splintered pile of bones below?

"Let's see where this leads," Craig called.

Craig's light was below the drop-off at the end of the ledge. Alex was incredulous that he would be climbing down the wall. He was about to shout for Craig to climb back up when he noticed that the end of the ledge was not an abrupt drop after all. Below were a series of narrow stone slabs that stuck out from the wall, forming steep steps.

From far below, Craig waved for him to follow.

Alex inched his way down the steps, hardly daring to breathe for fear of losing his balance. At one awful point, the steps came to the tiniest of landings before doubling back in the other direction. By the time he reached Craig, Alex's legs were trembling uncontrollably.

Craig sat with his back to the wall. Before him was a narrow arch that crossed the center of the shaft. At its top was a small circular platform.

"Isn't an arch always stronger than it looks?" Craig asked hopefully.

"Forget it – I'm not crossing that thing."

Alex pulled a piece of chalk from his pocket and flung it over the edge. They leaned forward, listening. Alex held his breath, counting silently. At fifteen, he stopped, having heard nothing.

Craig pulled back. "It can't be bottomless . . . can it?"

Alex held up his hand. "Listen."

From far below, they faintly heard what sounded like moaning. Alex felt his neck hairs rising. It was similar to what he had heard when he'd gone searching for Vanessa.

"It's them," Craig said, frightened. He drew up his knees. "Do you think I hit a ghoulie with my chalk?"

Alex's attempt at humor fell flat. Wide-eyed, Craig suddenly leapt up. Arms outstretched, he scampered up the narrow arch.

"Wait!" Alex scrambled to catch him, but partway up, his legs started trembling, his eyes lost their focus, and the arch wavered. Alex dropped to his hands and knees and took to crawling.

The eerie sounds from below were becoming stronger. They resembled the babble of thousands of people speaking at once, rising up, coming closer – close enough for Alex to imagine that at any moment ghoul-like creatures would claw at his feet. A shriek shattered the air. Alex leapt up, running the rest of the way up the arch. At the top, Craig was standing stock-still on the circular platform.

"Get down!" Alex prayed the platform would offer some shelter from what lay below. They curled up and pressed their hands tight against their ears to block out the awful noises. It was futile – the cackling, shouting, moaning, and shrieking were all around them. In the grip of an ice-cold fear, Alex watched ghostly gray shadows flash up and vanish. Nonsensical words leapt out from the roar, as if all of humanity swirled and spun around them. There were flashing moments of joy and unbearable screeches of pain. Contorted, shadowy faces and figures emerged and disappeared in seconds: a chalk white, screaming newborn with the face of a bat; a severed hand that twitched; leering faces with menacing eyes.

Alex felt that it was not the gray shadows, but him and Craig who were spinning, bucking, heaving among the howling masses. The watery ceiling Alex had seen earlier as a tranquil shimmering surface was now a twisting vortex, a multicolored cyclone. It seemed to be slowly descending on them – or were they rising up to it? Alex no longer knew if it was him or his surroundings that were moving, spinning, rising, falling; if the shrieks were from the shadows around them, or from Craig, or from himself. Numb with shock, Alex saw the howling whirlpool vortex spin around them. Then, mercifully, all went dark and still.

PART II

A Change in Time

8

WITHIN DARK FORESTS

Alex felt as if he were awakening from a very, very, deep sleep.

Wherever he was, it was warm and bright. He slowly raised his head and squinted against the sun. He was on a grassy knoll of an otherwise rocky hilltop, where the blue horizon stretched out in all directions and where clouds drifted lazily overhead. Curled up beside him was Craig. Alex gently shook his shoulder.

"Where are we?" Bewildered, Craig blinked slowly, as though, with each blink, he thought all this would go away and he would be back in a dark cave, or maybe even back in his bed waking up from a bad dream.

"I have no idea."

"Where's Annie?"

Alex frowned. "She's probably going back through the caves to get help. If we can get from here to the coast fast enough, we might meet her when she comes out."

"Won't she be surprised!" Craig managed a small chuckle.

Alex tried to spot the ocean past the surrounding hill-tops. He wished he had Annie's compass. Everything they'd brought was left with Annie. But where were the caves and that circular chamber, and how did he and Craig get from there to here?

Alex scuffed away some tufts of grass and moss, thinking that perhaps they'd been blasted up from somewhere far below. But there were no openings in the ground anywhere near them – not even so much as a rabbit burrow. The rock under them looked completely solid.

Alex and Craig climbed a crest and were overjoyed to see the ocean sparkling off in the distance. Between them and the sea was a densely wooded valley that was nestled between rocky, tree-studded hills.

"Anything look familiar?" Alex asked hopefully.

Craig shifted his gaze from up and down the coast to inland. "I didn't even know there were forests in this part of Scotland," he said. "Maybe we'll figure it out when we get down to the coastal road."

"That one?" Alex pointed to a small dirt road that came out from between two distant hills and disappeared in the forested valley.

"No, of course not – that's just a country lane. The coastal road is, you know, paved. It has a yellow line in the middle and signs on it like STRAITH MEIRN, 2 MILES."

"I don't see a coastal road."

"It's got to be there. It goes up and down the whole coast."

Alex shrugged. "Well then," he said, "let's head for the coast."

After looking for the best route, they decided they had no

choice but to climb down the side of the hill and follow the country road right through the forest.

"Look!" Alex pointed to where the sun glinted off some riding helmets. There were about a dozen people riding horses two abreast.

Craig shaded his eyes. "Looks like fox hunters – they're going at quite a clip."

They watched the riders pound down the winding dirt road until they rounded a bend and disappeared into the forest.

Alex worried that they might not get to the coast in time to meet Annie. "Let's hope there's traffic on that road," he said. "Maybe we can wave down a car and find out where we are, or maybe even get a ride."

"We shouldn't ask strangers for a ride – it's dangerous."

"Well, we certainly wouldn't want to do anything dangerous, would we?" Alex's sarcasm was lost on Craig.

Slowly they picked their way down the hillside. To cross a shallow, swampy section, they had to hop from rock to rock. Soon they lost sight of the ocean behind the hills; then their view of the valley was blocked by trees.

Alex was relieved when the terrain became less rocky. Surely the road could not be much farther. Once they found it, he estimated that, even on foot, they might make it to the coast in an hour or so.

<hr>

Suddenly out of nowhere leapt a wild man with matted hair, dirty rags for clothes, and a nasty glint in his eye. He landed on the path, his arms outstretched to block anyone getting past.

Alex shrieked. He turned to run, but another foul-looking man leapt onto the path behind them, blocking their escape.

"*Hee, hee, hee* – got ye." The first man laughed evilly, revealing stumps of rotted black teeth. The two men moved closer.

Craig bolted. One of the men caught him by the arm and cruelly twisted it behind his back. Alex jumped onto the man, grabbing his hairy arm to pry Craig loose. He felt a hard blow on the side of his head, followed by another from his face hitting the ground. When he struggled to get up, a kick to his side knocked him back down into the dirt.

Craig was screaming. One of the men barked, "Shuddup, shuddup," and there was the sickening sound of a fist hitting flesh. Craig, tossed to the ground, fell silent. Alex tried to reach Craig, but he felt a tremendous weight stomp on his back and another hard cuff to his head.

"Don't ye move," one of the men growled.

Alex could taste blood. A terrible pain throbbed in his head and in his back, where one of the men continued to press down hard with his foot.

"Damn noise was enough for Wallace's men to hear," said one in a low voice. "Kill 'em if they make another sound."

"We might get some ransom money for these two," said the other. "Seems to me someone'll pay for 'em. They're no sons of peasants."

Alex felt rough hands pull out the contents of his pockets, including some chalk and loose change.

"Look at this silver – and look at their breeks 'n' what else they're wearing. I say these two are from some visiting nobility."

"It's too risky trying to git ransom money from nobility," the other said. "We'll have a whole bloody army after us. Let's club 'em and be done with it."

A cold clammy chill went through Alex. Lying pressed to the ground, he saw the foot of one of the men not far from his face. His shoe was no more than a piece of leather tied to his foot. Knowing he had nothing to lose, Alex lunged and sank his teeth as hard as he could into the back of the man's ankle. The man shrieked and jerked his foot away. Catching a glimpse of a gnarled club swinging down at his head, Alex let go and pulled back. The club missed and hit the dirt with a thud. But Alex knew it would come down again at any second. He desperately tried to squirm out from under the man's foot, tensing for a blow that would end it all.

Alex heard a short gasp. A heavy weight fell across his back. There was a gurgling sound. He wriggled out from under the twitching weight and scrambled to his feet. One of the men was sprinting away. The other was on the ground, a look of amazement in his eyes as he stared down at an arrow protruding from his chest. The man made another gurgling noise, and bubbles of blood appeared in his gaping mouth. Then he lay still, his unblinking eyes staring blankly at Alex.

"Craig!" Alex dropped to his knees and put a hand on Craig's shoulder. "Are you okay?"

Craig slowly rolled his head to one side. "Are they gone?" He looked up at Alex. Under his puffy eye was a nasty black bruise.

"Sort of." Alex spoke as calmly as he could. "But don't worry. They won't hurt us anymore."

Off to one side, Alex noticed a movement. A tall lean man with dark hair stood quietly watching them, his head tilted quizzically. The longbow tucked under his arm had an arrow loosely notched in position. Alex eyed him warily, wondering if he was another thief, perhaps a rival of those who attacked them. The man dressed strangely: his jacket and trousers looked like they were made of green-dyed deerskin, vaguely similar to the deerskin jackets Alex had seen in the United States – except there, the jackets had fringes under each arm to shoo away mosquitoes and blackflies, and had buttons or zippers. This man's jacket was closed by laces, which crisscrossed up the front. He also wore a peculiar cap with flaps that hung loosely down the sides, looking like they could be tied under his chin if his ears got cold.

Alex helped Craig to his feet. The boys edged away from the body. Alex stared at it in morbid fascination. It was unsettling that the thief, who just a few moments ago was so full of life, was now some inert thing. This was not one of the casual deaths of his daydreams; this one gave him a queasy sensation, and he had to breathe deeply to keep it down. There was a curious buzzing in his ears. Feeling dizzy, Alex put a hand on a tree for support and gulped in air.

The deerskin-clad man bent over the body and abruptly yanked out his arrow. "I don't like killin' these rogues," he said, casually wiping the blood from his arrow onto the dead man's clothes. "Most of them are doing no more than trying to feed their own bairns the only way they know how. God knows it's hard enough to make an honest living without the likes of Hesselrigge making it damn near impossible."

Alex's nausea rose each time he looked at the dead thief, so he turned to face the other way. "Thank you for saving us, sir," he said timidly.

The man looked sharply at Alex, his eyes dwelling briefly on his clothes and shoes. "Ye speak strangely, m'lad, and your garments are unlike any I've seen. Where are ye from?"

"Canada."

The man stared at him blankly.

"I'm here to spend the summer with my aunt, but she's sick so I'm staying with the McRaes."

"McRaes, ye say? And what's your name?"

"Alex Macpherson, sir. And this is my friend, Craig McRae."

"Very good." The man nodded in apparent satisfaction. "Sir Ellerslie's my name. I'll send some men out to your clans. They'll be glad, I'm sure, to learn that ye two are safe. Now, tell me, what brings ye boys here wandering about these woods?"

"My mother disappeared," Craig said. "And, long ago, Alex's parents disappeared too. We're looking for them."

"Disappeared, ye say?" Sir Ellerslie clicked his tongue sympathetically. "I'll no be surprised if Hesselrigge's behind it. Has there been a demand for ransom?"

Alex and Craig glanced at each other. It had never occurred to Alex that his parents might have been kidnapped. And there was that name – Hesselrigge – again. Where, oh where, had he heard that name before? Alex shook his head. "Not that I know of, sir."

Sir Ellerslie turned away. "Ah well, no need to fear the worst."

Alex was convinced Sir Ellerslie thought his parents were dead.

Sir Ellerslie grabbed the dead man's ragged tunic and dragged him off the trail. "I'll send one of my men around to dig him under," he said, giving the body a heave to roll it beneath low-hanging branches. "If the wolves don't get to 'm first."

He gestured into the woods. "Come. I'll take ye to our camp."

There didn't seem to be anything else to do. Confused and hesitant, Alex followed Sir Ellerslie, Craig at his side. He did not understand why the man would want to have the body buried, except maybe to keep animals from eating it before the police came. No, that did not make sense: it would not take long for the police to come – once they'd been called. Surely he wouldn't be trying to hide the body; surely the police would understand that Sir Ellerslie killed the thief only to save Alex and Craig? Alex wondered if Sir Ellerslie was wanted by the police. He *was* a bit strange, referring to himself as "Sir" Ellerslie as if he were some kind of nobility. . . .

Once deep in the forest, they were quite secluded. Sir Ellerslie did not follow anything that even remotely appeared to be a trail, yet he led them without hesitation. The forest seemed to go on forever. They wound around gnarly, sticky pines, over moss-covered boulders, and through ravines with tiny creeks filled with slippery rocks.

Alex was relieved when they finally came upon a road.

He hoped they could catch a ride with someone, or, at the very least, make faster and easier progress. At the edge of the road, Sir Ellerslie stopped abruptly. He had them stand still while he listened. Satisfied no one was coming, he had them quickly cross the road and wait while he used a pine branch to carefully brush away any sign of their footprints. To Alex's dismay, they then headed into even denser forest.

For the most part, they hiked in silence. Sir Ellerslie had told Alex and Craig to avoid stepping on thin twigs that snap underfoot. At long last, Alex spotted a break in the trees. Craig wiped his brow with relief.

Sir Ellerslie knelt on the forest floor and motioned for Alex and Craig to come nearer. "I need to have a spy at Hesselrigge's castle before we head to our camp," he said. "I'll need ye to follow close behind me and do what I do. Above all, be very, very quiet – your lives depend on it."

As he crept from tree to tree, Craig exaggeratedly copied Sir Ellerslie's every movement. Sir Ellerslie didn't seem to mind, so long as Craig made no noise. The last few yards, they squirmed on their stomachs to the edge of the forest. Carefully, they parted the foliage.

Alex gasped. Perched high on shoreline cliffs was a fully intact medieval castle, complete with flags fluttering from its many turrets and armored soldiers standing guard on tall battlemented walls. Behind it sparkled a bright blue sea.

Alex gazed in awe, trying to imagine how, in an age prior to cannons, any army could take such a castle by force. Mere arrows and spears, or even catapults, could not possibly be a match for its massive walls.

The countryside about the castle bustled with people. Farmers hoed small, irregular gardening plots. Carts trundled down dirt paths – some pulled by hand, others by oxen. Thatched dwellings clustered about an intersection where a meandering coastal road met the road coming from the forest.

Surprisingly, despite the presence of so many in peasant and soldier costumes, there was no sign of tourists. Alex cupped his hand over Craig's ear. "Where are we?"

Craig raised his palms and shrugged. "I don't know. . . . The cliffs look familiar though."

Now that he mentioned it, they did look a lot like the cliffs near the McRaes' farm. It appeared as if the castle had been built atop the very ruins of the former Duncragglin Castle. Even the harbor looked similar. Although he could not see over the edge of the cliffs, Alex would not have been surprised to find a beach looking just like the one where he had found the carved board.

The double doors of the central blockhouse suddenly swung outward, and armored horsemen burst out at full gallop. Two abreast, they thundered over the drawbridge and down an earthen ramp to the roadway below. Sweeping through the main gates, they charged down the road, ignoring the plight of those who struggled to pull their carts and oxen out of the way.

Craig edged further back into the woods. "Are they coming to get us?" he asked nervously.

Sir Ellerslie gave him a reassuring smile. "Nae, m'lad. We're too far for them to have seen us."

"But, they could have seen us with binoculars," Craig said, his fear growing as the horsemen drew nearer.

"With what?" Sir Ellerslie looked puzzled. He pulled Craig down. "Wait right here 'til they're past."

Alex felt his heart pounding as the armed horsemen rounded the bend and came to within yards of where they lay. The horsemen scanned the forest, occasionally appearing to look straight at them. To Alex's great relief, they stuck to the road, rounded another bend, and disappeared into the forest.

"Knight James Barr is with them," Sir Ellerslie muttered grimly. "Off, cap in hand, to plead to King Edward Plantagenet for reinforcements, I suspect."

"Reinforcements?" Alex was confused. First they find themselves with an archer who saved them from robbers, but appears to be on the run from the authorities; now they find a castle where knights in armor are charging out to ask a king for more troops. This all appeared to be some kind of grand historical re-enactment.

"Aye, Hesselrigge's spies would have told him that an uprising is imminent. He'll want reinforcements to help him stamp it out. Better to take him now, before Barr makes it back with more men."

"An uprising?" Alex no longer expected an answer that made sense.

"And a bloody great uprising it will be too. The people around here have had enough of this murderous pawn of the English. It's time to put things right." Sir Ellerslie got up. "Come, let us tarry here no more; there's work to be done."

Once again, Alex and Craig found themselves in dense forest, running to keep up with Sir Ellerslie as he slipped soundlessly through the woods ahead.

Craig had trouble keeping up. Alex, too, was getting tired. He was also hungry and thirsty. They had not eaten since before they left Annie, and that felt like a very long time ago.

Thinking about Annie all alone in the underground chambers gave Alex an ache of fear. He tried to reassure himself by remembering how resourceful and organized she was and how she could follow the string back the way they came – but it didn't work. All sorts of things could have gone wrong for her . . . terribly wrong.

They crested a hill and spotted a clear blue loch tucked snugly in the surrounding hills.

Craig stopped dead.

"What now?" Alex asked.

"That's . . . that's our loch, Loch Karins." Craig's hand trembled as he pointed. "But there's no farm . . . and all these trees . . ."

Alex had to admit, the loch did look a lot like the one next to the McRaes' farm. *Lochs kind of look alike*, he thought.

Craig, however, could not be shaken. "It's the same," he mumbled. "Every rock . . ."

"These trees can't have grown overnight." Alex impatiently tugged on Craig's arm. "Quickly now, we need to catch up."

Sir Ellerslie held up a hand for them to stop and be silent. He stood listening carefully and hooted softly three times. With a chill, Alex saw archers materialize on all sides, their taut longbows pointing straight at them. Alex slowly dropped the stick he was carrying.

Sir Ellerslie stared directly into the archers' arrows with no sign of alarm. "I hate haggis," he announced.

"That'll be the password." A bowman signaled for the others to lower their bows.

"Why, look, it's Sir Ellerslie!" exclaimed another. "It's about time ye made it back. We'd almost given ye up for dead."

One bowman kept his bow up. He scowled from behind his stringy, dirty-blond hair. "Who be these charges?" he demanded. "Have ye taken hostages?"

Sir Ellerslie laughed. "Dinnae be daft, Rorie. These lads are from the McRae and Macpherson clans. I found them on the other side of the forest, looking for lost parents. Had I been a few seconds later, robbers would've left 'm for the crows."

The first bowman walked slowly around the boys. He stroked his pointy beard, examining them with great interest. Grasping the collar of Alex's shirt between his fingers, he leaned in closely. "The McRaes and the Macphersons must be doing very well to garb their young ones so. Have ye taken a look at the stitching in their fabric? I've never seen anything like it – so small and so perfect."

"Aye, Malcolm, it's strange," Sir Ellerslie admitted. "Their speech is peculiar too."

"These clans must be in with the English." Rorie pulled his bow back to full extension. "We cannae take chances."

Sir Ellerslie moved in front of the boys. "These lads are under my protection," he stated flatly. "And you are to put your bow down."

"But, they could be spies," Rorie persisted.

"I know they are not." Sir Ellerslie's eyes narrowed. "And that should be good enough for ye, Rorie."

Malcolm stepped between them and brushed aside Rorie's bow. "Let us be more courteous to these lads," he said lightly.

"I do believe that the McRae and Macpherson clans are on the right side of this conflict, but we can hardly expect them to come to our assistance if we mistreat some of their own."

"Aye, and Groenie will be glad of the help that these lads can provide." Considering the matter settled, Sir Ellerslie put a friendly hand on Malcolm's shoulder and turned his back to Rorie. "Good to see you, old friend. Come, let's get back to camp. I've a lot to tell Wallace."

The bowmen accompanied them through the forest. They passed close by the small loch, and Alex found himself picturing where Mr. McRae's farmhouse would be.

"Just over that ridge is a hollow," Craig said. "My guess is, that's where they've set up camp."

Alex gave Craig a skeptical glance. He could barely see that there was a ridge up ahead through the trees, much less a hollow somewhere past it.

"You'll see. We get to it through the split rock."

Alex was worried. It had been a difficult day (to say the least) and Craig seemed to be cracking under the strain. They appeared to be on a movie set for *Robin Hood*. Perhaps the actors were just practicing their roles. If so, Alex was not amused. He resolved to get away from these strange people at the earliest opportunity and to set out in the direction of the sea. Surely he would come upon a road. He remembered that the coastal road from the airport to the McRaes' farm had yellow emergency telephones every mile or so. He needed to reach one and call the police. . . .

"There." Craig had a look of triumph. "Do you believe me now?"

Alex stared in amazement. Up ahead, there was indeed a split rock – a very big split rock. It looked as if the hill itself had been cracked open. They followed a path between the towering jagged halves. Alex looked up and spotted more bowmen on either side.

"I hate haggis!" Malcolm bellowed. The guards lowered their bows.

The passageway opened into a small hidden dale, much as Craig had described. A central clearing contained many tents and bustled with more movie-set material. Target practice was taking place on one side, with archers firing at straw men. On the other, men clashed in mock fights with wooden staffs. Everyone was wearing long pullovers of some scratchy material bound up by a sword-belt. There were no jeans or T-shirts in sight.

A surprisingly tall, broad-shouldered man threw back the flap of one of the bigger tents and strode forward to greet them. He had a keen and commanding air.

"Sir Ellerslie! Welcome!" The big man extended a large hand. "What word have ye from the outlying areas?"

"The Foster and the McLeod clans to the west stand ready to join ye, Wallace," Sir Ellerslie replied. "I've yet to reach the McRae and Macpherson clans to the north, but suggest we do so now and ask whether they be prepared to send their men-in-arms. We can also tell them that two of their young sons are safe with us, although we know not the fate of the parents they seek."

Wallace turned to Alex and Craig. "I am sorry to hear that y'r parents are missing," he said. "If Hesselrigge is behind this, we will either have 'm freed or have their vengeance, for Hesselrigge's days are numbered."

"If I may, sir," Alex began hesitantly. With this meeting, the events of the past day came sharply into focus, leading him to an impossible-but-inescapable conclusion. "But would you be Sir William Wallace?"

"I'm no Sir William, but Wallace I am, in person." He gave Alex a friendly mock bow.

"Can you please tell me what year this is?" Alex asked.

"What an odd question. Why, it is the year of our Lord 1296, of course. Why do ye ask?"

"Because, sir," Alex replied slowly, thinking carefully of what he had read, "I want to know if your greatest victories are still to come, or if they are behind you."

"And tell me, young lad," Wallace said, "what are my great victories?"

Alex flushed. "I do not know them all, sir, but I know there are many." He paused, not sure where to begin. "There's the defeat of the English at a narrow bridge – half of the English army crosses and your men charge over a hill and catch them by surprise."

"What a tremendously good idea! I know just the bridge to try that, should the English be foolish enough to cross it." Wallace laughed. "And when all is said and done, who rules Scotland?"

"The Scots, sir, but not before –" Alex stopped abruptly, his face turning red.

"Before what?" Wallace demanded.

Alex tried to speak, but his throat was too tight. Stuck in his mind was the awful image from his comic book of Wallace being executed and butchered by the English. He shook his head.

"That bad, is it?" Wallace said grimly. He straightened, reached over his shoulder, and drew a huge sword from the scabbard across his back, giving Alex a terrible fright.

"Ye heard the lad," he roared, holding his great sword high. "Scotland will be ruled by Scots. For liberty!"

Metal flashed as everyone around them drew their swords and raised them high. "For liberty!" they cried out.

"To victory!" Wallace bellowed, thrusting his sword higher still.

"To victory!" the men roared in reply.

"Come." Wallace slid his sword back into its scabbard and placed his arm around Sir Ellerslie's shoulders. "Let us plan for war."

9

Captives of a Rebel Camp

"Take 'm to the hold," Rorie demanded.

A guard stepped forward, but Malcolm blocked his way. "There's no need for that," he snapped. "Ellerslie has vouched for these lads and said they'll be put to good use."

A short, stout man with a large apron wrapped around his sizeable middle raised his hand. "I could use some help."

"Well, then, Groenie, these lads are your new assistants." Malcolm clapped both Alex and Craig on the shoulder. "Treat 'm well, and may they last longer than the other assistant we gave ye."

Groenie scowled. "It was no my fault Sandy cut off his thumb."

"Give 'm some dinner, for starters, and make 'm a bed. They've had a long hard day. In the morn, they'll be ready to assist ye with your tasks."

Malcolm leaned in. "Groenie is our cook," he said to Alex and Craig in a low voice. "He'll make sure you're not idle during y'r stay with us, but do keep out of his way, especially when he gets in a temper – and *do* be careful with the knife." Malcolm laughed and shoved them toward Groenie. "We don't need extra bits in our stew."

Still scowling, Groenie led them around the far side of the tent. Staked and roped poles held up a long canvas awning that sheltered benches and tables. They passed a partly butchered deer. Its head hung limply over the edge of a table, a bucket catching the blood that dribbled from a wide slice across its neck.

Groenie thrust bowls into their hands. Then he plunged a ladle into a large cauldron, which hung suspended from a tripod of poles lashed over a small fire, and poured some strong-smelling brown stew into their bowls. Grunting for them to sit, he tossed them each a piece of crusty bread ripped from a large loaf.

Under normal circumstances, Alex would never have eaten such a foul-smelling stew, not even were he under the wrathful glare of his uncle. However, he was ravenous, and he knew his chances of getting anything else to eat were zero-to-none. He raised a spoonful and sniffed it cautiously. Alex knew that the gristly chunks were animal bits, but could not tell which parts of the animal they came from. He wondered numbly if Sandy's thumb was in the pot.

"Offal," Alex mumbled.

"You're right." Craig gave an extraloud slurp. "Awful good."

"No, offal. That means parts of an animal other than meat; you know, like the brain or something . . . oh, forget it." Craig was too busy slurping to listen.

Hunger got the better of Alex – he took in a small spoonful. It was chewy and tangy, but not too bad. He tried another.

Before he knew it, both he and Craig were looking down at empty bowls. Still hungry, he glanced over at the cauldron, then at Groenie, who was busy chopping greens. With some trepidation, Alex got up, bowl in hand, and approached Groenie. He was acutely aware of what happened to the Oliver Twist of his comic book when he was in this situation.

"Please, sir, can I have some more?" Alex asked timidly.

Groenie swung up his cutting knife. "How dare ye! That stew has to feed a whole army, and none of the men ever ask for more."

Dejected, Alex slumped back down.

"Alright, alright, here ye go, then." Groenie roughly slopped another ladleful into their bowls. "Just this once." He held up a hand. "Dinnae thank me, I'm going to make ye work double hard for it. See all them buckets? When ye are done stuffing y'r greedy guts, ye can each use a yoke to carry two at a time to fill 'm down by the loch."

Alex glanced at the buckets. He could do that.

For now, the only sounds were the distant voices of the men, the occasional snort from a faraway horse, the chopping and scraping of Groenie's knife on the cutting block, and the puffing and slurping of Alex and Craig cooling and eating their stew.

Craig looked up from his bowl. "What's William Wallace doing here? Didn't he live long ago?"

"Don't you get it?" Alex wiped his mouth, his hunger finally satisfied enough to talk between sips. "That chamber we were in, the one you thought was a spaceship launcher, it teleported us back in time over seven hundred years."

"So, we're not even born yet?"

"Of course we're born – we're here, aren't we?"

They mulled this over in silence. Craig picked a gristly bit out of his mouth and laid it carefully next to his bowl. "I wonder if my mum or your parents are here."

"Who knows?" Alex sighed. He was tired of trying to make sense of it all. Even if his parents were here, how would he find them? What if they were teleported back even further and were really old now? How would he recognize them? The effort to think through these questions made his head hurt. It occurred to him that they might never find a way to get back to their own time . . . that he and Craig might become two more missing persons, never to be heard from again. . . .

———— •·•·• ————

"Water! Now!" Groenie punctuated every word with a stab of his knife.

Alex felt a surge of anger. He considered refusing, but because Groenie'd given them the extra bowl of stew, he stumbled to his feet.

The meal had made him feel sleepy. He wanted to curl up somewhere, just about anywhere, tuck a blanket under his chin, and fall asleep. He forced himself to investigate the yoke. It was no more than a long stick with hooks on either end. There was a flat section in the middle to rest across his shoulders.

The boys headed for the loch, empty buckets swinging from their yokes, and approached the split rock. Abruptly, two burly guards stepped forward, barring the path with their spears. "Halt! Where do ye think ye're going?"

"We're off to get water." Alex thought this must be obvious, seeing how they were carrying empty buckets, but the guards did not move. "Groenie sent us," he added.

One of the guards hesitated. He jerked his head in the direction of the path and lifted his spear out of the way. "Off ye go, then."

The other guard protested. "Rorie said no one was to leave camp. No exceptions is what he said."

"Dinnae be daft. Groenie needs water to cook. D'ye want a meal at the end of the day or no? Besides, he'll cut off their thumbs if they come back empty-handed."

"Aye, true." The guard chuckled. "We don't want any more of 'm in our stew."

"Keep an eye out for any scouts Hesselrigge may have running about," said the first guard. "If ye're no back in ten minutes, we'll send some men out to look for ye."

The other guard laughed. "To look for what's left of 'm, ye mean to say."

Alex spotted more guards high up on the rocks overlooking the trail. He felt their watchful eyes following them as they passed. Well along the path, Craig stopped and pointed into the woods. "Let's take a shortcut – the loch is just over that rise."

Trudging through the dense forest, Alex tried to keep his buckets from banging against trees. The noise made him nervous. He recalled his encounter with the thieves all too well.

Once over the rise, sure enough, the loch came into view. The late-afternoon sun flashed off windblown ripples. They came to the water's edge at a rocky section, where they could lower and fill their buckets without getting their feet wet.

"My favorite hiding place is around that bend." Craig nodded towards a steep embankment. "Let's check it out before we head back."

Stepping-stones in the water allowed them to follow the shoreline past the embankment. About to round the bend, Craig stopped and pulled back abruptly.

Alex bumped into him, waving his arms to keep from slipping into the water. "Watch it, will you?"

"*Shh!* There are people over there."

"People? What do they look like?"

"Soldiers. They're wearing armor and they have swords and shields."

"Let me see." Alex squeezed past Craig and peered around the embankment. Horses were grazing on clumps of grass at the water's edge. Several soldiers sat with their backs against the trees, watching over them. From behind the tree line came flashes of sun reflecting off metal. Men were moving about within the forest.

Alex's eyes fixed on one person – a man who wore a red-dyed deerskin jacket. The man turned and stared, as if aware of being watched.

Fearing he was spotted, Alex scrambled back quickly, leaping from stone to stone.

"What about the buckets?" Craig called.

"Forget about them. Run!" Alex said, heart pounding.

Alex and Craig sprinted back up the trail. They knew the guards would be watching from high up on the rocks. Sure enough, they stood with their bows drawn.

"I hate haggis," Alex gasped without slowing down.

Panting heavily, they ran up to the tent where they had last seen Wallace and Sir Ellerslie. They tried to rush past a guard at the entrance, but the guard grabbed them roughly by the arms and held them back.

"Into the hold with 'm!" he roared.

Two other guards rushed forward and seized the boys.

"Sir Ellerslie!" Alex shouted. "Help!"

A cuff to the side of his head cut him off. Before he could get a breath to yell again, a gloved hand roughly covered his mouth and turned his head about.

"Be still, or I will have ye gagged," the guard hissed.

"But we saw soldiers, down by –" Alex's protests were cut off by another blow to the head. Numb and confused, he allowed himself to be marched away. They came to the far side of the sprawling camp, where iron manacles hung from a log lashed high between trees.

A scrawny, hunched man with long greasy hair emerged from a small lean-to. "Captives!" he cackled, breaking into a nearly toothless grin. He rubbed his gnarly hands together. "It's about time someone brought me some captives."

Chuckling gleefully, he snapped manacle irons tight around their ankles. He roughly raised Alex's and Craig's arms and snapped manacles onto their wrists, leaving them standing with arms stretched uncomfortably high over their heads.

The guard rubbed his big nose on his sleeve. "Keep a close watch on these two, Jack. They were caught trying to force their way into Wallace's chambers. If they babble any lies about soldiers and the like, make sure they regret it."

A second, older guard spoke up: "But don't get too

excited, Jack. No decision has been made on what to do with 'm. They came into camp under Sir Ellerslie's protection, so ye'd best not start flogging 'm yet."

A look of disappointment spread over Jack's face. "What? Am I to just sit here and watch 'm, then?" He pulled back clumps of hair with his dirty fingers. "We're fighting a war with Hesselrigge, and this is the best ye can bring me by way of captives?"

"Patience, Jack, patience," said the older guard. "We'll get ye more captives before long. Wallace may want a confession flogged out o' these two yet. But lower those wrist chains so they can lie down. I don't want to get into trouble with Sir Ellerslie. We'll have to wait and see what the morn may bring."

Jack turned to the other guard for support, but he scowled and looked away. Reluctantly Jack climbed onto a crate and cranked long spokes that stuck through the log. The log turned, slowly unwrapping the coiled chains.

"A wee bit more, Jack," the older guard ordered quietly.

Cursing, Jack cranked the spokes until the wrist chains almost reached the ground. "That does it!" he grumbled, as he stiffly stepped off the crate. "That's as far as it goes. I hope ye bring me better news the morrow. I didn't become a jailer to be sitting about with bairns. I suppose I'm to feed and water them and give 'm blankets too? *Bah*." Jack spat.

The ratty blanket Jack threw them stank. When Alex looked at it closely, he could see tiny bugs scurrying about in the dirty weaves. Still, it was a cold night and he and Craig had little choice but to use it, lying back-to-back for warmth, their manacled hands dangling a foot off the ground.

They chose not to touch the moldy dried chunk of bread Jack flung at them, nor did they drink the dirty water he placed barely within reach in a battered metal bowl. Alex shifted his weight to avoid a rock that was digging into his side. He hoped it would not rain, doubting very much that Jack would give them shelter.

The night passed slowly. Alex heard the sounds from the camp gradually die down until there was only the occasional snort of a horse and far-off snores. His head lying awkwardly in the dirt, Alex hoped Sir Ellerslie would come to help them. He wished very hard to try to make it happen. Sometimes, when playing cards, wishing very hard would make the right card come up. Someone once told him if you want to win, you have to learn how to wish.

Alex could feel Craig's back shaking and knew he was crying. He wanted to console him, to say something – anything – that might cheer him up, but nothing came to mind. Wishing someone could hear his wishes, he thought the night would never end.

———◆———

Alex must have slept as he suddenly noticed it was light. There were noises all around him, loud noises. He raised his head from the dirt and painfully turned his neck.

It was Groenie. He was in a right state. "What's going on here?" he shouted. "These two were given to me. I cannae do all the cooking by myself all the time. Let 'm loose."

"Ye know I cannae do that." Jack gave Groenie a rude gesture. "Go away."

Clutching his carving knife with a white-knuckle grip, Groenie turned on Alex. "Where are my buckets?" he shrieked. "Where did ye good-for-nothing vermin leave my buckets?"

"I don't know," Alex replied dully.

"What do ye mean, ye dinnae ken?" Groenie roared. "Tell me now, or I'll carve ye like dinner."

"Ask Malcolm." Alex wearily closed his eyes and pretended to fall asleep. He kept them shut even as he felt Groenie's boot nudge him, rocking him back and forth.

Groenie looked up at the jailer. "What did ye do to 'm?"

"Not a bloody thing. Maybe today they'll let me make 'm talk."

"When they do, find out where they left my buckets."

Groenie stomped away. Jack shuffled back over to his lean-to. Chains rattled as Craig sat up behind him.

"Good morning, Craig." Alex tried not to sound miserable. "Nice day, isn't it?"

Craig's chains rattled some more as he rubbed his eyes. "It's a beautiful day in the neighborhood."

In spite of everything, Alex managed a laugh. He sat up stiffly and stretched, looking around their open-air jail. "So," he said, "how are we supposed to find the toilet with all these chains on?"

Craig pointed to the bucket Jack had left next to the water bowl.

"What, no toilet paper?" Alex threw up his hands in dismay.

"Where do we wash our hands?" Craig asked. "What would Mum say?" The smile slowly faded.

108 A CHANGE IN TIME

"I think she would say, 'Thanks for trying to find me, Craig,'" Alex said quietly.

"Who would have thought we'd end up here?" Craig smiled wryly, holding up his manacled hands.

"Well." Alex took a deep breath. "I wonder what's for breakfast." He looked about as if expecting to find it sizzling in a skillet somewhere nearby.

Craig raised a finger. "How about we put in an order for scrambled eggs and toast?"

"Good idea!" Alex spoke to an imaginary waiter. "And can I also have some freshly squeezed orange juice, please?"

They sat cross-legged, tucked imaginary napkins under their chins, picked up pretend cutlery, and dug into the breakfast of their dreams.

"This French toast is the best." Eyes closed dreamily, Alex took another bite of thin air. "Pass the maple syrup, please."

The talk of food was making Alex hungry. He glanced over to Jack's lean-to and wondered if they would get anything other than the moldy chunk of bread that still lay in the dirt next to the toilet bucket and the water bowl. Perhaps if they got rid of it, they would get something else. Alex stood and kicked it into a cluster of bushes.

Jack's blood-chilling voice came from behind. "Ye don't want my bread, now do ye?" Somewhere in his voice, Alex detected a note of intense pleasure. "I gi' ye a piece of my bread out of the kindness of my heart, and ye just kick it away." Jack sauntered over to the bushes and stooped to retrieve the bread. He spat on it and smacked it down on a stump, well out of reach.

"The time will come when ye will be begging me to gi' ye this piece of bread – seeing how it's the last food ye'll get!"

With a gleeful snort, Jack headed back to his lean-to. He stopped to look toward the camp interior and squinted. Alex followed his gaze and felt his heart leap. Malcolm was striding purposefully in their direction, his pointy beard hitting his chest as he walked.

Alex was delighted – his plan had worked! Groenie must have demanded that Malcolm tell him where the buckets were, and Malcolm then learned that they were jailed.

Jack stepped forward to block Malcolm's way. "What's your business here?"

"Don't bother me, Jack." Malcolm shouldered him aside without breaking his stride.

He stopped before Alex and Craig and folded his arms. "So, m'lads, a fine pot of trouble ye find yourselves in." Malcolm's frown was gone, but no smile replaced it.

"I was only trying to see Sir Ellerslie to tell him –" Alex began.

Malcolm held up his hand. "That's not the issue here." He shook his head somberly. "Our emissary is back from the Macpherson and the McRae clans and he brought us news. The clans will join us in our efforts to overthrow Hesselrigge and are mobilizing their men as we speak." Malcolm's hand fell. "But both the Macphersons and the McRaes disavow any knowledge of ye two. Now, what I've come to ask is, how can that be?"

Alex's heart sank. How could he explain to Malcolm that they did not know them as they were not born yet and would not be born for over seven hundred years? His mind raced as he tried to think of something plausible to say. A weak and obvious lie would only make matters worse, but so would the unbelievable, ludicrous truth.

Craig finally broke the silence. "Please, sir," he began hesitantly. "They don't know us as we have come from another time."

Malcolm's face grew dark, his eyes all but disappearing behind his bunched eyebrows. "Don't be telling me that ye be wizards, as these we burn at the stake." He stepped back. "Rorie's right – we have no choice but to leave ye here until we learn the truth." With that, he turned to leave.

"Wait!" Alex called. "I need to tell Sir Ellerslie something important . . . it's about Rorie."

Malcolm stopped dead. He spun and pulled a fistful of Alex's shirt so they were practically nose-to-nose. "Anything ye can tell Sir Ellerslie, ye can tell me. Begin."

Alex hesitated, wondering if he could trust him. "I saw Rorie with a band of Hesselrigge's soldiers."

Malcolm's eyes narrowed.

Alex felt blood pound in his ears. He knew that if Malcolm was on Rorie's side, he and Craig would soon be dead.

"Where?"

"We took a shortcut through the woods and spotted them down by the loch."

"How many?" Malcolm shot a glance at Jack, sitting disgruntled in front of his lean-to. He was out of earshot, but not by much.

"Hard to tell. They were mostly in the woods. We saw about a dozen horses down by the water."

"Are ye sure it was Rorie ye saw with them?"

Alex nodded.

"Rorie is a commander here. His men are everywhere. Repeat what ye have said to no one, or ye'll be dead before ye can finish y'r sentence. I'll be back as soon as I can."

Malcolm released Alex with a light shove that made him stagger and strode away.

Jack watched him go. Malcolm did not appear to be intervening on behalf of the boys. If anything, he was angry with them. Perhaps he would soon authorize a bit of persuasion. Jack looked at Alex and Craig and broke into a gummy grin.

"What was that about?" Craig asked, disappointed to be left in chains.

"I'm not sure," Alex bent toward Craig, adding in a low voice, "but I think Rorie and some of his men are kind of double agents for Hesselrigge. If they knew that we know, we'd be dead in a second."

"Know what?" Craig looked puzzled.

"Exactly – make sure you keep it that way."

They waited several long hours while the sun rose higher and they got hotter and thirstier. Jack sat reclined before his lean-to, passing the time by slipping knots into the ends of the thongs of a cat-o'-nine-tails whip. Finally, several guards came stomping into view, among them the older guard that had brought them here.

Jack looked up, startled, and broke into a hopeful grin. "So, it's time, is it?" He got up eagerly and gave his refurbished whip an experimental flick. All nine tentacles crackled.

"Sorry, Jack. I'm told the Macphersons and the McRaes wish to deal with these impostors themselves. I believe they will get the usual treatment for those who make false claims as to their parentage."

"Ye mean beheading and disembowelment?"

"Aye, although I'm no sure in which order."

"Can we no ask them a few questions first?" Jack displayed his whip. "It'll no take long."

"There's no time, and besides, I need them fit for walking." The guard gestured impatiently. "Release them, Jack. Now! Get moving."

Jack reluctantly gathered up his ring of keys. He slowly flicked through them, one by one, his eyes firing angrily. He roughly twisted a key in each manacle, prying them open.

Alex's legs felt weak. Pretending to examine the red sores the rings had left on his wrists, he looked for a way to escape. There were woods not too far away. . . .

"Move it!" The older guard gave Alex a shove.

Alex and Craig were marched through the camp. It struck Alex as wrong, somehow, that the bustle of sounds around them continued as if everything were normal. Horses snorted on their tethers; birds chirped from the trees. A rhythmic clanging rang out. Sparks flew as a man with a thick leather apron and gloves used a short sledgehammer to pound a red-hot piece of metal against an iron block.

Alex wondered how everything could carry on as usual when it so clearly was not. The entire world should be stopping to see their predicament. Birds should be silent and sad in their trees; horses should watch with big sorrowful eyes.

The blacksmith should stop his pounding and gaze sympathetically as they passed.

None of this happened. The world appeared ready to let them die with barely a glance. Tears springing to his eyes, Alex felt crushed that the loss of his life could mean so little.

10

THE BATTLE AT LOCH KARINS

Alex and Craig were brought to a large tent. The older guard pulled back the canvas flap and gave the boys a wink. "Ye'll be alright now, lads," he murmured. "Rest assured."

Confused, Alex stumbled into the tent. A group of men standing about abruptly stopped talking. As his eyes adjusted to the light, Alex spotted Sir Ellerslie and Malcolm.

Wallace stooped to be closer to Alex and Craig. He rested his big hands on their shoulders. "Sorry for the rough treatment, lads. Don't be too angry with me. Rorie's men are all about. We had to fool 'm while we got ye out of there."

"No problem," Alex said weakly. "Think nothing of it. . . ."

Wallace gave Alex's shoulder an affectionate squeeze. "Excellent work, tipping us off regarding Rorie. I've had suspicions about him for some time." Alex winced from the pain in his shoulder and was glad when Wallace stood to address the group.

"We'll be leaving on horseback, with these lads bound

and on foot," Wallace said. "To Rorie's men, it will appear that we're off to meet the Macpherson and McRae clans to hand over the impostors. Once in the woods, we'll meet up with the others and have these lads lead us to the enemy. I've no taken the chance of having our scouts find their camp for fear they'd be spotted and we'd lose the element of surprise."

He turned to Malcolm. "Are your men in position?"

"Aye! They're waiting in the woods for our arrival."

"Excellent! And, Sir Ellerslie, have you organized and briefed the men here in the camp on what they're to do?"

"That I have. Those we know we can trust have been told. They await our word. I'll remain here to lead them."

"Very well." Wallace appeared satisfied and resolute. "At my signal, we will take down both the enemy camp and the traitors here in our midst. With luck, we'll capture Rorie in the process."

While Wallace continued his instructions, Sir Ellerslie led Alex and Craig to a table with long benches, where a large pitcher of water, some bread, and a small stack of dried meat were laid out. "Grab something to eat, lads," he said. "But be quick. We'll be departing soon."

The water tasted *so* good that, having downed several goblets and his stomach feeling full to bursting, Alex still wanted more. He had gotten so parched chained out in the sun that almost no amount of water could quench his thirst. He lay back down on the bench and felt his insides gurgle. He had left no room for food and could eat no more than a few nibbles of bread.

Alex idly stared at a fold of canvas that swept down from a ridgepole. His eyes slipped out of focus and the fold doubled.

Voices blended together into a low roar, punctuated by the occasional exclamation or laugh. He felt as if he were gently floating downstream, bobbing and twisting with the current.

The next thing Alex knew, his name was being called over and over again from far away. He opened his eyes slightly and saw two Sir Ellerslies floating before him. Sir Ellerslie's two faces drifted closer together, spread back apart, then snapped together as one.

Alex lifted his head. "What is it? Where am I?" He struggled to sit up.

"Relax, relax," Sir Ellerslie said, gently helping him up. "We've let ye sleep as long as we could, but it's time we were off."

Alex stared in dismay. Craig was being led from the tent, his hands tied behind his back. The rope traveled up, knotted around his neck, and hung before him like a long leash.

Sir Ellerslie nodded approvingly. "That'll fool the bastards." He spotted the look on Alex's face. "*Och*, don't ye worry . . . we'll have these ropes off ye lads as soon as we're in the forest."

"What! Me, too?"

With considerable misgivings, Alex allowed himself to be tied. As he expected, the rope chaffed his neck. Worse, he had to keep his arms high behind his back to keep it from choking him.

Outside the tent, horses neighed.

Wallace leapt to his feet. "It's time. Let's be off!"

The tent flaps were flung open and Wallace strode out, followed closely by Malcolm and a number of his lieutenants. A bowman roughly pulled Alex and Craig behind him as if they were livestock. He knotted their ropes to his saddle.

Wallace gave his horse a jab with his heels. It shot forward and settled into a trot.

"Ready?" Malcolm called out, one arm in the air. He waited as his lieutenants and bowmen settled their skittish horses. Then he swung his arm down. "Let's go."

Alex felt the rope jerk tight around his neck. He staggered forward. Arms still high behind his back, Alex stumbled down the uneven forest path, desperately trying to put some slack in the rope. Craig ran beside him, bumping into him as he dodged obstacles. While Alex understood that this was all to fool Rorie's men, he wondered irritably why they had to put on such a good show.

Sentries on the hillside over the split rock waved and let them pass. Momentarily distracted, Alex caught his foot on a root and pitched forward. Unable to use his arms to break his fall, he hit the ground with a hard thud. Rolling onto his side, he tried to scramble back up before the rope went taut. It jerked his neck painfully and he almost fell onto his face again, but caught his balance just in time. The sentries whooped with laughter.

They passed a few bends in the trail when Malcolm motioned everyone to stop. He cupped his hands over his mouth, hooted, paused, and hooted again. After a few moments, a single hoot come from somewhere in the trees, followed by two more. Shadows were moving in the woods. One by one, several dozen bowmen silently slipped out of the forest.

Wallace dismounted and led his horse into a secluded area. "We shall leave the horses here and continue on foot."

Craig and Alex were untied, and they led the others through the forest. Everyone took great care not to rustle branches or step on twigs. Before long, they caught sight of water shimmering through the trees. The buckets lay where Alex and Craig had left them the day before. In a low voice, Craig explained that the soldiers' camp was around the embankment. Wallace and Malcolm conferred quietly.

Malcolm had a group of men follow him back the way they came, and Wallace waved for the remaining men to come close.

"Malcolm and his men are circling around to the other side of the camp," he explained. "We will get into position by climbing yon ridge. Rorie might have posted sentries, so we'd best travel in groups of three. Spread out, and advance quietly. If ye find a sentry, kill him and be quick about it. Once we reach the high ground overlooking their camp, lie low and wait for Malcolm's signal. He'll start the attack from his side and draw them out. Once they're all headed for him, he'll signal us with his horn and we'll attack. Be careful not to overrun the enemy and fire upon our own men on the other side."

The men fidgeted. They flexed their fingers and tested their bowstrings.

Wallace ordered the boys to stay put. "It's no likely, but in case one of Hesselrigge's men makes it past us, I want ye to keep hidden in yon bushes."

Alex wanted to say "good luck," but Wallace and his men had already moved on, leaving Alex and Craig eerily alone in the deceptive calm.

They made themselves a semicomfortable hiding place

in the bushes by twisting off a few branches for extra camouflage. There was nothing left to do but wait. Hours later, they finally heard it: Malcolm's horn.

"It has begun." Alex and Craig listened intently, but heard only a few distant shouts. The silence surprised them, but then arrows make little sound. They waited, as ordered.

Alex was about to get up when he heard a crashing in the trees. Peering cautiously through the foliage, he saw movement: shapes, legs, feet running. Several men, panting heavily and wheezing, were coming closer and closer. Alex and Craig ducked down and covered their heads. The bushes around them shook.

"Wait fir me, will ye, man? For God's sake," puffed one of the men. "There's nobody at our heels."

The rustling through the undergrowth slowed and stopped.

"That bastard Wallace sure surprised us back there," gasped a voice that sounded like Rorie. "Someone must have given away our position. When I find out who, I will carve out their eyes with a dull knife."

Alex hardly dared breathe.

"Are ye sufficiently rested? We need to be off to Duncragglin for more men. Sir James should be back with reinforcements from King Edward ere long. We'll rout that bastard Wallace from his lair and put an end to his treachery once and for all."

"Aye, on the end of a swinging rope –"

"If he doesnae feel my steel twixt his ribs first."

The crunching footsteps and voices receded and faded away.

Alex shifted uncomfortably. "This is not good."

Craig scrambled to his feet. "We've got to tell Wallace."

"No, wait! We were told to stay here." Alex tried to hold Craig back, but it was too late: Craig was gone.

Cursing, Alex left the hiding place, crouching in the undergrowth. He ran after Craig, up the slope towards the enemy camp. Craig leapt to clear an obstacle, but Alex fell over it, sprawling face-first on the ground. Raising his head, he looked in horror at a mop of blood-soaked hair: a soldier. Judging by the split in his head, the soldier was done in by a hard blow from a battle-ax.

Craig wrinkled his face in disgust.

Alex gulped air. He had that annoying buzzing in his ears again. "This must have been a sentry," he gasped.

A small crossbow lay discarded near the corpse. Craig picked it up and gave the drawstring a tug. It barely moved. Undaunted, he lay the front of the bow down on the ground and stepped on it, placing his feet on either side of the shaft. Teeth gritted, Craig pulled up on the drawstring with all his might to extend it far enough to hook onto its catch.

"*Phew*, that is tight," Craig said, inserting one of the arrowlike bolts that lay strewn about. Holding the crossbow up like a rifle, he sighted along the stock and pulled the trigger. The drawstring twanged and the bolt shot like a bullet, thudding a split second later deep into the trunk of a nearby tree.

Craig's jaw dropped. He slowly lowered the bow.

Alex was impressed. "That thing might come in handy . . . can I have it?"

"No way."

Alex gathered up all the bolts he could find. Most lay in

a heap, where they had fallen from the dead soldier's quiver.

"Give 'm here." Craig held out his free hand, the other still clutching the crossbow.

"No!"

Craig's face turned red. "Those arrows are no good without the crossbow."

Alex held the bolts out of reach. "They're not arrows, they're bolts, and that crossbow is no good without them. Hand it over."

They glared at each other. Finally, Craig broke the impasse. "Fine!" he said. "We'll share, but I get the first turn."

"Deal." Alex held up his little finger. "Pinkie swear?"

"What's that?"

"A promise that can't be broken."

Alex and Craig linked their pinkie fingers and touched thumbs.

"Can you carry the bolts for me?" Craig asked.

"Sure, no problem."

With the crossbow tensioned and ready to fire, they continued their ascent far more cautiously than before. Alex did not want to stumble over any more sentries, dead *or* alive. Now and then, they stopped to listen for sounds of battle, but all was quiet except for the birds chirping cheerfully as ever.

From the top of the ridge, they could see all the way down to the enemy camp. Motionless shapes lay scattered about the forest floor. Emerging from behind one tree to quickly scurry behind another, Alex and Craig slowly closed in on the camp. The shapes were people . . . motionless people . . . dead people. Anxiety welled up inside Alex. He could so easily end up like them. It took only one bolt. . . .

Some shapes were bristling with arrows that stuck out from just about everywhere, so Alex tried to think of them as porcupine people. Ketchup people were the ones with ketchup dribbled around the arrows, spilling over the ground around them. Others were Lego people, without limbs or a head attached. Lego people were also ketchup people. As Alex and Craig stealthily approached the camp, they tried to stay away from each of these people, giving them furtive glances in case one of them moved.

Hearing a thump behind a collapsed lean-to, they scrambled behind a tree, tripping over each other in the process. Craig thrust the crossbow at Alex. "Here! It's your turn."

Alex ducked. "No way! You shoot them."

Craig dropped the bow at Alex's feet and turned away. Reluctantly, Alex picked it up.

Craig was shaking. "Let's go back."

"Go back where?"

"To the bushes where we were hiding. We can wait there."

It was tempting. What if that noise came from a dying soldier? Should he shoot him to put him out of his misery? But what if the bolt didn't kill him and only made matters worse? What if it was Malcolm . . . or William Wallace?

Alex had no idea what to do, but knew he had to do something. He couldn't leave and not know what made the noise. Peering down the crossbow shaft, finger on the trigger, he crept forward.

11

Hare Today

Sweat beaded on Alex's forehead and the collapsed lean-to slipped in and out of focus at the end of his cocked crossbow. He decided against a direct approach as he wouldn't be able to see what lay behind the lean-to until he was almost upon it. It was better to make a wide circle around to the other side.

Placing each foot carefully, Alex tiptoed from tree to tree, thankful for the chattering sparrows. Several dead soldiers lay in his way, sprawled facedown in the dirt. Arrows protruded grotesquely from their bodies. He gave them a wide berth.

Craig stuck close by him. Whenever Alex hesitated, he dropped onto his stomach and covered his head.

Hearing voices, Alex ducked behind a tree, Craig scrambling on all fours after him. Alex listened hard. He could make out bits of what was being said.

"I told you we should have gone back to get help, but noooooooooo, you wouldn't listen."

Remarkably, it sounded like a girl.

"It's not *my* fault," replied a boy, who sounded annoyed. "How was I to know we would end up like this?"

Craig leapt up. "It's Annie and Willie! Annie, Willie, it's me, it's me!" he called joyfully.

Two heads popped out from behind the collapsed lean-to. Craig was on them in a flash, hugging Annie and slapping Willie on the back, happy tears rolling down his face.

Alex felt a flood of relief. "Are you guys alright?"

"We're just fine," Willie said, overcome. "At least, we are now."

"I'm so glad we found you!" Annie said.

"How did you get here?" Alex asked.

Annie explained that after they were separated in the cave, she'd waited as long as she could for them to return, then found her way out at the next low tide. She bumped into Willie, who had woken up feeling better, saw that Alex and Craig were missing, and ran out to find them.

"I saw where you and Craig were on the wall before that big monster-head lowered," Annie said. "But I couldn't be in both places at the same time. The head lowers only if both levers are pulled at once."

"Did you get blasted out of the spaceport?" Craig's eyes glittered.

"That's no spaceport," Willie said somberly. "It's hell. We've been to hell . . . and back."

"To hell and back *in time*, you mean," Alex said.

Willie looked up, startled. "No way!"

Alex gestured all around. "Did you think this is all one

big costume party? Did you think someone planted a forest when we weren't looking?"

Willie scrunched his brow. "Maybe we're in another dimension."

Annie looked at him. "What?"

"Another dimension is another universe happening at the same time, in the same place." Willie spread his arms dramatically. "Another time, on the other hand, is the same universe happening in the same place, but at a different time."

Annie stifled a snort. "Did you read that in one of your space comics?"

Alex rubbed his chin in his best imitation of a thoughtful professor. "Can one dimension be the past or future of another and, if so, what's the difference between being in another dimension and being in another time?"

"If this is another dimension," Craig asked, "then what is William Wallace doing here?"

Annie gasped. "He's here? William Wallace is here? Are you sure?"

"Of course we're sure, we met him," Alex replied. "Maybe you saw him too – he and his men attacked this camp."

"But why would he want to attack these nice soldiers?"

"Nice soldiers?"

"Yes," Annie continued. "They were going to take us to the castle. They said their boss, some Lord Hessel something-or-other, was a friend of the McRae clan and would want to meet us."

"Are you sure you weren't hostages?"

"I don't think so. . . ."

"Guys . . . GUYS." Willie waved his arms to get their attention. "Look around. Don't you think that we could have this conversation somewhere else? Whoever gets back here might not be in the best of moods."

"Let's go to Wallace's camp," Alex suggested.

"I'm not going back there!" Craig held up his hands in protest. "First, the cook was going to cut off our thumbs and put them in the stew, then we got chained up by this creepy man who wanted to torture us all the time. Then they wanted to have us beheaded, then they tied ropes 'round our necks and dragged us behind a horse –"

"But, Craig, don't you want to warn Wallace about the reinforcements coming from Duncragglin?"

"I do, but . . . but . . ." Craig's face contorted. "What if we don't get to see him and they chain us up again? I *really* don't want to be chained up again."

"I still think we should be having this conversation somewhere else," Willie said.

"Let's go to the coast and see if we can find a way back into the caves," Annie said. "We've got to try to get home."

No one argued. Alex retrieved the crossbow and slung the quiver over his shoulder. Willie fitted himself with a longbow nearly as big as he was tall, and Craig strapped on a belt with a dagger that, in his small hands, appeared long enough to be a sword. Removing the belt from a dead soldier was unpleasant, but Craig was determined to have it. Willie and Alex rolled the body back and forth while Craig loosened the belt from its loops.

"Good grief, you guys," Annie said, as she emerged from a partially collapsed tent. "People are more likely to shoot at us if you carry all that around. What are you planning to do with it, anyway? Kill somebody?

"Now here is something useful." She thrust a sack into Alex's hands. "There's one for each of you."

Opening the sack, Alex found bread, smoked meat, a pot, and a blanket. He slung it over his shoulder.

They left camp in the direction of Duncragglin Castle. The route took them past the spot where, hundreds of years later, the McRae farmhouse would stand.

Willie slapped the trunk of a large tree with thick spreading branches. "I think this one is right in the middle of our house," he said.

Craig skipped back out from under the tree. "Careful! Don't stand under the toilet . . . something might be happening in another dimension."

"Do you think people in another time or dimension see us as ghosts?" Alex looked up to where the bedroom window would be. "Do you think we might have seen *ourselves* moving about a few nights ago?"

"Let's say hello to ourselves." Craig jumped up and down and waved his arms.

"Oh, look." Alex laughed. "Craig's hiding under the bed."

Willie sauntered behind a cluster of bushes. "I sure hope no one can see us 'cause I need a little privacy right about now." His head lowered from view.

"Don't use stinging nettle leaves," Annie called out, "or you'll be sooorrrry."

They made it to the coast "nae bother," as Willie put it. A cool sea wind was blowing over the cliffs, flapping their clothes and tossing their hair about. From their high vantage point, they could see far down the winding coastline to where the towers of Duncragglin Castle rose over neighboring rocks.

Annie pushed her hair back from her face. "The tide is too high for us to find our tunnel into the caves."

"When will it be at its lowest?" Craig winced in anticipation of bad news.

"Could be today, could be weeks from today. There's no way to know till we've watched a few tides come and go."

"So, what will we do?" Alex asked. "We can't go wandering along the coast in broad daylight. Guards are bound to be patrolling the area."

"See that point way down there, the one that comes out the farthest?" Annie stood close to Alex and pointed to a distant rocky outcropping. "Over there's a rock slab that sticks up like a lean-to. It's there in our time, so it's got to be there now. We call it Fort McRae. When we're in it, we can see anyone coming for miles."

"Let's go," Craig said.

No one needed convincing. They turned away from the castle and trudged along the edge of a high plateau. A sudden movement caught Alex's eye. He turned in time to see a brown hare bound away between tufts of tall windswept grass.

Willie dropped his sack and fumbled with an arrow, but by the time his longbow was pulled, the hare was gone.

"Alex, go left," he said. "Annie, you and Craig spread out and keep him from escaping. I'll circle 'round to the other side."

Annie hesitated. "You're not really going to shoot that poor wee thing, are you?"

"Darn right," Willie said, his eyes bright. "We can't just be eating your dry bread."

"I packed smoked meat too. . . ." Annie protested, though she knew there was no stopping Willie once he got going.

Keeping his longbow half drawn, Willie crept in a wide arc to where they last saw the hare. Alex tensioned his cross-bow and followed suit, circling around the other way. He stepped gently, all the while squinting down the stock of his bow. Opposite, he saw Willie approach, slowly closing in with his bow drawn tight.

Suddenly he caught a glimpse of a brown, floppy-eared head. He aimed and pulled the trigger. The bow twanged and an arrow thudded into a grassy mound next to him.

Alex stared at the arrow, confused. It was pointing in the opposite direction than he had shot from. It was pointing, in fact, at him. He looked up.

"Whoops." Willie gave a sheepish shrug. "Sorry about that."

Alex angrily pulled the arrow out of the dirt. "You could've killed me."

"I know, I know. It was an accident – I said sorry, didn't I?" Willie kicked about in the tall grass. "Did you get him, by the way?"

"How am I supposed to know? At least I didn't get *you*."

Parting clumps of grass, they looked around for Alex's bolt, both with their bows ready. Alex was careful to stay within arm's reach of Willie's bow. He hoped he would not have to finish off a wounded hare.

Alex wearily sat on a grassy knoll. "I give up. That bolt could be anywhere. Besides, I've got plenty more."

"Over here! Look!" Willie waved excitedly. "A rabbit hole. Perhaps he's in there."

Alex got down on his knees and peered into the dark opening. "Great. What do we do now? Crawl in after him?"

Willie sat back on a mound. "We wait. He's got to come out sometime. We can hide behind the tall grass and get him when he sticks his head out."

"That might take a long time." Alex sighed.

"It's what hunting is all about," Willie said. "Sometimes it takes hunters all day to make a single kill."

"But we haven't got all day. Anyway, don't they have a back door to their burrows?"

"Of course!" Willie twisted. He froze, eyes wide. Only thirty feet away was the big brown hare, up on its hind legs, watching them.

Very, very slowly, Alex raised his crossbow. Both sights along the stock lined up against the brown furry shape, and he ever so gently squeezed the trigger. Feeling the bow recoil, he saw neither bolt nor hare.

"You've got him!" Willie shrieked, leaping over to where the hare had sat watching.

Alex rose slowly, reluctant to see what he had done. "Is he dead?"

"I think so." Willie looked down into the tall grass. He lowered his bow and prodded something with his foot.

A brown form lay on its side, its hind leg twitching. Alex was horrified to see that it was still alive and suffering. He fumbled to put another bolt into his crossbow, but before he could get it tensioned and ready to fire off another shot, the twitches became slower and less frequent. They stopped. He heard swishing noises in the grass from Annie and Craig running up behind him.

"Brilliant," Craig roared. "What a shot! Right through the middle."

"The hare doesn't think it's so brilliant," Annie noted dryly.

Willie gave it a nudge. "Take a look. The hare does not think. In case you haven't noticed, it's dead."

Annie stared sadly at the hare's black lifeless eyes. "I hope it doesn't have any babies to look after," she said.

"If it does, they need to look after themselves now," Willie retorted. "That's life."

"No, it is not." Annie glared fiercely at Willie. "That's death. There's a big difference."

"Save it." Willie wriggled the bolt out of the hare and handed it to Alex. "That's simply the way it is. The only thing you need think about now is dinner."

Imagining a bowlful of steaming hot, chunky rabbit stew made Alex realize how hungry he was. He told himself there was no reason to feel guilty. And who was Annie to be critical? He would rather have lived the short life of that rabbit than be one of the animals on the McRae farm, left to stand in its own poop for most of its life.

He wiped the bolt against the grass, purposely leaving some blood on the shaft. He wanted to recognize it as his lucky bolt so he could pick it next time they were hunting.

It was a good-sized hare. Willie tied its hind feet together and used the same rope to sling it over his shoulder. The hare's dangling front paws slapped the tops of Willie's legs as he walked.

12

FIRE

Annie looked out over the rocky point and marveled how little had changed. "If you're a rock, seven hundred years is just a blink in history," she said.

Willie bent and picked up a stick. "Let's collect some firewood to take with us," he suggested. "That way, we won't have to come back out."

Alex raked around for dry bits of kindling. A thought occurred to him. "Do you have anything to light this with, Annie?"

"Don't you?" Annie suddenly looked concerned.

Willie glanced back and forth between them. "Having raw rabbit was not what I had in mind," he said nervously. "Please tell me we have something to light a fire."

"I think so," Alex said, looking doubtfully at his handful of dry moss, leaves, and dead pine needles. "But . . . it will take some doing."

They piled twigs and branches into each others' arms so high that it blocked their view. Staggering and stumbling all the way to the rocky point, they gratefully dropped their armloads into a single large heap.

Alex straightened and had a look around. Tall rock formations cast long shadows down to the water's edge. Behind him loomed a huge slab, one end sticking up high enough to offer shelter. Annie ducked under it and pulled a blanket from her sack.

"Aren't you worried it might fall?" Alex asked.

"I used to be," Annie said, "especially when Willie's friends would climb up top and jump while we were under it, but not anymore."

"Why not?"

"Well, if it's still standing over seven hundred years from now, it can't very well fall on us now, can it?"

Alex felt silly. "I guess that's true." He sighed and slung down his sack. "I will sleep better knowing that." He held out his hand. "Can I have your dagger please, Craig?"

Craig hesitated and Alex wiggled his fingers.

"C'm on, let's go. I need it to make a fire starter. We've got to hurry if we're to get a fire going before sundown."

Craig watched as Alex painstakingly whittled bark off a curved stick and attached a sack drawstring to each end.

Willie stopped to watch, tilting his head skeptically. "How's that supposed to work?"

"Easy. We spin a stick with this bow until the bottom gets really hot and ignites."

"You've done this before?"

"No . . . but it can't be that hard. I saw them do this at an Aboriginal village once."

Willie rolled his eyes and Alex angrily threw down his

sticks. "Do you think I'm doing all this for fun? Do you have a better idea?"

"Flint."

"Flint. Oh, why didn't *I* think of that?" Alex mockingly slapped the side of his head. "You idiot, teeny tiny sparks aren't going to light a fire! Don't waste your time."

"*This* is the waste of time. C'm on, Annie, let's find some flint. There's sure to be some along the shore." Willie stomped away.

"I bet I'll start a fire before you do," Alex called after him.

Willie turned. "You're on. The loser has to be a slave for a whole day."

"Deal!"

"You'll be fetching my food, slave."

Alex quickly got to work. He pressed down on the stick while twirling it back and forth with the bow. The bottom emitted a rhythmic squeak.

He heard a *clink, clink* off to one side. Willie was smacking two rocks together over a handful of dry moss.

"Careful you don't get your fingers caught," Alex sang out merrily.

Willie mumbled something and gave his rocks an extra-hard bash. One landed in his little pile of dried moss and scattered it about.

Alex choked back a laugh. "Have you ever done this before?"

Furious, Willie reassembled his moss, turned his back, and renewed his efforts. Craig and Annie burst into a fit of giggling.

Willie raised a fist. "Watch it!"

"*Ooh,* I'm scared." Alex giggled. "Annie, save me."

Willie hunched over his pile of moss with his rocks. Sparks flew and he bent to puff gently onto the moss.

Worried, Alex tried to make the bow move faster. The string kept slipping, so he made a new knot. Again, it slipped. Fumbling another attempt to tie it tighter, he flung the bow away.

Annie picked it up. "Let me try." She picked apart the tangled bundle of overtied string and reattached it with a simple loop knot.

Alex tried again, vigorously pulling and pushing on the bow. Craig helped by pressing down on the top with another stick. The twirling stick hummed, its rounded end rubbing a smooth dent into the base.

Willie took up a new technique, smashing a large rock down on a smaller one. Bigger sparks flew, but none made any lasting impression.

Alex's arms ached. He pressed on and on until, with one extrahard push, the fire-stick slipped and clattered to the ground. He put his finger to the dent it had made in the wood, quickly pulling back. "It's hot!" he exclaimed.

Excited, Annie knelt opposite Craig to help him hold the stick. Alex worked the bow again, sweat trickling down his face.

"Give me that." Willie suddenly caught the end of the moving bow.

Alex looked up, alarmed.

"I didn't have the right kind of rocks," Willie mumbled, his eyes averted.

Working together, they made the stick twirl faster.

Fascinated, they watched as a small blackened ring of sawdust formed around its base.

"Do you smell something?" Annie sniffed hopefully.

"That was just me," Willie retorted gruffly. "Pay it no mind."

"No, I smell something burning."

"Smoke!" Craig burst out gleefully.

"It's working!" Willie put on an extra burst of speed. The base of the stick emitted an unmistakable gray hint of smoke.

"Don't . . . ease . . . up," Alex panted, his arms feeling like they were about to fall off.

The sawdust flared and died. Annie sprinkled shavings. There was another flare-up. Tiny flames flickered and the shavings became a red glow. They watched breathlessly as more ignited. Never before had such tiny flames brought them such joy.

"We did it! We did it!" Craig jumped up and down.

They sprinkled larger and larger shavings on the flames, followed by twigs propped over the growing fire. Before they knew it, they were all dancing madly around flames, which shot up as high as their shoulders.

"Fire! We make fire!" Willie hopped heavily from one foot to another.

Even the normally reserved Annie did twirls, arms raised to the sky. Finally exhausted, tired of clapping each other on the back and giving high fives, they collapsed into a heap beside the crackling flames.

"Guess what?" Annie said. "We've used up all the firewood."

Alex looked over to where the pile had been and rolled back with a groan. There were but a few small twigs – not enough to keep the fire going overnight. And beyond the flames, everything was black.

Alex scrambled to his feet. "We better get more before it's too dark to see! Annie, you and Craig go back to the forest; Willie and I can check the shoreline for driftwood."

"No way!" Craig looked to the dark menacing forest in dismay. "I want to go with Willie," he said.

"Okay, I'll go with Annie, but we get to take the crossbow." Alex slung the quiver over his shoulder. "And try to bring back some big stuff – we'll need it!"

———————◆———————

Up ahead, the forest was no more than a black silhouette – one that Alex knew could contain all sorts of hidden dangers. Crossing the bare open rock, he couldn't shake the feeling that there were eyes in those woods – eyes that were watching them, following them. He trained the crossbow on a random spot, shifting it quickly to aim it at another. "Maybe we should skip the forest and check the shoreline instead. A couple of big pieces of driftwood are all we'll need."

Impatient, Annie strode on ahead. "We know there's wood in the forest, so let's go," she said. "And stop making me so nervous!"

Alex lowered his bow. Heart pounding, he kept step with Annie as the black wall of forest loomed over them. *There's no one there, there's no one there, there's no one there,* he repeated to himself.

Once the forest had actually swallowed them up, Alex felt better. Now they were hidden too, and nothing had gotten them yet. But once Annie piled firewood into his arms so high he could barely see over it and sent him back across the exposed rocks to camp, he felt more vulnerable than ever.

A few branches fell from his pile and clattered onto the rocks. "Forget about them," Alex pleaded, but Annie put down her branches and painstakingly reloaded each of the fallen sticks.

Alex tried to reassure himself that if anyone was there with a bow trained on his back, surely they would have shot him by now. Finally, the forest well behind them, he regretted having been so scared, especially when Annie'd been so brave. Alex dumped his wood near the fire.

Craig sat huddled by the warmth of the fire, his back to Alex. He did not turn to see what Alex had brought.

"What's the matter, Craig? Scared by the bogeyman?" Alex reassuringly put a hand on Craig's shoulder. "Don't worry. I was spooked out there too."

The small form stirred and looked up.

Startled, Alex almost fell over backwards. It wasn't Craig!

13

THE UNLUCKY RABBIT'S FOOT

"Please don't hurt me," squeaked the intruder. A teary face appeared briefly before disappearing behind thin folded arms.

"Alex, put that thing away!" Annie waved her arm angrily. "Can't you see it's just a frightened wee lassie?"

Alex lowered his crossbow, shooting nervous glances to the darkness past the flames. "Is there anyone else out there?" His voice shook.

"Th-Th-They're gone. They're all gone."

"Who's gone, my dear?" Annie sat next to the little girl and gently stroked her tangled hair.

"My family – my mama, my papa, Wilfie, Susie . . . they're all gone."

"Gone where?"

"Heaven. They've all gone to heaven," the little girl wailed, burying her face once again.

"What happened?" Annie dreaded to ask, but the question popped out.

"They burned down our house." The girl clutched her

knees and turned herself into a little ball. "They wouldn't let anyone out. Papa tried, but they shot him so he went back in."

"Your family was burned alive?" Annie blurted out, horrified. "Who . . . who would do such a thing?"

Her voice sounded small and distant: "Soldiers."

"How could they . . . why would anyone . . . ?" Alex fumbled for words. The magnitude of what he had heard left him numb and dazed.

"It wasn't true." The girl rocked back and forth. "Papa wasn't an enemy of the castle lord; Papa just didn't have enough money to pay them. He paid them all he could, but they kept coming back for more. Papa said he needed to feed his family, and they said he was an enemy, but it wasn't true!"

A heavy silence fell over them. Alex thought of terrified children screaming, smoke stinging their eyes; the hacking, coughing, gasping; the flames. . . .

The little girl leaned into Annie.

"Poor, poor dear." Annie held her gently. "You must be exhausted."

Alex went to make her a bed. He wished they had brought back pine bough cuttings to use for a mattress. Tomorrow they would get organized. Tonight, however, he was not going to venture back into that forest.

Choosing an area close to the fire, Alex stretched out his blanket. He folded it twice, so it was a quarter of its original size, figuring that the girl could sleep on three layers and have the fourth over her. He did his best to bunch up a sack into a pillow.

Footsteps crunched on the gravel-like stones. Alex recognized Willie's voice and Craig's laugh. Seeing the girl,

Willie hastily dropped his firewood and strung an arrow. Alex blocked his way, then explained what had happened.

Willie slowly lowered his bow. "Good God! Hesselrigge and his men are worse than we thought," he said.

Annie tucked the sleeping girl into the bed Alex had prepared. Firelight shadows flickered over her dirty little face. Shooing the boys to the other side of the fire, Annie said, "She's exhausted; let her sleep, poor thing. Her name's Katie. She's been hiding out here on the coast living off clams and bits of seaweed. Imagine being only six years old and out here all by yourself for days – no fire, no blanket, cold and black nights."

"What are we going to do with her?" Craig asked. "Can we take her back home with us?"

Willie snorted. "She's no stray cat," he said. "We need to send her to a neighbor."

"We can't." Annie pulled a blanket from her sack. "She told me that her neighbors are afraid that Hesselrigge's men will come looking for her."

Alex placed a piece of heavy driftwood across the fire. Willie knelt to arrange his blanket.

"We're going to have to share these blankets," Annie said pointedly. "We no longer have one for everyone."

Willie opened his mouth to protest. Instead, he got up and walked away. "You figure it out."

Annie spread out the largest blanket and covered it with two smaller ones for them to share. She rolled her sack into a pillow and promptly lay down in the middle.

"Not bad," she declared. "It's a bit hard, but I think I can sleep like this."

"I get the middle too." Craig plopped himself down next to Annie.

That left the outsides. Alex placed his bow next to his pillow, loosely inserting a bolt. Willie snuggled in and pulled the blanket he was sharing with his sister up to his chin. "Rabbit for breakfast," he reminded everyone.

"Where is that rabbit?" Annie asked.

"I put it in a crevice with the rest of our food. I rolled some big rocks in front so nothing can get at it while we're sleeping."

Craig lifted his head. "Like what?"

"Werewolves," Willie answered, without hesitation. "We'll have to keep an eye out for them. They like to eat little boys."

Craig disappeared under the blanket.

"Don't be silly, Willie," Alex said. "There are no were-wolves out here. Can't you see it's not a full moon?"

"It's almost a full moon."

"Not good enough; they come out only when the moon is completely full. We won't have to worry about werewolves for two or three days."

The top of Craig's head and eyes slowly emerged from under the blankets. "Are you sure it's only when the moon is completely full?"

"Absolutely sure," Alex said. "It's the same with vampires."

"Vampires?" Craig disappeared under the blanket again.

"Aren't they far away in Transylvania?" Annie asked.

"They fly, remember?" Alex replied. "Vampires spread all over Europe. It took people a while to figure out how to kill them."

"You mean, by driving a stake into their heart?"

"Precisely. There's no other way to prevent them from turning into vampire bats at each full moon and biting people, who then also become vampires. They had trouble figuring out who were the true vampires, so they probably hammered stakes into the hearts of a lot of innocent people."

Craig stared up into the black night. "You guys are kidding, right?"

"No," Alex said.

"Shouldn't one of us stand guard?" Craig suggested. "We could take turns."

"Good idea," Willie mumbled sleepily. "You first."

Silence finally settled in and Alex gently drifted off to sleep.

"What was that?" Craig cried out.

"What? What was what?" Alex and Willie scrambled for their bows.

All they could hear was the peaceful sound of waves lapping against the rocky shore and the faint hooting of an owl.

"I don't hear it anymore," Craig whispered finally.

"What did it sound like?"

"Like something was moving about out there."

Willie grew irritable. "Are you sure you heard something?"

"Yes, yes, I'm sure. It was out there somewhere." Craig waved vaguely in the direction of the northern shoreline and shifted uncomfortably.

"It's your own fault for telling him about werewolves," Annie said. "Now let's get some sleep. I'm tired."

Willie lay down and tugged on the blanket. "Annie, don't be such a hog!"

Annie pulled back. "You've already got more than half."

"Craig, stop kicking!" Alex asked irritably.

"I'm just trying to get comfortable." Craig kicked some more.

Finally they all fell asleep on the hard rock under the huge stone slab on the desolate rocky peak. They slept without stirring until well after dawn, even though the rising sun shone brightly into the angled slab, warming them and the surrounding rocks.

———◆◆◆———

Alex lifted his head. Shading his eyes, he looked around. No, it was not all a dream. He was really hiding out in a dangerous place seven hundred years before he was born, and he really had to find his way back. . . . The others had something to return to: a home on the farm with people to miss them. Alex, though, couldn't think of a reason to return, except that where he came from was not as nasty and deadly as this.

He looked out to see if his hard-won fire was still going and found himself staring into the apprehensive eyes of a grubby little girl squatting next to the smoldering fire.

"Good morning, Katie," he croaked.

She watched him warily, a stick of firewood in her hand.

"Did you keep the fire going?" he asked gently.

She nodded.

"Good girl! It was hard work to make that fire. Are you hungry?"

She hesitated, then nodded vigorously, eyes averted.

"Me, too! C'm on, everyone. Let's get up. It's breakfast time!"

Beside him, bodies stirred and stretched.

"Morning already?" Annie yawned, her tousled brown hair half over her face.

Willie groaned. "I don't think I fell asleep until dawn."

"Don't just lie there," Alex said. "Katie is hungry and we've got to cook some rabbit."

Annie immediately sat up and looked around. "There you are, my dear. Hungry?"

Katie nodded.

Annie tossed off the blanket, exposing Willie's back. "Where did you hide that food?"

"Over by those rocks, there." Willie reached out from under the blanket and pointed.

"Well, go get it then," Annie said, shooing him along. "Rabbit-chopping is your job."

"Says who?" came a mumble from under the blanket.

"That's the way things are, Willie-boy." Annie stood, whisked the remaining blanket off Willie's still huddled form, and folded it into a tidy square. She stretched, reaching way up to the rock slab above, and rolled her neck. "What I wouldn't do for a change of clothes and a toothbrush." She grimaced as she ran her fingers through her long tangled hair.

"Why don't you take a great flying leap into the ocean?" Willie suggested. Shivering, he pulled a sweatshirt over his head.

"I might do that later," Annie retorted, unfazed. "It looks like a nice enough day."

Willie slapped the dead rabbit down onto a flat boulder. "Okay, let's do this." He surveyed his furry task. "Where do you think I should start?"

"Maybe you should cut off the head," Craig offered.

Willie looked up. "Why the head?"

"It looks gross staring at us with those ants crawling across its eyeballs."

"And it won't look gross if I cut the head off? Maybe *you* should do it!"

"Slice it up the belly," Alex suggested.

Willie rolled the rabbit onto its back and hovered the knife over its furry white underside. "Do you want me to take the guts out?"

Alex snorted. "No, you don't gut it. It's not a fish. You need to skin it."

"The whole thing?" Willie looked at Alex blankly.

Alex sighed. "Let me try." He took the knife, lightly rubbing the blade against the skin, but he could not bring himself to slice through.

"Excuse me," said a little voice.

"What is it, Katie?" Alex spoke gently so as not to frighten her. He shifted to block her view of the dead rabbit.

She wriggled past him impatiently and took the knife from his hand. In a flash, she had pierced the rabbit's loose fur and sliced it open from head to tail.

Annie gasped. The boys stared, their jaws gaping.

Katie flipped the rabbit inside out and rapidly sliced off strips of muscle, dropping each one into the pot Annie had hastily provided. Once she finished with every possible scrap of meat, she carved out a few morsels that were also dropped into the pot.

"What are those?" Alex asked hesitantly.

"I think that dark red one is the heart." Annie looked slightly pale. "The gray ones, I think, are the liver and kidneys. Don't ask me what the others are."

There was not much left of the rabbit when Katie was finished with it. Even its little black eyeballs were missing. Nor was there much left of Alex's appetite.

Katie held up a furry appendage. "Who wants a lucky rabbit's foot?"

"No, thanks, you keep it, Katie," Annie said quickly.

"I've already got one." She reached down her top and fished it out. "It's really lucky."

"I'll take it," Alex said.

Katie beamed and tossed it over. "There, now you will be lucky too!"

Alex's appetite returned when he smelled the hot bubbling stew. Annie had topped it up with fresh water she found trickling down a crevice. Katie had sprinkled in handfuls of forest greens, and the stew smelled delicious. At least Alex knew there were no thumbs in it.

Alex set himself the task of carving a wooden spoon. The bottom round part was easy, but hollowing out the inside was challenging. When he was done, it was far from smooth, but it did hold a decent sipful of stew. Everyone gathered around to take turns having a slurp from it. Katie sat next to Alex, who kept a close watch for a rabbit eyeball. Finally he lay back contentedly, with an arm flung over his face.

14

NEVER UNDERESTIMATE

"I think the stew needs a bit of crab," Willie said, stretching lazily. "Later, much later, when the tide is out, let's go crab-hunting."

Alex propped himself up on one elbow. "When will it be out far enough to find our tunnel?"

Annie was sitting cross-legged, looking over the shore. "Can't tell yet," she replied. "By tomorrow, we'll be able to see which way it's going. When the tide reaches the highest watermark, the lowest tide will be about six hours later."

Alex sat up. "If the lowest tide is only a few days away, we don't have much time to get ready. We'll need to get our hands on a torch, or an oil lamp, or whatever the farmers around here use for light. Even candles would be a help."

"But how will we get these things?" Annie asked. "There are no shops around here, and we have no money."

"Looks like we'll just have to steal what we need," Willie replied.

Annie waved a finger at him. "Do you know what they do to people caught stealing around here, even if it's only a loaf of bread? They hang them, just like that."

"*Phew.*" Willie wiped his brow. "I thought they'd do something bad, like cut off their hands or something."

Annie sighed. "I've had it with all you stinky people. Before we do anything else today, let's get cleaned up. I've found a perfect spot to wash our clothes and have a bath."

"Just what are we to wear when our clothes are drying?" Willie asked.

"Sacks," Annie replied. "We'll wrap sacks around ourselves like skirts – or like kilts for you boys."

"I don't need to wash," Willie grumbled.

"Look at yourself! You're filthy. I can smell you from here."

Willie inspected his blackened hands, slowly turning them over to see the dirt caked under his fingernails. "You've got a point." He grinned, exposing fuzzy teeth. "But lassies go first."

"Right, then." Annie bundled up her sack. "Let's go, Katie."

Startled, Katie looked up from where she sat on her blanket.

"It's alright, Katie." Annie held out her hand. "It's not going to hurt a bit."

Reluctantly, Katie put her hand in Annie's and let Annie lead her away. She glanced back to Alex, silently pleading for him to save her.

Craig waited until they were out of earshot. "She sure is a grubby wee lassie," he said.

Willie snorted. "Speak for yourself, you grubby little boy."

Craig shot him an angry look. "I'm not as dirty as she is. She looks like she hasn't had a bath in years."

Alex passed away the time by whittling a comb from a strip of bark while Willie and Craig lazed about. The sun was high in the sky, and the stew had made them contentedly full. Waves lapped gently against the pebbly beach near their feet.

"Do you know what I would like right now?" Willie said, propping one dirty foot upon the toes of the other. "I would like an ice-cream sandwich bar."

"*Ooh*," Craig moaned. "You should not have said that."

"With some whipping cream dabbed on top . . ."

"And I would like a chocolate sundae, with nuts sprinkled on top," Craig said, lazily waving an arm at Alex. "Go get me one, will you?"

"Sure, no problem." Alex picked up a rock and pretended to shake some nuts on top. "Is this enough?"

Craig nodded. He took the rock and used a short stick as if it were a spoon. "*Mmm*, you have no idea how good this is."

"Where's my ice-cream bar?" Willie demanded.

"Coming right up," Alex said, passing down another rock.

Willie nibbled on it. "This is a bit harder than the ice cream I remember – still pretty good though."

"What is pretty good?" Annie's voice came from somewhere behind them.

Alex turned and watched a sack-clad Annie step into view, hair dripping wet. Behind her, an equally wet-haired Katie followed. She wore Annie's jacket like a dress, her hands poking out of rolled-up sleeves.

Annie dropped her bundle of wet clothes onto a rock, carefully adjusting her sack under her arms. "Just what are you boys doing?" she asked.

Willie held up his rock. "Having ice-cream bars and chocolate sundaes, of course; what does it look like we're doing?"

Annie rolled her eyes. She shook out her clothes, one by one, and laid them out flat. Katie's dress did not look clean, but it did look lighter.

"You know, that sack looks pretty good on you, Annie." Willie gave Alex a nudge. "What do you think, Alex?"

Annie flushed and shot them an angry look. "Let's see how good you lads look in a sack. Go on, get going. And do a good job scrubbing out your underwear."

Willie opened his mouth to retort, but his eyes fell upon Katie. "Very well." He got to his feet. "No peeking."

"Don't worry, you've got nothing worth peeking at."

Katie looked up wide-eyed, first at Annie, then at Willie. She let out a little giggle.

"And how would ye be knowing this?" Willie demanded.

"I'm your big sister, silly." Annie gave him a smug smile. "I know everything."

"Too true," Willie muttered, sack slung over his shoulder.

As Alex and Craig followed him around a bend, they heard another giggle from Katie.

———◆———

The bathing area was a hidden pool set into high surrounding rocks. Water trickled down from a crevice.

Craig prepared to get undressed. "Don't look."

"Dinnae be daft," Willie said. "We're all boys here."

"I don't care, don't look," Craig insisted.

Humoring Craig, Willie and Alex turned their backs. Willie let out a giant whoop and leapt, fully dressed, into the pool. He surfaced, spitting water into the air, and turned to splash Alex.

"Cannonball!" Alex bellowed. He took two big steps, leapt, knees tucked up, and kerplunked next to Willie.

Craig abandoned his plan to get undressed and ran to the water's edge. "Is it cold?" he called out.

Willie swept an arc of water at Craig. "Feel for yourself."

Craig squealed and jumped back. "Don't do that!"

Willie removed his trousers underwater. He smacked them down hard on the surface, first on one side, then the other. "Die . . . die!" he shouted.

Craig was finally waist-deep in the water. "How do we get clean without soap?" he asked.

Alex looked up from scrubbing his shirt between his hands. "We don't – we only get rinsed off, but it's better than nothing."

Willie motioned for silence. "What was that?" he hissed.

"What was what?" Alex tried to follow Willie's line of vision.

Willie pointed to a ridge. "I thought I heard something over there."

Willie and Alex climbed dripping from the water to retrieve their bows. Craig sank further into the pool and glided under some overhanging rocks.

Alex hastily wrapped himself in a sack. He was sure no opponent would take a skinny, naked boy with a crossbow seriously.

Clad only in his underwear, Willie tiptoed towards the ridge, longbow drawn and ready. Alex hesitated, thinking they should go the other way, away from the sound. But he couldn't leave Willie advancing on his own. Alex tensioned the crossbow, inserted a bolt, and reluctantly followed.

Willie flattened himself against a boulder, then slowly crept around it, his arm trembling from the effort of holding back the bowstring. He whispered hoarsely, "On the count of three, ready? One, two, three . . ."

They leapt past the edge of the boulder. Alex landed in a crouch and swung his crossbow back and forth. There was nothing except more rocks, cliffs topped by forests, and a shoreline stretching far to the south.

Willie relaxed his bow. "There's nobody here." He sounded disappointed.

Alex placed his bow down on the rocks. "It's a good thing too; my sack was about to fall off!" As he spoke, the sack did indeed drop to his feet.

Willie hooted. "He would have fallen down laughing. He would have been laughing so hard, he wouldn't have been able to put up a fight."

Alex stood naked, fists on his hips. "And what would have been so funny?"

"I surrender." Pretending to be the enemy, Willie rolled on the ground in convulsions of laughter. "Don't shoot, I surrender." He wiped tears from his eyes.

"That was very funny, boys." The voice came from up above them.

Willie and Alex frantically scrambled for their bows.

"Settle down, settle down" came the voice again. "Don't ye hurt yourselves."

"Sir Ellerslie!" Alex was delighted to see the familiar figure perched on the ridge.

"It is I." Sir Ellerslie landed with a soft thud next to them. "Ye lads need to learn a thing or two about stalking. Two quick arrows would've been the last of ye both."

"What are you doing here?" Alex asked, hastily tying his sack.

Sir Ellerslie winked. "Scouting, m'lad." He waved to Willie. "Hello. Would ye be any relation to wee Craig? I do see a bit of resemblance."

"He's my younger brother." Willie slowly released the tension on his bow. "But I think you're mistaken: there's no resemblance."

"Indeed! So there are lots of ye McRaes wandering through these dangerous lands then. And how is that wee rascal, Craig?"

"Oh, fine – he's probably shaking with fear behind some rock right now. We may have trouble finding him. . . ." Alex looked around in bewilderment. "Now, what did I do with my crossbow? Didn't I leave it –"

"Hands up!" came a squeaky shout from behind them.

Shocked, Alex raised his hands, as did Willie and Sir Ellerslie. Slowly, they turned around. Craig was pointing a drawn crossbow at them. He was shaking with fear and struggled to keep the weapon steady.

"Craig!" cried Alex. "It's us . . . and Sir Ellerslie."

Craig lowered the bow. "Sir Ellerslie?" A smile spread over his face. "I'm so glad it's you. I thought we were captured."

"Nae, it was you who captured me. Well done, m'lad. There's no many who can say they've done that."

"It seems, Sir Ellerslie," Alex said with a mischievous smile, "that you still need to learn a thing or two about stalking."

Sir Ellerslie gave Alex a gentle shove. "True!" He laughed. "The lesson I will take from today is to *never* underestimate my adversaries – or my friends." He put a hand on Craig's shoulder. "Thank you, Craig, for asking me to put up my hands rather than shoot me. That was good of you."

Craig blushed. "I wouldn't have wanted to shoot you, Sir Ellerslie."

"I'm glad to hear that. There are far too many people out there who do."

"Did you win the battle?"

"Which battle? There have been so many. Do you mean the one with Rorie's men? Yes, I did survive that, although they put up a better fight than we thought. I suspect they were a special force of Hesselrigge's best men, on a mission to capture or kill William Wallace."

<hr />

Back at the bathing pool, the boys quickly finished scrubbing their clothes and bundling them up. Clad only in sacks, they led Sir Ellerslie to their hiding spot. They found Annie, now in her mostly dry clothes, picking through Katie's tangled hair with the comb Alex had carved. At the sight of Sir Ellerslie, Annie hastily reached for a rock and Katie sprinted out of sight.

"It's okay, this is our friend, Sir Ellerslie," Alex called out.

"Pleased to make your acquaintance, lass." Sir Ellerslie gave a deep bow.

Alex explained who he was, and Annie lowered her arm. It took several minutes, however, for Katie to peer out from behind a boulder.

The boys set about spreading their wet clothes over rocks. Sir Ellerslie sat near the fire. He glanced about the camp, nodding approvingly.

"You're well hidden and sheltered here. How'd ye find such a lovely spot?"

"We were lucky, that's all." Annie lifted the lid of the warm pot at the edge of the fire. "Would you like to have some stew?"

Sir Ellerslie leaned forward to have a look. "*Mmm*, that smells mighty fine, but I don't want to be taking your food." He settled back.

"But, I insist." Annie gave the pot a stir. "We have plenty, and tomorrow we're going crab-hunting anyway, so it's best we finish up the remains."

Sir Ellerslie relented. He took the wooden spoon, ladled up some stew, and had a sip. Alex watched carefully, but by the time Sir Ellerslie was finished, he still hadn't spotted either of the rabbit eyeballs.

"Can you tell us, Sir Ellerslie," Alex asked, "where we might be able to get our hands on some torches, or perhaps some oil lamps?"

"We've got lots back at our camp. But why would ye be needing them?"

"To find our way through the caves," Craig blurted eagerly.

Sir Ellerslie paused. "Caves?"

Craig covered his mouth. "In case we find one," he added quickly.

"Where are these caves?"

There was nothing to be gained from lying. "Down by the castle," Alex said, and he told Sir Ellerslie of the entrance that could be reached only at the lowest tide. Sir Ellerslie laughed when Alex described how it led up a shaft they thought might have been a toilet. Then he suddenly looked serious.

"Tell me, do these caves lead into the castle?"

"I think so, but we haven't been that way."

There was a gleam in Sir Ellerslie's eye. "The castle is almost impenetrable in a frontal assault, and we fear much loss of life," he said. "Should this be a back door to the fortress, we might have the answer." He continued to press them for details. Finally satisfied, he rose to his feet.

"Well, lads and lassies, I must be off. Low tide is but a few days away, and there is much to prepare."

"Can we come with you?" Craig asked.

Sir Ellerslie ruffled Craig's hair. "I havenae the time to be traveling with wee rascals. Besides, I think it would be better for ye to stay here. Ye should be safe enough until I return with Malcolm and a band of his men. Soldiers do, however, make patrols, and I strongly urge that any time any of ye venture from this hiding spot, ye keep a close eye out for them."

Sir Ellerslie looked to Katie. "I am very sorry to hear about what happened to your family, Katie. I will personally see to it that ye are looked after properly, when all is said and done."

Katie dropped her eyes. "Thank you, sir." She gave a small curtsy, her lip trembling.

"I'll be back within two days." Without a further word, he departed.

Craig said what everyone was thinking: "I wish he didn't have to go." It felt safer when Sir Ellerslie was with them.

Now a sense of nervousness and anxiety came over them all.

"He'll be back, don't worry. He knows where we are now," Alex said.

———◆◆———

The rest of the day was spent waiting for clothes to dry, tending the fire, and contemplating what was to come. Annie finished combing out Katie's hair. She had transformed her from a scruffy urchin with matted hair into a little girl. She was still reluctant to meet anyone's eyes for more than a second or two, but Alex often noticed her watching him. Wherever he went, Katie was never far away.

At dinner, they almost finished the rabbit stew and ate the last of the dry bread and biscuits Annie had salvaged from the soldiers' camp. Alex wondered what kind of crabs they would catch the next day and whether he could possibly bring himself to eat something that looked so disgusting.

As the sun set, they rearranged the blankets. To accommodate Katie's wish to sleep between Annie and Alex, Craig ended up between Annie and Willie and he was quite happy about it. He made no bones about not wanting to be on the outside edge. This left Willie and Alex on opposite ends again, each with their bow within reach, and Annie where she wanted to be, smack in the middle.

Satisfied with this arrangement, they settled into sleep, no longer plagued by the prospect of werewolves and vampires. Alex felt Katie snuggle into his back. He was her big brother now, the only one she had. And she was the little sister he never had. He tugged the crossbow closer, wanting nothing bad to ever happen to her again.

Flames lapped up the sides of a large piece of driftwood. The fire's faint pop and crackle and the hypnotic tongues of flame soon lulled him into a deep and restful sleep.

15

THAT'S NO MY SON

"Where's Katie?"

Annie shook Willie. "Katie's gone. Get up, hurry!"

Willie pulled his blanket up over his head. "Don't worry," he mumbled sleepily. "She'll be back soon. She went crab-hunting."

"When?"

"I don't know . . . it was early . . . the sun was barely up."

"That was ages ago! We have to go look for her. Oh, how could you let her go on her own? You heard what Sir Ellerslie said about soldier patrols. . . ."

"Don't blame me! I told her to go back to sleep, but she wouldn't listen. She said it was the perfect time to catch crabs and away she went."

The weather had taken a turn for the worse. A cool, light drizzle misted them as they clambered over the rocks to the water's edge.

"Where can she be?" Annie fretted. "The tide is too far in to be catching crabs."

"What's that over there?" Craig asked. Something half-submerged was bumping into a distant rock with each rise and fall of the waves.

"Katie!" Annie shrieked.

Alex felt a clammy chill. *Please let it not be Katie.* They raced to the shore. It was only a sack rolling about in the waves. A swell brought it up within reach.

Craig dragged it out of the water and held it open. "There are a couple of crabs in here," he said. "But why would Katie have left it?"

They looked fearfully up and down the coast. There was no sign of her.

"Spread out and keep looking," Annie said.

Alex rounded a point. Seeing movement, he threw himself down flat. Not more than a half a mile down the coast was a small band of four or five men on horseback. He raised his head to have another look. His worst fears were confirmed – they had seen him. Several were pointing in his direction and spurring their horses into a gallop.

Alex ran back around the point to where Willie, Annie, and Craig were searching for Katie. "Soldiers are coming! Quick, get back to the hiding place. They're on horseback and they're almost here!"

Willie froze. "What? Are you sure?"

"Yes," Alex shouted. "They've seen me and they're coming fast."

Craig began to run, tripped, and sprawled. Annie helped him get up, and they both sprinted for the hiding place.

Alex stopped. The realization of what he had to do came with a numbing chill.

"I'm going to the forest," he called. "They don't know you're here and they'll follow me. I'll lose them in the woods."

Willie started after him. "I'm coming with you."

Alex waved for him to stop. "No, no, no! You need to look after Annie and Craig. GO! Quickly, before they see you."

Alex ran the other way, scrabbling up a slope. Stopping for breath, he looked back and saw the horsemen down by the shore drawing near at a steady gallop. One spotted him and gestured to where he stood. They drew up their horses, conferred briefly, and turned inland. The horses picked their way around rocks and headed up a steep gorge.

Good. Annie, Craig, and Willie will be safe . . . for now.

Alex made a quick calculation. The gorge led up to the cliff plateau. From there, they could shoot down on him or chase him anywhere. He simply had to make it to the plateau and into the forest before they could intercept him.

He scanned the cliff. There was no trail, so he decided to climb straight up. The further he climbed, the steeper it became. The drizzle made the rocks slippery. Alex squinted against the rain and looked for new handholds. Finding fewer cracks and crevices, he feared he would reach a dead end.

He was up so high that a single slip would mean certain death. There was no time to climb back down and try elsewhere.

His arms and legs trembling, he reached for far-off finger grips and toeholds. He pictured the soldiers looking down at him from above, laughing as they casually strung their bows. He wondered if it would be better to jump or wait for the arrows. He gritted his teeth. *I've got to make it, I've got to. . . .*

Each time he thought there were no holds left, a stretch enabled him to reach another. Finally, he reached a fissure covered by tall grass. He scrambled up the remaining slope, careful not to slip on the crumbly earth. His head popped over the top edge. Before him were rolling, grassy hills that ended at a solid green wall of forest. He glanced in the direction of the gorge. The horses had not made it up yet.

Alex sprinted through the open fields. *Must reach trees; must reach trees; must reach trees.* Suddenly, to his dismay, there they were, galloping across the field, each hunched in his saddle. They were approaching fast.

Alex fought back tears of rage. *Is this just a big game for them?* He wished he had his bow, so he could stop and aim.

But he did not have a bow, and to stop would be to die – of that, Alex was certain.

The forest looming ahead, Alex put on extra speed despite the severe pain in his chest. He heard the thunderous hooves drawing near, shaking the ground as he ran. An arrow streaked by him. Then he was among the trees. The underbrush quickly thickened. He dove under bushes, their thorny branches scratching him and tearing his clothes.

The soldiers dismounted and followed. They were not exhausted from running and would be able to run him into the ground. The pain in his lungs, his sides, and his legs was too intense to go much farther. His breath came in ragged gasps.

Alex searched for some way to turn, some way to take a last stand, however futile. Above was a twisted tangle of branches. He climbed, pulling himself high up through the limbs until he was shielded from the ground by a thick leafy cluster. There, he waited as quietly as he could while still gasping for air.

The soldiers drew nearer. He heard rustling, their voices, someone cursing. "Damn it all, ye had a clear shot back there. How could ye have missed?"

"Stop your complaining. We'll get him yet."

Alex held his breath when the soldiers passed under his tree. He braced for the worst, but they crashed on into the woods without slowing. Alex could hardly believe his luck, but he knew the soldiers would soon be back. A bold plan came to him, but could he do it?

I have to, Alex thought grimly. He forced himself to leave his hiding place and drop from branch to branch to the ground. He ran back the way he came, past the same sharp thorny bushes that had scratched him a few minutes before. He ran and ran until he was at the edge of the forest, where the soldiers had left their horses.

Alex had been on a horse only once before. A schoolmate in Canada lived on a hobby farm. There, Alex had brought a horse to a trot, bouncing awkwardly in the saddle while trying hard to get the hang of moving with the horse's rhythm. He wasn't good at it, but he'd managed to stay on.

The horses snorted as he approached and watched him warily. There was no time to waste. Alex untied the reins of each horse and turned them about. Any hope he had of a quick and merciful death at the hands of the soldiers was eliminated by what he was attempting to do; they would now be angrier than ever.

Alex picked the most docile-looking beast of the lot, quickly adjusted the stirrups, and swung up onto its back. Still holding the reins of the other three, he dug his heels into the horse's sides. To his dismay, it did not move. It simply put its head down and munched on grass.

"C'm on, giddyap, GO!" For good measure, Alex gave the horse a slap. Nothing, only the a swish of its tail.

Alex heard a shout, and an arrow whizzed past his shoulder. He slouched as a second and third arrow passed over him. The soldiers were closing the gap. Pleading with his horse to get going, he saw a soldier stop to fire off an arrow. It went astray and stuck deep into the rump of one of the horses. It reared, with a loud shrieking neigh. Bucking and kicking, it bolted, frightening the other horses into running too.

Alex's horse broke into a furious gallop. He flew right out of the saddle, but managed to hang on. The frightened beast thundered across the field.

Alex spotted the remaining horses: one galloping alongside, the one with the arrow in its flank stomping and rearing, but no longer running. The last had resumed grazing.

Alex's horse slowed. He dug his heels into its sides to keep it going, but it ignored him. A soldier leapt onto the grazing horse and spurred it on. Infuriated, Alex saw the soldier's horse instantly obey. He shook his reins, yelled giddyap, and even tried to kick his horse, but to no avail. His horse merely shook its head and stopped altogether. Frustrated and feeling a deep rage well up within him, Alex leaned forward and sunk his teeth hard into his horse's twitching ear.

That did it! His horse surged forward. He attempted to direct it inland towards the woods. To his amazement, the horse responded. Soon, trees were flashing by. But as the horse galloped along a narrow forest trail, it brushed so close to the trees that some almost caught his legs. It ran headlong under low branches, making Alex flatten and slide to one side to avoid being hit. Several times, the horse jumped over fallen tree trunks. Each time, Alex flew from the saddle and almost lost his grip.

The hard-whipping soldier was close behind. Alex shouted, "Yeah, yeah, yeah," to keep his horse on its careening gallop. It ran over an embankment, deciding to charge down a dry creek bed. That was fine with Alex, as long as it kept going. When the creek bed ended at a small loch, the horse hurtled along the shoreline. Alex barely had time to register that the water to his left was the loch of the McRaes' farm – the loch near William Wallace's camp – before his horse plunged back into the forest, following yet another narrow trail.

Suddenly the soldier's horse fell, tumbling head over hooves as if shot dead in midstride. The soldier was flung into the air and landed in a flailing roll. He sprang to his feet, drawing his sword, only to suddenly turn into a porcupine person, arrows protruding everywhere. He fell to his knees, then onto his face, and lay twitching.

Alex frantically reined in his horse, trying not to fall. "I hate haggis, I hate haggis!" he cried, throwing up his hands.

Its reins slack, Alex's horse snorted, shook its head, and stopped. Bowmen materialized all around, their bows drawn.

"That be the old password," one said.

"Take me to Sir Ellerslie . . . or William Wallace," Alex pleaded. "I have important information."

The bowman stretched his bow. "We take no captives."

"Sure you do!" Alex was desperate. "Why else have you got Jack, the jailer? Also, Groenie will be unhappy if you shoot me – I was his helper."

The bowman hesitated. "This lad knows us all."

"Is he not among those impostors they were to bring to the McRae clan?" asked another.

"That was a trick to fool Rorie," Alex pleaded. "Ask Malcolm; he knows."

Another bowman stepped forward. "Aye," he said. "We'd best do that. Down ye get."

Alex slowly dismounted. Several bowmen were retrieving arrows from the soldier, now motionless. A rope was stretched taut across the trail at knee height. Either his horse saw the rope and cleared it, or the bowmen sprang the trap after his horse had passed. Miraculously, the soldier's horse was now on its feet again, appearing none the worse for its tumble.

Several bowmen swung the dead soldier by the wrists and ankles and heaved him over the rump of his horse. His head swung back and forth as they trekked towards the camp.

Alex concentrated on the trail ahead, trying not to look at the body. He saw the split rock. The bowmen waved to barely visible sentries. "Eye of the storm," one called out. Alex presumed it was the new password.

Judging by the number of men in the camp, Wallace had found more recruits. One large group was engaged in a mock battle, clanging their swords.

A group leader called out, "What news? Has there been a battle?"

The clanging of the swords died, and Alex's party became the center of attention.

"Nae." A bowman thrust Alex forward. "We have merely caught this young lad here leading a soldier to our camp. Maybe Jack can get the truth from him."

Alex's protests fell on deaf ears.

The swordsmen stood aside for a familiar, pointy-bearded man. "Alex, lad! Good to see ye safe and sound."

Malcolm waved off the men's protests. "This is a friend and an ally. Don't ye worry; I'll commend your actions in keeping this lad safe to Sir Ellerslie. I'm sure he'll want to thank each of ye personally for this good work." He heartily put his arm around Alex's shoulders. "Now come, we must tell Sir Ellerslie you're here. He told me of your encounter with him on the coast."

Malcolm steered him to a large tent, where guards stood aside upon Malcolm's approach. Alex strained to see in the dark interior, lit only by an oil lamp.

A dark form rose. "Alex! What brings ye here, lad?" The voice was Sir Ellerslie's.

"The soldiers found us." Alex tripped over himself in his haste to tell him everything. "They've got Katie – we have to save her. I barely got away when the soldiers came. We've got to hurry!"

"Not so fast, m'lad; slow down and tell me exactly what happened." Sir Ellerslie motioned for Alex to sit and poured him a mug of water.

Alex took a deep breath and recounted the events of the day, starting when he woke with the others and discovered that Katie was missing. Sir Ellerslie and Malcolm shook their heads in amazement as Alex described climbing the tree to evade the soldiers. They burst out laughing when he told them that he'd escaped by stealing their horses.

When he finished, Sir Ellerslie turned to a large person seated beyond the glow of the oil lamp at the far end of the table. "We may need to advance the timing of our attack," he said. "Particularly if Hesselrigge thinks to have the lassie interrogated. She knows our plan to use a tunnel."

"I am no convinced of this plan." Wallace's deep voice rumbled down the length of the table. "I am no convinced that diverting a team of my best men to finding tunnels and caves that might not even exist is a good idea. These men will be needed in our assault."

"Aye, I understand your concern," Sir Ellerslie said. "But if the tunnel does exist, and if we do manage to open the main gates from within . . ."

"Those are a lot of 'ifs.' Tell me . . ." Wallace leaned forward and addressed Alex directly ". . . this tunnel ye say can be reached only at the lowest of low tides, what makes ye say it connects with the castle?"

"I was told this by a professor who has studied the history of this area," Alex replied. "He said that battles over the castle were won and lost because of the caves."

"A professor? Be that one who professes knowledge?"

"Yes, he is a learned man – a scholar."

Wallace turned to Sir Ellerslie. "There will be no rescue if ye fail. Ye will be vastly outnumbered within the castle, and heaven help ye if ye are caught: Hesselrigge will show no mercy, far from it in fact." He pulled Sir Ellerslie aside and continued in a low voice. "Are ye quite sure to put so much confidence in the word of this lad? As I've said before, he does appear to be a bit soft in the head, does he no?"

Sir Ellerslie smiled. "I'll stake my life on it," he said simply.

"That is precisely what ye are doing." Wallace picked up his gloves. "Very well; this bizarre plan is a long shot, but worth a try. However, ye will get no more than a half-dozen men. Our main force will begin the assault of the castle one hour before the second dawn – whether ye have successfully penetrated the castle or not."

Bursting with excitement, Alex struggled to maintain restraint as he said, with his head bowed, "Thank you very much, sir."

Wallace looked at Alex quizzically. "Quite un-expectedly, we now have a lot riding on ye, m'lad. Fate can never be foretold and forever surprises. Be off now, and Godspeed."

Malcolm followed Sir Ellerslie from the tent. "We'll need to bring five of your best men," Sir Ellerslie said, "and *only* your best. We'll also need torches, ropes, and picks."

"Aye, Sir, I know who to choose." Malcolm gave a half-salute. "Give me one hour."

"Very good." Sir Ellerslie gave Malcolm a nod of farewell. "Alex, I have some affairs to attend to. I suggest ye get some-thing to eat from Groenie."

———◆·◆———

Alex was left alone to explore the camp. He stayed well clear of the area where men were practicing, clashing swords with vigor. He didn't want to get in their way.

Alex hoped to make it past the kitchen lean-to unno-ticed, but Groenie spotted him, calling out with surprising joviality, "Alex, m'lad, ye're back! From the dead, it would appear! Would ye be here to help me this time? I've been so busy with all these extra men."

"I'm sorry, Groenie. I am to depart on an important mission with Sir Ellerslie and Malcolm within the hour."

Groenie scrunched his brow. "It's always the same." He took up a dirty scrub brush. "Ah, well, never mind. Come and have some grub before ye go. I've baked a new batch of bread, and there's some venison stew ye can dip it into."

Alex gratefully accepted the offer. He sat at the long wooden table while Groenie ladled it out. Placing the bowl and a hunk of fresh bread before Alex, Groenie looked at him with a glint in his eye. "Whatever your mission, m'lad, do me one favor: *Win*. Defeat the enemy. The sooner they're defeated, the sooner I get to go back to my land and see my wife and bairns."

Surprised, Alex watched Groenie resume his pot-scrubbing. He had not thought of Groenie as a man with a family.

Alex finished his meal and had some time on his hands, so he decided to stroll about the camp. Passing the black-smith's workplace, he noticed racks of shiny new swords, shields, and breastplates. It appeared Wallace had plans for enlisting even more recruits.

A solitary older man was wheeling a squeaky wheel-barrow down a bumpy trail. The wheelbarrow's contents were covered by a dirty cloth. Curious, Alex followed, catching up to him on the outskirts of camp, where the man was struggling to push the heavy load up an embankment. Failing at his first try, the man backed up to take another run at it.

"Can I help?" Alex offered.

"Aye, can ye carry my shovel for me?" The man carefully set the ends of the wheelbarrow down on the uneven ground. "It keeps falling off my 'barrow when I go over bumps."

Alex took the long-handled shovel. "Do we have far to go?" He did not want to be late for his scheduled rendezvous.

"Nae, just over this wee rise here." The old man wiped his sweaty hands on the back of his trousers. Pulling up on the wheelbarrow handles, he ran at the hill, the load bouncing and thumping with each bump. The cloth cover shifted and a bare human foot protruded from under the folds.

Alex stopped dead in his tracks.

"C'm on, then," the old man called back over his shoulder. "Here's the spot."

Ahead was a ridge of freshly dug earth. Reluctantly, Alex followed as the old man pushed the wheelbarrow over the last crest. The man set the wheelbarrow down before a trench, put his hands on his hips, and stretched. His backbone popped and crackled.

"I'm too old for all this haulin' about," the old man grumbled. "I should be home sittin' before the fire with my pipe, havin' my bairns and their bairns tendin' to my needs."

"Why don't you do that?" Alex asked, from ten paces away.

The old man's eyes lost their focus. "Aye, laddie, why indeed. At one time, I thought that is how I would live out my old age. Me and my missus worked hard on the land all these years; we had enough to share, and share we did. Those were good days. We had four sons and two dochters that grew to be big – and a few more that didn't, mind ye. Then the dark days came. As the price for staying on my land, the purser demanded more and more of my crop 'til there was no enough for us. We grew more and more hungry, and there was nothing I could do. My wife, my dear wife of so many years, got sick. I had no money to pay for a healer – I pleaded with the lord's men to give me a reprieve on my taxes so we would have enough food . . . so I could take my wife to a healer and pay for some medicine. . . ."

The old man was no longer talking to Alex; he was talking to himself. His voice was strained. "I miss you, Lizzie. I will to my dyin' day."

Alex did not dare interrupt.

"My dochters have married good lads, but they cannae make enough to live. Their wee bairns cry out in hunger. Two of my sons were taken to be soldiers. Before the soldiers could come for my other two sons, I met the good William Wallace, who told us we could fight – aye, fight and win!"

The man paused and looked intently at Alex. "To me dyin' breath, I shall fight. It's better to die spittin' on the dead of your enemy than living with them spittin' on ye every day, don't ye think?"

"What happened to your sons who became soldiers?"

"I've never seen 'm again." The old man abruptly pulled up on the wheelbarrow handles. The wheelbarrow's nose dug into the dirt and the grisly contents slid out and tumbled into the trench.

The man squinted at the twisted corpse. Although all his armor had been removed, Alex recognized him as the soldier that had chased him.

"That's no my son," the old man said, with a tired note

of relief. "Now, lad, ye know why I have this job. If I do find my missing sons, I will want them to have a proper burial."

"Where are your younger sons?" Alex handed the old man his shovel.

"They're no so young. Big strappin' lads they are, and they're here fightin' with William Wallace." The old man flung a shovel of fresh earth down into the trench. It landed with a dull thud, splattering dirt over the white dead face.

"I just hope they don't meet their older brothers on the battlefield. And if they do, I hope they won't know it."

The old man flung down more shovelfuls until the corpse was but an outline in the dirt. Only the toes of one foot protruded. Waving away the persistent flies, Alex noticed there were many more outlines in the dirt, each covered with squiggling, whitish gray shapes – clusters of feasting maggots! Suddenly, Alex knew why the air about him had such a strong sickly-sweet odor. He felt the now all-too-familiar sensation of blood draining from his body.

Waving away the flies, Alex said weakly, "Good-bye. See you again sometime, Mr. . . ."

"Bruford," the old man said with a smile. "Alan Bruford's my name, and y'rs?"

"Alex."

"I thought so. My son has told me much about ye already."

"He has? Do I know him?"

"Aye, ye've met him a few times. Malcolm's his name. Say hello to him for me. Hurry off now."

Alex raced back down the embankment. He was still stiff and sore from having run so much earlier that day, but he did not want to be late.

16

THE MISSION

Alex jogged through the entire camp without finding Malcolm and his men. He did not know where they were to meet and was worried that he might not find them.

Heavy clouds had rolled in, bringing a bout of drizzle and mist. The damp took the enthusiasm out of the war games. Men sat clustered near their tents, playing games of chance and dexterity with small sticks, ready to take refuge should the rain come down harder. They shouted and threw back their heads with great bellows, exchanging coins whenever someone won.

A tent flap flung open and Sir Ellerslie appeared. Relieved, Alex was about to shout and wave when he noticed, barely visible in the darkness of the tent, a woman in a long dress. Sir Ellerslie turned back and they embraced. Alex kept going, not wanting Sir Ellerslie to catch him watching.

Horses neighed in the distance. Alex explored the out-skirts of camp and found Malcolm with a small group of men, leading the horses from paddocks. The men were dressed entirely in black. Their horses snorted impatiently, sensing a hard ride ahead.

"Everything ready?" The voice came from behind him. Alex looked over his shoulder and saw Sir Ellerslie approaching. He was alone.

"Aye, Sir." Malcolm slapped a saddlebag. "We have torches in watertight bags, with flints to light them, rope to help us climb, and picks to hack our way past underground obstacles. We have a few skins of water also. Beyond that, we'll have to live by our wits – and the sword."

"That we will do – well done, Malcolm." Sir Ellerslie ran an appraising eye over the men. "And tell me, who have ye chosen to join us?"

"The best!" Malcolm said, holding out his arm toward a slight, fine-featured man who, at first glance, seemed better suited for the ministry than part of a crack assault team. "Reagan here is an expert climber. He spent much of his youth in the Highlands and was renowned for his ability to climb sheer cliffs – even when they sloped forward over the climber. He can hang out over nothing. I thought his talents would be useful to us."

Reagan finished tying a coil of rope to his saddle and made a small bow.

Malcolm gestured to an intent-looking man with neat, oily-black hair. "Neil, on the other hand, is a champion swordsman. He can swing a sword so quickly that before his opponent can counter a move to one side, Neil has him on the other."

Neil's eyes never left Sir Ellerslie's, even as he gave a slight nod.

Sir Ellerslie suddenly made as if to draw his sword, but before it cleared the scabbard, Neil's sword was under his chin. Sir Ellerslie swallowed and slid his sword back. "Nicely done."

Neil put his sword away and bowed.

Malcolm carried on to the next – a tall man with several daggers protruding from over his shoulder in a modified quiver. "Hugh here is good with a sword too, but what distinguishes him is his ability with a dagger. He can throw one with such force that it sinks to the hilt, unless, of course, it's stopped by a rib."

Sir Ellerslie rubbed his chin. "That's an unusual talent. Can we have a demonstration on yon tree?"

Hugh reached back over his shoulder. There was a flash of spinning steel and a dull thud.

Sir Ellerslie let out a low whistle. "That would be very effective in confined quarters – if ye can strike a spot with no armor."

"I've seen him skewer an apple thrown into the air. Now George – that large muscular man there – is the best at unarmed combat. He can outwrestle any man I've ever met and can snap a person's neck at will. But when he's not agitated, he's the gentlest man around. Aren't ye, George?"

George tipped his cap and bent to pick up a heavy saddle. Seemingly without effort, he swung it high and lowered it gently onto his horse's back.

"He loves animals and playing with children. When he stands with his arms out, children pretend he's a tree and climb all over him."

There were a few smiles, but no one laughed. They knew better than to laugh at big gentle George.

"And who's that man with the unusually short bow?" asked Sir Ellerslie.

A barrel-chested man not much taller than Craig looked up from tightening his horse's saddle.

"Yon's Donald. We have many men who excel with the longbow, even more that are good with a crossbow, but none who fire a short bow like Donald. He can fire one arrow after another so quickly that the second is airborne before the first has struck."

"Short bows are hard to pull – and hard to shoot straight," said Sir Ellerslie.

"Aye, but they're good for short-range conflict, such as we may encounter in caves or a castle," Malcolm said. He gave Donald a nod.

Following a flash and a blur, two arrows quivered in the tree, one on either side of Hugh's dagger.

"Hey!" Hugh protested. "Ye could have damaged my dagger. That handle is finely carved from deer antler –"

"Calm down, Hugh," said Malcolm, stepping between them. "If Donald wanted to hit your dagger, he would have."

Hugh looked unconvinced, but retrieved his dagger from the tree. He hesitated, then pulled out the arrows and handed them to Donald.

"Well, this is an excellent collection of talent ye have assembled here, Malcolm." Sir Ellerslie gave a playful smile. "So tell me, what speciality do ye bring to the team?"

Malcolm did not hesitate. "I lead, Sir. I apply the talent where and when it's best used."

"Then we truly have everything we need for success."

Sir Ellerslie clapped his hands and raised his voice so everyone could hear.

"This will be a difficult mission, one where we will face grave danger and near impossible odds. But when we succeed, and succeed we will, Hesselrigge will swing from a gibbet, and we will have gained a great victory in our fight for liberty. It is also a secret mission. Once I tell ye of what we are to do, there is no turning back. Should any of ye wish to decline, tell me now."

Reagan spoke up. "We're with ye, Sir Ellerslie. I believe I speak for us all."

"Aye, I'm with ye as well." Neil's pronouncement was followed by nods from the others.

Sir Ellerslie smiled. "Very well, let me tell ye of our mission. We will be penetrating the castle by way of secret caves. Once inside, we will disrupt the defenses and find a way to facilitate a main assault, which will commence before sunrise the day after the morrow, approximately thirty-six hours from now."

The men murmured their surprise.

The questions came in rapid succession:

"Where are these caves?"

"Are they guarded?"

"Will we have to dig our way in?"

"Who is this lad?"

Sir Ellerslie raised his hands.

"This is Alex." He had Alex stand before him and face the men. "The first time I saw this lad, he was lost in the woods and about to become intimately acquainted with the working end of a robber's club. He is a bit of a mystery to us. He speaks strangely, and no one is sure from where he comes, although he claims to be of Macpherson lineage.

"Alex is not alone. Every time I find him, he's with young folk, all of whom speak strangely, though none as strange as him. The others claim to be of the McRae clan, but none of the McRaes have knowledge of them. He has told us of a secret tunnel that is rumored to access caves beneath the castle. It's our job to find it."

Sir Ellerslie paused for this to sink in and gently clapped Alex on both shoulders. "Tell the men, Alex, what ye know of these caves."

"The caves are old," Alex began hesitantly. "They were here before the castle was built. Not many know they exist. Some who found them went in and were never heard from again. . . ."

The men rolled their eyes.

"It's true!" Alex tried desperately to sound more convincing. "My parents were among those who disappeared in those caves, and I'm going to find them –"

Sir Ellerslie cut him off. "We will be searching the caves only to find a way into the castle. But I do commit to ye, Alex, that when our battles are over and Duncragglin is ours, we will do what we can to help ye."

Sir Ellerslie turned to address the men. "Our first task is to find the tunnel. If we do not succeed, we will have lost no more than a day's effort. If we do, the game is on." He put his foot in the stirrup and swung onto his horse. "Let us be off."

The men headed out, leaving Alex to scamper up the horse Malcolm had prepared for him. As Alex caught up, his horse slowed to a steady canter. The men let the horses find their own pace, and before long, they were down to a brisk trot. Alex bounced painfully in the saddle until he got the hang of the new rhythm.

The path narrowed rapidly, and the horses moved into single file. Alex found himself right behind the swordsman, Neil, whom he recognized by the oily-black shiny hair that protruded from under his deerskin hat.

Ahead was a hazy mist. Branches brushed past when the horses maneuvered turns. After being slapped in the face by a wet leafy branch, Alex learned to watch Neil's back and duck and weave when he did.

As if to better assault the riders, mist particles banded together to become a chilling, penetrating drizzle. The light rain soon pasted Alex's hair to his head and sent trickles of water down his neck. He fumbled to button up his jacket with one hand, the other holding the reins of his trotting horse. Although thankful that his jacket held back most of the rain, he wished it had a hood, or that he had a hat like the others . . . or better yet, that it would stop raining.

By the time they reached the coast, the rain had become an outright downpour. They took shelter under the canopy of large trees, but cold splatters of water continued to find them. Soaked all down his back, Alex sat shivering, hunched in his saddle, feeling miserable. Here he was, seven hundred years from his own time, his friends captured or dead, no place to call home. . . . Unexpected tears mixed with the rain that trickled down his face.

Through the din of rain crashing through the forest, Alex heard one of the men speak. "Good thing it's coming down like this," the man said. "Less likely for soldiers to be about."

"Aye, it will send them dashing back for the shelter of the castle," said another. "Besides, it can drizzle for days, but rain usually stops after a downpour."

Sure enough, it was not long before the steady roar became lighter and the rain stopped altogether.

Malcolm dismounted and signaled for the others to stay put. Sprinting across the wet grassy plateau, he kept low to the ground all the way to the cliff edge, where he scanned the base of the cliffs and the shoreline.

"No sign of soldiers," he reported. "But some might still be lurking about, so proceed with caution. There are many wee coves and inlets that I couldn't see into."

They followed a soggy path along the edge of the forest, keeping a close eye for patrols now that they were in open view. Their horses had recovered from the long run through the woods and clopped along at a brisk trot.

Alex did not know where he was. The forest all looked the same to him: trees, trees, and more trees. He did not recognize the place where he had stolen a horse until they were riding right past it.

"Here! Here's where I left the other soldiers."

Malcolm reined in his horse and led the men into the trees. Alex showed them where the soldiers had tied their horses and then impatiently turned his horse about.

"Annie and the others should be in our hiding place," he said. "I gave them plenty of time to hide. Let's hurry. We should be able to bring our horses down that gorge."

Sir Ellerslie grabbed the reins of Alex's horse. "Wait just one moment here, young lad. We cannae just go blundering along. The soldiers might still be there, hiding – waiting for ye to come back."

"So what do we do?"

"We ambush the ambushers." Sir Ellerslie shifted in his saddle. "Malcolm, have Reagan go down the cliffs. Donald and Hugh can take up a position along the top ridge to the south. From there, they will have a good view of the shoreline and can fire down on any soldiers they see. Neil can go with ye down the gorge to the north to cut off any possible escape. Alex and I will draw them out. We'll circle back to the water's edge far to the south. The tide is on its way out and there's plenty of beach. As we proceed along the water's edge, they'll see us coming and think we're alone. We'll be out of the range of their arrows, so at a certain point they'll make a move. Once they're out of hiding, your men can take them down."

Malcolm grinned. "That's no unlike how we defeated them at Loch Karins. A fake to the left followed by a shot from the right. Do ye think they'll ever learn?"

"Aye, they might. And we'd best be prepared for that too. Keep an eye out."

Sir Ellerslie gently tugged his horse's reins. With a jerk of his head, he motioned for Alex to follow. They set off back the way they came.

Winding along next to gently lapping waves, their horses'

hooves muffled by the firm wet sand, all was calm and still. The setting sun peeked out from behind dark clouds, casting warm rays over Alex's wet clothes. He rocked back and forth on the saddle. For the first time in hours, he felt relaxed. *Wouldn't it be nice*, he thought, *if our ride ends at a log cabin, with a crackling fire, a table set with a hot cheesy-pasta dinner, pumpkin pie for dessert . . . with Annie, Willie, Craig, and Katie all there with me, laughing and joking about their adventures?*

Sir Ellerslie's quiet voice brought him back. "We're getting close; be alert."

Alex recognized the stretch of sloping rocks sticking out into the sea and he felt his heart quicken. He strained his eyes to detect movement. *Which of those distant sloped rocks is their shelter?* The shoreline looked completely deserted.

Even as they drew nearer to the point, there was no sign of anyone having been there. Alex recognized where he had searched for Katie. They were close to the hideout now, but still no sign of anyone. *Please let the soldiers be long gone*, he prayed, *please let Annie and the others be here*.

Sir Ellerslie drew in his horse and signaled for Alex to halt. He scanned the rocks, bow ready.

The first soldier Alex spotted came out from behind rocks further up the coast. He was soon accompanied by another, then another, until a half-dozen soldiers blocked their way.

"Those are not the same men . . . ," Alex began.

From behind nearby rocks, more soldiers leapt out and, battle cries ringing, charged.

Alex tugged hard on his horse's reins to turn it around. His horse reared, flipping Alex off its back onto the wet sand. His horse screamed and kicked madly, an arrow protruding from deep in its rump.

Suddenly an arrow lodged directly in Sir Ellerslie's back. Fighting to retain control of his horse, Sir Ellerslie did not fall. Instead, he kicked it into a gallop.

Alex did the only thing he could think of – he ran straight into the ocean. Water splashed around him, slowing him as he ran. When almost waist-deep, Alex dove, holding his breath. He kicked hard and breaststroked with all his might, until his lungs were screaming for air.

Gasping, Alex surfaced and swam straight out to sea. Arrows splashed into the water next to him, bobbing up to float harmlessly on the surface. He took another gulp of air and went back under. Within seconds, out of breath, he surfaced. He swam farther and farther from shore until, too exhausted to continue, he flipped over into a float.

Arrows were no longer falling around him, nor did it appear that anyone was coming in after him. Rising and falling with the ocean swells, Alex tried to see what was happening onshore. It had become dark. He listened intently, but could hear only distant waves upon rocks. Every now and then, he thought he heard a shout.

Alex was afraid that they might as yet set out after him and knew he could not stay for long in this numbingly cold water. He started swimming. The only stroke he could maintain for any length of time was the apple-picking sidestroke, and then only on his right side. He decided to fill bushels of one hundred apples each. He measured his progress in bushels and by the slow passing of a black peak silhouetted by an orange and red sky. His apple-picking was taking him north, towards the castle, towards more soldiers . . . towards the caves.

Cold racked Alex's body. Soldiers or no soldiers, he had to head in. *Seventy-eight, seventy-nine, eighty apples.* He remembered which bushel he was filling by concentrating on a particular finger. As he was now on the pinkie finger of his left hand, he must be filling his tenth bushel. The picking was getting slower. He shuddered each time he stretched out for yet another apple and felt himself sink further each time he passed the apple back. It took greater and greater effort to reach out. His body seemed determined to curl into a ball, but he knew he had to stretch out into the cold again, he had to . . . or he would sink.

Alex took in a gasp of water. He kicked hard, spluttering, coughing, flailing. . . . He tried to hack his airways clear. Lungs screaming, he sucked in convulsively and felt more water coming in. Everything was spinning, and he could no longer tell which way was up. Blackness swirled around him. His twitching became weaker, his gasps for air futile. A wave of darkness swept up and receded, followed by another and another. And then a last large wave of blackness flooded over him . . . a wave that did not recede.

PART III

A Change in Duncragglin

17

THE CAPTIVE IN MALCOLM'S HOME

Alex woke to find himself in a bed under snug covers. A small coal fire flickered shadows over a sloped plank ceiling. Lifting his head, he discovered to his delight that the bundle next to him was Craig, sleeping soundly the way he usually did: head tilted back, mouth slightly open, making gentle gurgling noises.

"*Shh!*" An ancient, wrinkly woman was raising her finger to her lips. "He's been awake for hours, watching ye, asking over and over if ye're alright," she rasped. "Let him sleep."

"Is Annie here, and Willie?"

The woman shook her head, her piercing eyes fixed on Alex. His heart sank.

"Are they . . . are they . . . ?" Alex could not bring himself to say the *D* word.

"They're missing." The woman drew her loose shawl up around her shoulders. "Sir Ellerslie thinks they were captured and taken away before ye got back."

"Sir Ellerslie's alive?" He thought of Sir Ellerslie, struck by an arrow. "Is he here?"

No sooner had Alex spoken than Sir Ellerslie appeared, his tall lean form looming up behind the elderly woman. Alex could see fresh white bandages bound across his chest. In several places, splotches of red had soaked through.

Alex gasped.

Sir Ellerslie laughed. "Aye, they got me good." He held up a rustling, metal tunic. "I knew this coat of mail would come in handy one of these days. The arrows didn't go in very far . . . still hurt, though."

"Malcolm? And the men?"

"I'm here, laddie." Alex instantly recognized the gruff voice. Malcolm emerged from an adjoining room. He gave Alex an affectionate clap on the shoulder. "Ye gave us a right fright. If big George wasn't such a strong swimmer, we'd have lost ye for sure."

Alex was bursting with questions. He sat up, careful not to disturb Craig. "What about the soldiers? And the others? How did you –"

"Settle down, settle down," Malcolm said, pulling back a chair. "All in good time. Let's get some hot soup in ye and I'll tell ye the rest – it's no all good news, mind." He looked grim.

Alex clambered half out of bed before discovering, to his horror, that he was wearing nothing at all. He pulled the covers back up all the way to his chin.

"Dinnae be silly." The old woman smiled as she shuffled over to the fireplace. "I've raised four boys of my own and they were no shy."

She felt a few of the dark shapes hanging before the fire. "These'ns are dry," she said, lifting them off the hooks. "I'll need to dig out a coat and boots though. Yours were lost to the sea.

"Have ye ever seen anything like these wee breeks?" She held up Alex's underwear to show Sir Ellerslie and Malcolm, giving a tentative tug on the elastic waistband. "They have some magical weaving about the waist."

"They're truly wondrous." Malcolm gave the band a little pull. "I wish I had wee breeks like these. Then I wouldnae feel such a breeze under my tunic."

Alex felt his face flush. "Excuse me, but can I have my clothes please?"

"But, of course." Grinning broadly, Malcolm handed the underwear back to the elderly woman. "Pass these to Alex, would you please, Gran?"

Gran? Alex's eyes widened.

"Aye, that ruffian is my grandson." The woman's eyes twinkled as she handed Alex his clothes. "I helped my son raise him after his mother died, God rest her soul."

"That's my old bed ye're in. I shared that with my older brother. . . ." Malcolm looked away.

Alex suddenly remembered the words of Malcolm's father, Mr. Bruford, when he said: "That's no my son."

"Me'n my three brothers shared two beds here in this room. Ma and Pa and my two sisters had the other room, yonder," said Malcolm.

Alex dressed under the covers, drawing smirks from the others.

"So, tell me what happened." Still buttoning his shirt, he sat at a rough plank table, where Malcolm's grandmother had placed several bowls of steaming hot soup. "How did we get away from the soldiers?"

"It was them that had to get away from us." Malcolm picked up his bowl and took a loud slurp. "They were clearly not expecting to see us. Sir Ellerslie's plan worked, although there were more of them than we thought. Those we didn't kill ran for their lives. . . ." Malcolm stared into his soup. "They got Neil though . . . the poor devil got run through."

"He's dead?" Alex gasped.

"Aye, sad to say it's true. He was bristling with arrows, but still managed to get out his sword and carve a few. . . ." Malcolm blinked back tears.

"He died the only way he would have wanted to – his sword stuck through the last foe he faced," Sir Ellerslie said quietly. "Without his heroic efforts, all might have been for naught."

"Aye, he broke their offense."

"He did more than that," Sir Ellerslie said. "He broke their spirit. Once they saw the kind of men they were up against, they knew all was lost."

They sat hunched over their soup, each lost in private thought – a moment's silence for Neil.

"Well, that's it then," Sir Ellerslie said. "We'd best return to Wallace's camp to join forces for the main assault on the castle."

Alex was aghast. "What about the caves? And the plans to get into the castle and open the main gates for the attackers?"

"The tide'll no be at a low point again until tonight. I don't think that gives us enough time. Besides, with the capture of your friends, they may know of the caves and be waiting for us there."

"Annie and Willie wouldn't tell them about the caves!"

"Ye don't know Hesselrigge and his men, Alex," Sir Ellerslie said gently. "They have . . . methods. I've seen them snap many a strong man."

"All the more reason to go after them."

Sir Ellerslie and Malcolm were unmoved. They stared into their soup.

"I'm going alone, then," Alex said.

"Dinnae be daft," Malcolm said flatly. "Ye'll be captured or killed."

"It's better than doing nothing."

"No, it is not," Malcolm said. "Sometimes, the best thing is to do nothing."

"You can do nothing all you want. But I will not – not when my friends are in so much trouble."

"We cannae let ye go, Alex," Sir Ellerslie said firmly. "I'll tell ye why: simply put, ye know too much. If ye were caught and Hesselrigge's men got ye to talk –"

"So I'm a captive now, is that it?" Alex banged the table angrily.

Storming away, Alex returned to his bed and pulled the covers up over his head. He wanted no more to do with these people. He imagined himself, armed with a dagger and sword, charging through the castle in search of his friends. He killed every soldier he encountered. It was a bloodbath.

"Alex, Alex, are you okay?" A little voice penetrated the layers of thick covers.

He pulled them back just enough to see Craig peering anxiously at him.

Alex nodded. "And how are you, Craig? What happened after I ran away?"

Craig looked off into the distance. When he spoke, his voice was flat and expressionless. "The soldiers that chased you were only the first that came looking for us. We split up and hid in separate places. Annie found a hollow under a rock for me to hide in. She made me promise not to move, no matter what. I told her, 'Yeah, yeah, I promise,' but no, that was not good enough for her. She told me to pinkie swear like I showed her, then she gave me a hug and said, 'Really, really, promise, okay?' So I promised, and I did a pinkie swear, and I stayed hidden – even when the soldiers got really close. . . ."

"Yes . . . then?"

Craig covered his face with his hands. "She made me promise," he said, with a muffled sob. "I heard her screaming when they dragged her away . . . I heard Willie too. It sounded like they hit him pretty hard." Craig collapsed onto the bed and pounded it with his fist. "Why did you make me promise? Why did you make me do that?" he sobbed.

Alex sat frozen on the bed. He did not know what to do. He no longer expected things to get better.

Suddenly Alex knew he was prepared to die. But he would not die quietly – he would die fighting, railing, scream-ing, lashing out at all that opposed him. Rage shook him as he looked about the small cottage. They were alone. Sir Ellerslie and Malcolm had gone to the other room, closing the door behind them. Malcolm's grandmother had left some time ago, the early-morning sun briefly streaming through the cottage door as she went out. Alex got up and buckled a dagger belt around his waist. He did not bother with a broadsword, too big and heavy to be of use. Instead, he took a crossbow down from a shelf and slung a quiver full of bolts across his back.

Alex tugged the laces of the leather shoes Malcolm's grandmother had given him. They were too big, but Alex didn't care about things like that anymore. He didn't care that the coarse woolen jacket prickled him through his cotton shirt. All that mattered was what he had to do.

Without a word to Craig or anyone else, Alex unlatched the cottage door and stepped outside.

18

Prepared to Die

Alex blinked in the morning sunshine and tried to get his bearings. Around him were hills crisscrossed with low walls and dotted with thatched-roof cottages, not unlike the one he had left. Each cottage was surrounded by a few ramshackle sheds and animal pens. There was a distant bustle: the bellow of a cow, a clanging of buckets, the persistent crowing of a cock. The fields were dotted with people hard at work – stooping over crops, pushing wheelbarrows. One was in an animal pen, shoveling.

The smell of manure hung about like an invisible fog. Alex felt it stick in his throat and cling to his clothes. None of that mattered.

By the position of the sun, Alex figured left was east, and east was the direction of the sea. So that was the way he went, crossbow over his shoulder. The footpath he was on spilled into a muddy road, barely wide enough for two carts to pass. That road suited him fine. It headed, more or less, in the right direction.

The ruts in the road brimmed with water from yesterday's

rain. Puddles spread right across the road. To get around them, Alex climbed a bordering wall, crossed a muddy field, and rejoined the road farther down. He wished he could walk balanced on the stone walls, but the tops were too jagged.

It was not long before Alex's feet were so wet that puddles hardly mattered. It was no different for others Alex encountered. Having muddy wet feet appeared to be an accepted fact of life here.

Alex stood next to a low stone wall to make way for a small flock of sheep, ushered along by a woman with a swishing stick. Her dog dashed back and forth, yapping whenever one lagged. Alex smiled at the woman as she passed. In return, she gave him a wary glance.

Alex passed a man leading a fierce-looking bull, with a long and shaggy red coat. The man squelched his way through the ankle-deep mud.

"Excuse me, sir," Alex called out. "But, could you tell me if this is the road to Duncragglin Castle?"

The man gave Alex a suspicious sideways stare. "What business would ye have with Duncragglin Castle?"

"That would be my business, sir," Alex replied boldly. This was, after all, the day he was prepared to die. He might as well be brazen about it.

"Turn about and go back home. Nae good will come of ye at Duncragglin Castle." The man and his shaggy bull continued on their way.

Home, and where would that be?

The man said he was to turn about, which must mean that by not turning about, he would be going the right way. Encouraged, Alex quickened his step, splashing along through the mud.

He was further encouraged when the road joined another to make a wider but equally muddy road. *Roads would get wider closer to the castle*, he thought.

On this wider road, an ox-drawn cart tilted dangerously, one of its two large wheels sunk deeply in the mud. Its teetering load of hay and produce was ready to fall, but for a few puny slats.

A man struggled knee-deep in watery muck to insert a plank in front of the sunken wheel. It looked hopeless. The wheel had sunk in the ooze right up to its axle.

The man did not take heed of Alex until Alex stood next to the cart and asked, "Can I help with something?"

The man looked up angrily. Mud was spattered over his face and dripped from his beard. "I ask the heavens above for some help, and what am I sent – a laddie. *Bah!* Away with ye. I've got work to do."

Normally, Alex would have been quite stung by such a rebuke. But not on the day he was prepared to die.

"Why don't you use the plank to lever it?" Alex asked. "You might be able to raise the side of the cart enough to put some rocks under the wheel."

"Levering it will never work. Be gone, laddie, and leave me to my task." The man turned dismissively, resuming his efforts to wriggle the plank into place deep in the slippery, sloshing, water-filled rut.

Embedded in the mud at the roadside was a large rock that looked just the right size for a fulcrum. Alex shrugged. He could not leave the man like this. With a sigh, he slung off his quiver, leaned his crossbow against a stone wall, and looked around for something he could use to dig out the rock. He climbed over the wall and kicked about in the field. Finally, he found a stick. It was small, but looked sturdy enough.

It took awhile, but with a steady effort of scraping and scooping, Alex managed to remove enough dirt to loosen the rock. However, it was still in a hole and it was still a long way from the cart.

Alex dug a makeshift ramp. He got down low behind the rock to give it a push. Water seeped into the hole, making the rock slippery and hard to handle. Alex put his shoulder to it, even though that meant he had to put his knee right into the mud. Head down, he heaved and felt the rock move. To his astonishment, the rock lifted into the air. Looking up, he saw the cart owner struggle to carry it, his muscles popping. The man staggered across the muddy road and dropped the rock behind the cart, where it landed with a heavy thud.

"Let's try it your way," the man panted, his chest heaving.

"We've got to get it closer to the axle." Alex crawled under the listing cart and used his stick to scrape away some mud to make room for the rock.

"Get out of there!"

Hands seized Alex's ankles and pulled him backwards. He was no sooner dragged out from under the cart when it settled deeper into the mud.

"It's dangerous under there," the man said gruffly.

"Thank you for your concern." Alex looked dubiously at the mud that now caked his clothes right up to his chin.

The man chuckled. "We're a right mess, are we no?"

"I was fine until I met you," Alex said, dismayed at how wet and filthy he had become.

They wriggled the timber so one end rested squarely on the rock and fit snugly under the axle. The other end stuck high up the back of the cart. The man tried to push the end down, but the cart did not budge. He leapt and landed heavily, draping himself over the end of the plank. This time there was a slurping noise.

"It's coming, it's coming. We need more weight," he shouted.

Alex scampered onto the plank. More slurping noises came from under the cart. Alex shuffled up to the end of the timber, his arms outstretched for balance. In his enthusiasm, he stepped right up onto the man's back and jiggled his weight up and down.

"*Oof*," the man said.

The timber started moving, gathering momentum until it had lowered all the way down to the ground.

"Stay here. Keep it down." Alex leapt from the man's back. He scrambled to collect rocks to place under the wheel, wishing he had thought to do this beforehand. He searched further and further from the cart while the man continued to lie down in the dirt, puffing on the end of the timber.

"You can get up now."

Gingerly, the man pushed up with his arms and legs. The timber under him rose slightly as the cart wheel settled onto the rocks. He got up and slowly walked around the cart, stroking his beard. "Good job, laddie. Is there anything I can do to repay ye for y'r hard work?"

"That's okay." Alex gathered up his quiver and crossbow.

"Glad to have been of assistance. I think I'll be off." He balanced the end of his crossbow on his shoulder and turned to proceed down the road.

"Where would ye be going, lad?" the man called after him.

"The castle."

"I am also. I'm off to sell this hay and greenery."

Alex stopped, struck by a sudden thought. "Do they let you in?"

"Of course – how else could I unload?" The man stooped to pull his timber out from under the cart.

"Can I come with you? I'll help."

Surprised, the man straightened. "I don't need any help unloading. . . ." Seeing Alex's disappointment, he said, "Alright, alright. Ye can come with me. I'll tell the guards ye're my long lost nephew from o'er the east side of the Highlands . . . no, that won't do . . . I'll tell them ye were born with a strange way of speakin' . . . better yet, how about ye don't speak at all, boy. I'll tell 'm ye were struck dumb at a wee age."

"Thanks a lot . . . I think!"

"Don't mention it." The man held out a big paw for Alex to shake. "Donald Dundonnel's my name. My friends call me Don-Dun, that is, when they're being polite."

"Hi, Mr. Dundonnel." Alex grasped the huge hand the best he could and pumped it up and down. "I'm Alex, your dumb nephew from over the hills."

Don-Dun flicked a switch across the ox's backside. "C'm on, Rhua, go. *Hup*, let's go!"

The ox lowered its head and strained, its eyes bulging. The cart creaked and swayed, and its wheels started turning.

"Keep it going, Rhua, *hup*, *hup*. That's it, we're out of here!"

Rhua settled into a leisurely plod, the cart groaning and swaying behind him. The two travelers strode alongside, exchanging stories as they trudged down the muddy road. Don-Dun led the ox by a rope attached to a large ring in its nose, and Alex learned that the cart and the ox were all that Don-Dun had. From the farms up and down the coast, Don-Dun bought hay and produce that he sold at what higher price he could fetch from the cooks and stablemen of the castle lords and earls. Sometimes, Don-Dun said, he would end up being paid less than it cost him to buy. At best, he made a meager living off the difference. "Ah well, enough to buy an ale or two with dinner some nights. It would be nice, though, to save up a bit and buy a piece of land and have a missus and together have a few wee bairns . . . but I don't see how that's possible, the way things are these days."

The last time Don-Dun had saved up a bit of silver, he was robbed by soldiers. Two held swords to his throat while others searched for his purse. They tipped over his cart, laughing as they rode away. It took him half a day to right his cart and reload it. That was a year ago, and he had yet to earn enough to replace the silver pieces he lost that day.

"Oh, aye, they were Hesselrigge's men alright, but there's naught to be done about it. Who's there to complain to? Soldiers? They'd laugh in my face. It's no right, but what's to be done?"

For his part, Alex told Don-Dun about having come from

the future, where people could fly in big metal ships with wings, some of which could hold over eight hundred people.

Don-Dun smiled politely. "That's more than all the folk in Duncragglin Castle."

Alex knew Don-Dun didn't believe a word he said, but he didn't care. This was the day that nothing mattered, nothing except the mission he was prepared to die for – and he was getting closer: he actually had a way to get into the castle now! He didn't even have to use the caves.

Don-Dun shared his dry, crusty stick of bread. It took a lot of chewing for each bite to go down, but Alex was not complaining, far from it. The afternoon sun was beginning to dry their clothes, and Alex was able to pick some dried clumps of mud out of his hair. He felt better than he had in days.

19

BREECHING DUNCRAGGLIN

The traveling produce merchant with his dumb nephew, plodding ox, and cart full of the best greens this side of the Forth crested a high hill. Off in the distance were the imposing towers and walls of Duncragglin.

That was where he was going to die.

Alex felt a cold shiver pass through him. Each step was bringing him nearer. He closed up his jacket below his neck and shifted his crossbow from over his shoulder to under his arm.

"I suggest ye keep that thing under the hay," Don-Dun said. "That's where I keep my lance. If ye carry it out in the open anywhere near the castle, soldiers will take it away."

Alex reluctantly took his suggestion. The road was getting busier, with farm and trade folk going about their business, and he did not want to attract attention. They overtook a man who hobbled along, bent forward under a tremendous bundle of firewood. Coming the other way was a woman with a large basket of eels on her back, which were poking out from under the cover. The basket looked heavy.

Don-Dun gave a pleasant hello to those who passed. Some replied with a nod or a small wave, others ignored him. No one gave Alex a second glance. He was nothing but another dirty urchin – not an unusual sight on this road. Alex was careful not to speak when people were within earshot. To help him remember, Don-Dun suggested he think of his mouth as being sewn shut, "'Cause that's what might happen if they think ye're a foreign spy."

"Do they leave a little gap for food?"

"Only if ye're unlucky – ye live longer that way. Now *wheesht*, before someone hears ye babbling away in that strange way of yours."

They fell in behind a box cart drawn by a pair of oxen and led by a tall thin man in black. Alex noticed that although the man's clothes were black, they had not been black originally. And what looked like black gloves were not gloves at all; they were the man's own hands. Jumping up to see over the sides of the box cart, Alex saw it was full of coal.

They plodded along behind the coal cart in a silent convoy. Together, they rounded a bend and arrived at the arched gates of Duncragglin's outer walls. Beyond them, Alex saw numerous stalls and shops lining the castle's outer court-yard. Armored guards blocked the convoy's passage. Don-Dun pulled back on Rhua's rope for him to slow up and stop.

A guard slowly circled the coal cart. The blackened driver watched impassively as the guard knelt to look under-neath, then climbed the back end to prod into the coal with his lance. The guard then leapt to the ground, scowling and clapping black coal-soot from the front of his tunic. The sooty driver handed him something small.

The guard glanced at it and jerked his head. "Get on with ye," he growled. The driver calmly urged his oxen on through the open gate.

The guard turned to Don-Dun. "Move on up here," he barked. "What have ye got?"

"Hay for the stable master and greenery for the lord's kitchens," Don-Dun sang out. He stood stiffly, with Rhua's rope in his big hands as the guard slowly walked around him, eyeing him suspiciously.

Turning to the cart, with its towering mound of hay topped with a crown of green vegetables, the guard asked, "What else is in this cart?"

"Nothing," Don-Dun replied. "Just a few crusts of bread and a blanket to cover me at night."

Without warning, the guard stabbed his lance through the hay. Over and over, he stabbed at it, seeming disappointed that the lance point came out yet again with no blood on its end.

The guard turned to Alex. "Name."

"Alex!" Don-Dun shouted. "*Er*, his name is Alex."

"Let the boy answer for himself. What's your name, boy?"

Alex opened his mouth, but he thought about his lips being sewn shut and no sound came out.

"Answer me!"

"*Nnnaahhaa*," Alex croaked.

The guard angrily turned back to Don-Dun, who raised his hands apologetically. "The lad's been struck dumb at an early age," Don-Dun said. "That's the most I've ever heard him say."

The guard pointed to the cart. "Unload it."

"Oh, please, no!" Don-Dun fumbled for his purse. "Wait. Forgive me, did I forget about the toll? Here, I have a penny."

"A penny?" The guard eyed the coin coldly, making no move to take it.

Don-Dun pulled out a second penny. "It's the best I can do. I'm but a conveyor of hay. Sometimes I dinnae make more than a few pence for all my efforts."

"That's no my problem." The guard hesitated. Scowling, he snatched the pennies from Don-Dun's hand and jerked his head for them to move on.

———◆———

Once clear of the gates, Don-Dun pounded his fist into his palm. "Damned robbery. The way it works here, m'lad, is either ye pay them a bribe that ye call a toll, or they make ye spend the day unloading and reloading your cart. I couldnae have that. My hay would've gotten all muddy . . . besides, they would've found your bow."

"Does everyone pay them a toll?" Alex felt guilty.

"*Och*, no. They'd be too afraid to seek a bribe from the powerful. It's only poor folk like me who have to pay."

Grumbling, Don-Dun led Rhua past ramshackle market stalls that took up every available space bordering the courtyard. All manner of goods spilled out from under their crowded awnings. One had a pile of animal skins, each with earflaps and eyeholes. The thick cream-colored ones would be sheepskins. Alex thought they would make great Halloween costumes. "What are you?" a startled lady would ask, when opening the door to "Trick or treat." On her doorstep, she'd find a sheepskin-covered boy peering at her through the sheep's eyeholes. "I'm a wolf – a big baaaaaaad wolf," the boy would reply, with a *heh, heh, heh.*

Further down was a shop with large clay pots brimming with floury powder that made Alex think about baking bread, scones, or maybe even cake. *Ah, to have a bite of chocolate cake!* Alex suddenly felt hungry. He hadn't had anything to eat except for a few chunks of Don-Dun's dry crusty bread.

On the other side of the open courtyard was an imposing blockhouse, so large that most of the castle was hidden behind it. Alex could see only one way in and that was up a ramp, over a drawbridge, and through a large archway. He wondered why the drawbridge was up in the daytime. He hoped it was not because Hesselrigge had somehow got wind of William Wallace's intention to attack, which was planned for first light tomorrow. He worried that Hesselrigge had forced Katie, Annie, or Willie to tell what they knew of the rebels – their number, position, or plans. Horrible images of how Hesselrigge might do this kept crowding his mind.

Alex shut his eyes tight, trying to force the nightmarish images to stop. Surely his friends were merely locked up somewhere – cold and hungry perhaps, but otherwise okay. He doubted it. All he could do was hope and pray they were still alive and try to get to them as quickly as possible.

"How do we get into the castle?" he asked anxiously.

"*Wheesht.*" Don-Dun raised his finger to his lips. "We cannae have people hearing ye." He gave Rhua's rope a gentle pull. "Come."

They walked past a stall with skinless, bloody sheep hanging by their hind legs. Flies buzzed about, squiggling on the meat, crawling over lidless eyeballs. Alex lost his appetite.

Don-Dun stopped at a big wooden building at the far end of the wall, with double doors opening into a dark dank interior. Inside, the back ends of horses protruded from narrow stalls. All was quiet, except for restless thumpings against side boards and the occasional snort or neigh.

A tall boy stood vigorously brushing a horse. A younger lad was holding the horse's leg bent, picking at the underside of its hoof with a curved knife. Another was passing with an armload of straw or hay; Alex couldn't tell which until the boy deposited it at the back end of a horse.

"Ye, over there, where be the stable master?" Don-Dun called.

The tall boy took one look at the muddy and disheveled Don-Dun and Alex in the doorway and scowled. "Be gone; we have nothing here for ye." He went back to brushing the horse.

"I said, WHERE BE THE STABLE MASTER? Answer me, boy!"

The boy scampered to the other side of the horse and peered uncertainly at Don-Dun. "We havenae lodgings or food here – terribly sorry."

"I don't want to be eating and sleeping with the *horses*. I want to have a word with your stable master."

"That's me." The voice came from deep within the dark stable. Stepping out from the gloom came a man with long black hair tied back in a ponytail, a brown vest, and strikingly tall leather boots with cuffs. He stopped and slapped a loosely held leather glove onto the palm of his hand. "State your business."

"Outside is a cart full of the richest and greenest hay that can be bought on the coast. Hay that's fit for the king's horses . . . only seeing how the king is no here, I suggest it be for the castle lord's horses instead."

The stable master looked skeptical. "Show me."

He followed Don-Dun out of the stable, eyes widening as he saw the mountain of hay. He rubbed some ends between his fingers and gave them a sniff. "Is it the same the whole way through?"

"I'm no trickster," Don-Dun said, an edgy note creeping into his voice.

The stable master ignored him. "And what manner of greenery is that on top of your load? Horse feed?"

"Oh, no." Don-Dun laughed. "Those are the finest fresh vegetables, fit for the castle lord's dinner. They were grown in a valley well in from the coast with the best soil north of the River Forth. I aim to sell them to the master of the kitchen."

"I can take care of that too. Let me have a look."

Alex climbed the cart slats to where the vegetables lay perched high up on the hay and tossed down a leafy bundle. Don-Dun caught it and held it up proudly.

"Take note of these turnips, plucked from the ground not when they are the fattest, but when they are the tastiest. And what about these right braw cabbages? Have ye ever seen any-thing like 'em? The castle lord will sing the praises of any cook that presents him with a plate of these – they're the tastiest variety known to mankind."

The stable master gave one a squeeze. "Lord Hesselrigge is not in the habit of singing anyone's praises," he muttered.

"But how could he not? Let's not forget these fat fresh

beauties." Don-Dun split open a long green pod and scraped out a row of beans.

The stable master popped them in his mouth and chewed slowly. "How many have ye got?"

"There's ten twenty-pound sacks of beans, thirty-two heads of cabbage, and forty-three bundles of turnips." Don-Dun smiled broadly. "That's two hundred and twenty-six individual turnips, if ye wish to count them that way."

"Three groats," the stable master said abruptly.

Don-Dun's smile faded. "These fine vegetables are worth more than that. . . ."

"Three groats for the whole lot. Everything on your cart."

"What?" Don-Dun's brow furrowed. "Ye do me wrong. That's much less than I had to pay for all this. I need fourteen groats just to cover my costs."

"Four groats, and not a ha'penny more. I can buy this off any of the merchants who come this way."

Don-Dun shook his head. "That's no true. None but the growers of this valley I spoke of can produce such quality. Perhaps, seeing how ye do not have the good sense to recognize the difference, I should show it to the master of the kitchens instead."

"Without me, ye won't get to see the master of the kitchens," the stable master retorted. "He's in the castle, and the guards will not let ye in without me."

Don-Dun turned toward the blockhouse. The drawbridge was still up and about a dozen soldiers were stationed on the ramp. They did not look as if they would politely step aside and have the drawbridge lowered at the request of a muddy man with an equally muddy boy and an ox-drawn cart of hay.

Frustrated, Don-Dun scanned the rows of market stalls. "Is there no one here who can buy my vegetables?"

A smile flickered across the stable master's lips.

"Very well," Don-Dun said. "Take me to the kitchen master and I'll pay ye five percent of what he pays me for the goods. Only though," he hastened to add, with one finger in the air, "if ye buy my hay for two groats."

They finally agreed on one groat and three pence for the hay and seven percent of what the kitchen master paid for the vegetables. The stable master also offered to buy Don-Dun a pint of ale, once all was said and done. "And a cider for the lad," he added.

"Fair enough," Don-Dun said. The deal was sealed with a handshake.

The stable master called to the boy in the stable. "If anyone asks for me, I'm in the castle. Tell them I'll not be long."

Don-Dun turned Rhua and the cart in a tight semicircle. He steered him well away from a group of workers busily assembling a tall wooden structure that looked like it could be a frame for a market stall, but for its location in the center of the open courtyard. Only when one of the workers tossed the end of a thick rope over the end of a timber arm did the purpose of the structure become chillingly clear.

Alex tugged on Don-Dun's sleeve and pointed, not wanting to risk saying a single whispered word for fear of the stable master hearing.

The stable master noticed his interest. "Aye, silent lad," he said. "It's a gallows. It's where many a man has swung high and kicked his last." Lowering his voice, he spoke to

Don-Dun. "It's hard to know why people swing from this gibbet sometimes; the offenses that can lead to it are so many. They assemble these gallows so often, I don't know why they don't just leave it standing."

Alex watched the assembly with morbid fascination. He wondered how they actually went about the mechanics of having people hang by a rope from the neck until dead. *Did they have them stand on a chair, slip a noose around their neck, then kick it out from under their feet? How long would it take?*

With a fright, he discovered that Don-Dun, Rhua, and the stable master were nowhere in sight. *How could a huge cartful of hay just disappear?* Fretfully, he ran in the direction they were heading, spotting a swaying green mound emerge above stall awnings. They were climbing the ramp. Alex dodged through the market-goers and caught up with them when they were almost at the drawbridge.

The stable master called out to guards clustered about a game of dice. "Lower the bridge; we're coming through."

A guard paused, dice in hand. He turned and shouted a gruff command to the blockhouse.

The drawbridge descended in fits and stops, nudged along by wooden arms. It was hinged at the top and held up by heavy chains. Creaking and groaning, it connected with the ramp. From within the blockhouse, heavy portcullis bars lifted to clear a passageway into its dark interior.

Rhua's first step onto the drawbridge echoed with a hollow thud. He halted abruptly, eyes rolling.

"It's alright, Rhua. Let's go, let's go! *Hup, hup!*" Don-Dun flicked the switch across the ox's rump.

Rhua's pace quickened and the cart wheels rumbled loudly across the timbers. The bridge vibrated under his hooves. He pulled the cart faster than Alex had ever seen him move before, slowing only when they were past the huge entrance doors and onto the solid floor of the dark passageway.

Alex was hardly able to believe his luck – he had made it into the castle!

20

BARTERING WITH THE KITCHEN MASTER

D on-Dun led Rhua into a covered courtyard. The roof was staggered with slits that let in shafts of light. Overlooking the courtyard on all sides were long interior balconies, one above the other, six levels high.

For attackers, it would be a death trap. Should Wallace and his men somehow manage to storm the front gates and get past the drawbridge, they would find themselves squeezed through a narrow passageway into this courtyard, where defenders could fire down on them. Arrows, rocks, spears, hot boiling tar – the works – would rain death. Wallace's men would have to climb over an ever-growing pile of their own dead. Should the pile reach all the way up to the first balcony, the defenders would simply climb the ladders to the second. The courtyard would become a mountain of death.

"Go on ahead," a soldier said to the stable master. "Ye know the way."

"Aye, but I've also got some fresh greens," the stable master said. "C'n ye send for the kitchen master?"

The soldier shouted for a more junior soldier to convey the stable master's request.

Don-Dun and Alex followed the stable master through double doors into a two-storey chamber. Inside were large mounds of straw, hay, and grains. A ramp spiraled down, dried horse dung and straw dust clinging to its worn slats. Below, Alex could see stalls, where the horses of the castle lord and his high-ranking soldiers were kept.

Through a narrow slit in the rear wall, Alex could see a covered bridge connecting to more of the castle. Under it was the entrance to the harbor.

Don-Dun gestured to the top of the cart. "Up ye get, m'lad, time to unload."

Alex tossed the vegetables down to Don-Dun, who gently caught each one, stacking it against the wall. Then he climbed back down and looked about for a pitchfork to unload the hay. He sighed. It looked like a lot of work.

"Stand back, lad." Don-Dun unbuckled straps that secured the cart-poles to Rhua and pushed up, his arms straining. He brought the cart to a balancing position and gave it a further heave. The cart tipped, sending the entire mountain of hay sliding off the back to land with a great dust-billowing crash. Alex covered his mouth with his sleeve. From down below came the neighing and stomping of startled horses.

Don-Dun slowly raised his arms until they were straight out in front of him. "Didn't think that would work, did ye?" he said with a big grin.

Alex punched him on the arm.

Laughing, Don-Dun pulled the empty cart back down to

rest the pole straps across Rhua's back. His few possessions, and Alex's bow, remained secure in a sack tied to the cart's front slats, but his lance had slid to the floor with the hay. Don-Dun tossed it back onto the cart, hiding it in a gap in the boards and covering it with handfuls of hay.

The stable master frowned. "The soldiers would not be pleased to see that."

"There's no need for them to see it," Don-Dun replied grimly, "unless they give me cause."

"If ye're not going to be a bit smarter than that, ye too will be hanging under the rope tonight, together with the young foreign spies."

Alex's head jerked up. A terrible rushing sound filling his ears, he dimly heard Don-Dun inquire as to where these spies had been captured.

"Up the coast a wee bit," the stable master said. "It's said they speak with some strange dialect and are in these lands under no authority or permission. That alone is enough to hang, of course, but moreover they're accused of spying for the rebels."

Alex clung to the cart for support. *It cannot not be true; oh, let it not be my friends that are to hang tonight.* But every shred of hope crumbled the moment he held it. It had to be them. *What, oh what, am I to do?*

"Your lad appears rather pale," the stable master commented casually. "Is something wrong?"

Alex almost forgot to remain silent. He opened his mouth to reply, but only a few stammering sounds came out.

Fortunately, everyone's attention was diverted by a heavy potbellied man who stomped into the chamber, followed closely by a tall thin man with long gray hair. Alex thought the tall thin man looked familiar.

"Who is it," the potbellied man bellowed, his jowls jiggling, "that claims to have fresh greens of such quality that they warrant disturbing the kitchen master?"

Don-Dun replied haltingly. "That, *er* . . . would be me," he said. "These greens I laid out here for ye to see were grown in a fertile valley far from here . . . but they are fresh, I assure you. I brought them here with great haste and –"

"Duncan!" The kitchen master snapped his fingers for his companion to examine the greens.

The tall thin man strode over to where Don-Dun was proudly displaying his wares. He randomly flipped over some samples, holding a few to his nose. He took out a knife, carved into a tuber, and nibbled on its crunchy insides.

He nodded approvingly.

"Rubbish!" The kitchen master's heavy jowls quivered. "I can see from here that's naught but a pile of half-rotted rabbit feed."

The stable master cleared his throat. "Wait a moment," he said. "Even I can see that these are quality greens."

"Have ye been offered a percent of the sale?" The kitchen master sneered when the stable master averted his eyes. "Very well, ye have gone to the trouble of bringing him here. I'll be generous and pay a groat for all this."

He reached into a vest pocket and drew out a silver coin. He gave it a toss, and it fell with a *ting* on the floor.

Don-Dun made no move to pick it up. He stared at the kitchen master, his face turning a deep shade of red.

"Ye've been paid, now go – or do I have to call the guards?"

The kitchen master put his hand on the handle of a long dagger tucked into his belt.

Don-Dun's voice was flat and cold: "This is robbery."

"Have it your way . . . guards!"

Two burly armored guards burst into the chamber, swords drawn. Alex suddenly realized that the kitchen master knew he would need these guards; he'd planned this robbery from the start.

"Stop all this madness," the stable master protested, flapping his loose glove up and down. "It was in good faith that I brought this man here –"

"Be still, or I'll have ye clapped in irons also." The kitchen master raised his fleshy arm and pointed to Don-Dun. "Guards, take him away."

The taller of the two guards loosened wrist irons from his belt. "Come with us quietly, or ye die here," he growled.

Don-Dun edged back to the end of the cart.

The shorter guard raised his sword up over his shoulder and held it like a bat. Mouth twisted into a grimace, he took slow deliberate steps forward.

Alex had no particular plan, but knew he had to do something. He slipped the sack off the cart and pulled out the crossbow behind the cover of the cart wheel. Stepping on the bow with both feet, he pulled the drawstring back to its notch. Then he inserted a bolt.

Don-Dun's eyes stayed fixed on the guards while his fingers burrowed into the loose hay on the cart. "I've been robbed by the likes of ye before, but no more," he said.

"Don't do it!" The stable master called out too late. The shorter guard lunged and swung his sword.

Don-Dun raised his lance, deflecting the blow, and crashed the butt end against the guard's helmet. The guard spun and thrust with his sword, but it lacked the lance's reach. It caught him, point first, just under his breastplate, penetrating so far that its point made a tepee from the tunic on his back. The guard's grimace was replaced by a slack-jawed look of shock. He took a rasping breath, his sword clattering to the ground.

That frozen moment seemed to take forever, but it was over in the blink of an eye. Don-Dun gave the guard a hefty kick, but before he succeeded in wrenching his lance free, the other guard's sword came swinging down with a force that would have severed Don-Dun's unprotected arm were it not for the stable master, who whipped out his own sword and blocked it with a heavy clash of steel.

Their swords locked, the stable master roared for the guard to stand down. Far from obeying, the guard used his brute strength to force the stable master's sword down to one side. He attempted a release-and-thrust, but the stable master was quicker. He sidestepped and gave the guard a swift jab, catching him precisely in the gap between the bottom of his helmet and the top of his metal shoulder plates. Blood spurted through the guard's fingers as he clutched his neck. He staggered backwards, sword still raised, and collapsed on the floor.

The kitchen master slowly raised his dagger over the stable master's unprotected back as the stable master bent over the fallen guard.

Alex stepped out from behind the cart and raised his crossbow. "STOP!" he shouted.

The kitchen master's eyes flicked over to Alex. He

froze, dagger in the air, then stepped back, quickly returning it to its sheath.

"Don't move." Alex's finger was tight on the crossbow trigger. He looked straight down the stock to the kitchen master, his heart pounding in his ears.

"My back made a tempting target for ye, did it now?" The stable master's voice was low and threatening. He raised his sword to the kitchen master's chin. "But for this lad, ye might have had me there."

"Ye have attacked the castle guards," the kitchen master replied. "That's a capital offense."

The stable master jerked his thumb toward the two dead guards. "It seems to me that they did the attacking – something they clearly will do no more."

"It's this piece of scum who did the attacking." Don-Dun pointed at the kitchen master, shaking with rage.

The kitchen master fluttered his hand as if to ward off a pesky fruit fly. "How dare ye address me in that –"

"Shut your trap." Don-Dun leveled his lance with the kitchen master's big belly. "Ye're no worthy of a response. My days may well be numbered by what has transpired here today, but it gives me some satisfaction to know yours are over."

Don-Dun pulled back his lance. The kitchen master turned a sickly gray color and dropped to his knees. "No please . . . spare me . . . I'll do anything . . . I'll tell the captain that the guards killed each other in an argument . . . ye are free to go . . . I swear. . . ."

Alex held out his hand. "Wait! Stop!"

Don-Dun looked at Alex in surprise, his lance poised.

"Tell him to free my friends from the dungeons, and it's a deal."

"Your lad is not so silent now," the stable master said, a smile flitting across his face. "And that would be a foreign dialect I hear – would ye be a rebel spy too?"

Alex peered down the stock of his crossbow. "So what's your answer?"

"I cannae do that," the kitchen master pleaded. "I haven't the authority to go to the dungeons . . . but I can see ye out from the castle. I can help ye escape."

"He lies!" The outburst came from the tall thin man, who stood well back from the fray. "He uses captives from the dungeons as slave labor – chains them to a counter and has them prepare food."

Alex had heard that voice before. He lowered his bow. "Duncan?" he said, astonished. "Can you really be Duncan from Mr. McRae's farm?"

"The same." Duncan bowed his head in greeting. "I'm glad to have caught up with ye at last, Alex. We must tell the professor the good news."

"The professor?" Alex repeated.

"Aye, Professor Macintyre. Ye know him, do ye not? He tells me ye've met in the airplane."

"Oh, yes . . . of course." Alex's head was spinning. "The professor is here?"

"Aye, he and I have had quite the trials and tribulations since we embarked on our quest to find ye lot." Duncan broke into a wry smile. "We both needed to assume positions at this castle – not an easy thing to do, let me assure ye. I used my knowledge of growing vegetables to gain the employ of the kitchens, where I'm to ensure the finest of foods are bought and prepared for the castle lord and visiting nobles and dignitaries. The professor, on the other hand, has become the castle lord's fool."

"A fool?"

"Aye, and a fine job he does entertaining Lord Hesselrigge with his clever witticisms. It's a position with some prestige, and it gives him the run of much of the castle. We were hoping ye'd all get rounded up by Hesselrigge's men so we could take ye all to the kitchen as slaves one day and, from there, find a way to escape into the caves."

"One day! Don't you know? Annie and Willie have been accused of being rebel spies. Out in the courtyard, Hesselrigge's men are putting up the gallows. They're to hang tonight!"

Color drained from Duncan's face. "No! That cannae be –"

"The lad speaks true," the stable master said. "I was told of this firsthand by the master builder."

"We have no time to waste then." Duncan prodded the kneeling kitchen master. "We must compel this bag of dirt here to order the captain of the guards to bring the captives to the kitchens."

"Ye must know it's not that simple," the stable master said. "We cannae all be wandering about the castle without being challenged."

"The kitchen master and I can," Duncan replied. "And so can ye and Don-Dun, if ye put on the slain guards' armor. Alex we can bring along in irons."

The stable master looked with distaste at the dead guards. "There's no point in this," he said. "We're in enough trouble already for killing the kitchen master's guards. Freeing captives will only seal our fate."

"Not so," Alex interrupted. "When William Wallace captures this castle, he'll reward the people who fought against Hesselrigge."

The stable master impatiently slapped his loose glove against the palm of his other hand. "This castle is impenetrable – not even Wallace and his band of brigands can take it."

"With our help they can!" Alex replied.

"Oh, this is good!" the stable master said. "Now we are to somehow help overthrow Hesselrigge altogether. This is turning into a farce. It's not as if Wallace's men stand waiting for us outside the castle gates."

"But they do. I spoke with William Wallace only yesterday. He and his men will attack the castle at dawn tomorrow."

The enormity of what Alex said filled the room.

Don-Dun broke the silence. "Forgive me, Alex," he said gently. "But it's not every day that I meet a lad who comes from a future time, when ships fly in the air, and now claims to not only be on speaking terms with Wallace himself, but also to know what he will do on the morrow."

"Far-fetched, perhaps," Duncan said. "However, at this point, it seems to me that ye stand nothing further to lose and everything to gain."

Don-Dun sighed. "Well, I guess this is no time for half-measures." He turned to the stable master. "Help me with this, will you?"

The stable master grudgingly propped up a dead guard so Don-Dun could pull off the armor. It was sticky with clotted blood.

Don-Dun grimaced. "We'll need to rinse this armor in a trough before we put it on. What say ye?"

The stable master shrugged. Taking up an armload of bloody armor, he followed Don-Dun down the ramp, leaving the two dead soldiers crumpled on the floor.

The kitchen master's eyes darted towards the stable doors.

Duncan blocked his way. "Just try it – truly, I would *like* ye to try it. It would give me such pleasure. Or would ye like to call for the guards? It would be the last sound ever to come from your miserable throat." Teeth gritted, Duncan raised his dagger.

"No . . . please . . . spare me." The kitchen master collapsed at Duncan's feet, covering his head with his hands.

Duncan's lip curled. "Ye have no idea how hard it has been, Alex, to have been the servant of this cowardly specimen of inhumanity. If ye saw how he treated the poor, hungry, and tired slaves he brought up from the dungeons . . . nonstop work with no food or rest . . . the only thing keeping the slaves going was the constant threat of having a finger or a hand cut off by this monster. . . ." Duncan paused. "I'll no give ye more details, m'lad," he added, a catch in his throat, "except to say that to not fall into despair, I had to keep telling myself that surely this isn't the essential state of humanity; surely this is only an abhorrent example of what we are capable."

Alex heard the clink of armor and the pounding of heavy feet. He was sure it was Don-Dun and the stable master, but, nonetheless, the sight of two fierce armored guards clanking their way up the ramp gave him a fright.

Don-Dun removed his tight-fitting helmet and twisted awkwardly in his armor. "How on earth do they wear these things all day? I cannae even pull my shirt out from down my backside."

"Well, I'm not going to help ye with that!" The stable master snorted. He took the manacles from his belt, fastened one end loosely about Alex's wrist, and promptly gave him a shove.

Alex fell and glared up at him. "What did you do that for?"

"Practice." The stable master pulled Alex back up. "I'm the mean guard, remember?"

"How could I forget?" Alex rubbed his wrist. "Are you done practicing?"

"Almost." The stable master gave Alex another shove. "Remember to keep a still tongue in your head."

Alex stayed as far out of the stable master's reach as the manacle chain would allow.

"On your feet, vermin." Duncan pulled the kitchen master up by the back of his shirt and pressed the dagger point against the small of his back. "Feel that? Here it will be, awaiting the slightest wrong move on your part. Make sure ye say and do all the right things, or they'll be your last."

Don-Dun held open the stable door. Alex's heart soared. They were off to the dungeons to free his friends.

21

To the Dungeons

The kitchen master led the way, Duncan close by his side holding the dagger concealed against the small of his back. The stable master and Don-Dun clinked along behind them, dragging a scurrying Alex, who was ever watchful of catching a cuff from the stable master's heavy glove.

They passed under an ornate arch. Through narrow slits on each side, Alex caught glimpses of the sea and the harbor and realized they were traveling through the covered bridge that spanned the chasm from the blockhouse to the castle.

Along the way, they drew curious looks, but no one tried to stop or question them. Feeling cheerful, Alex wondered who would have believed, just this morning when he left Mrs. Bruford's cottage, that he would actually make it this far. He no longer anticipated his own death with heavy resignation. He had to succeed – the lives of his friends depended on it!

Once inside the castle, Duncan led them through dimly lit chambers. A curtain flung open in a nearby alcove, and a well-dressed blond man seated at a table with three soldiers glared at them.

Duncan pulled the kitchen master in close. "If they suspect us, ye'll be the first to die," he hissed. "Remember that."

The blond man rose. "Well, if it isn't the kitchen master. Where be ye off to this fine day?"

Alex's heart sank. Although he was cleaned up, his hair neatly combed back, the man was unmistakably Rorie – the traitor they had discovered in the soldiers' camp at Loch Karins. Alex hid behind the stable master.

The kitchen master held his back arched from Duncan's dagger. "We're off to the dungeons for some more kitchen workers," he grunted.

Rorie and his men stood before them to block their way. "Since when do ye pick your own kitchen slaves?" he asked.

"Oh, ye should have seen the last scrawny bunch they sent us, Sire," Duncan said hastily. "Couldn't get any work out of them – even after the kitchen master cut off a finger or two with his cleaver. One even went mad and played with two dead cocks, pretending one was Lord Hesselrigge and the other William Wallace. . . ."

"Silence!" Rorie held up his hand. "Do not speak unless spoken to, servant!" He tilted his head to see past the stable master. "What manner of captive is that cowering behind ye?"

"A miscreant," the stable master replied hastily. "Fit for naught but kitchen tasks."

Alex kept his face averted. Rorie's eyes narrowed and his voice was full of menace. "Well, well, look who we have here. I do believe this captive needs to join the others we have in for questioning."

"There's nae point in that." Don-Dun tried to sound

casual. "The lad is deaf and dumb, barely more than an animal. We've heard naught from him but a few grunts."

"We'll see how much grunting he does when we stretch him on the rack." Rorie laughed. "Indeed, he may have some interesting things to tell us."

The stable master stood stiffly at attention. "I would be pleased to escort this miscreant to the rack room for ye, Sire," he announced in an official voice.

"Aye, good idea. Let us all go to the dungeons together." Rorie turned to the kitchen master. "Ye can pick out your slaves and –" Rorie stopped to eye him suspiciously. "Is there something wrong?"

The kitchen master jerked his head back and forth.

"There's no need to be upset about me taking your captive," Rorie said with a small crooked smile. "There's plenty more in the dungeons."

"But none that are as fit, Sire," Duncan babbled. "There is much work to be done in the kitchens. Lord Hesselrigge will be displeased if we fall behind –"

"Silence!" Rorie's hand fell onto his sword. "One more word from ye . . . *servant*," Rorie spat, "and your tongue will be fed to the dogs. Do not presume to tell me what Lord Hesselrigge wants – he is not concerned with trifles."

Rorie tapped one of his soldiers. "Go up to Hesselrigge now and tell him we have another of the foreign spies in custody. He may well wish to question this one personally. This one I know to have been in Wallace's camp recently."

They descended, Rorie's torch flickering shadows down narrow dark spiral steps. The stairs ended in a cold damp alcove deep in the lower castle basements. Beyond an iron gate, a low arched corridor was dimly lit by a long row of smoky torches. There was a steady *plink, plink* of water dripping somewhere in the distance.

Rorie cupped his hands to call through the bars. "Gatekeeper!"

"Keeper, keeper, keeper" echoed back.

Rorie seized a rope that ran between hoops along the wall and gave it a pull. A bell clanged. He gave the rope several more impatient tugs.

Three shadowy figures emerged, the middle one bent and gaunt, half a head shorter than the others.

"Coming, I'm coming, hold your horses," the bent figure rasped. He shuffled nearer, the lantern in his hand casting eerie shadows. Two heavyset guards followed.

"Who's there?" The gatekeeper's speech was slurred from lack of teeth. He held up his lantern and squinted. "Oh, it's you, Sire," he said. "What brings ye down here again so soon?"

"We're off to the rack room with another of the foreign spies," Rorie replied. "The kitchen master is here to pick out some more workers."

The gatekeeper set his lantern down and held a large ring of skeleton keys to the light. "Let me see now. . . ." He swung one key after another around the ring. "Ah, here we are . . . no, wait . . . it's this one."

"C'm on, man, let me in!" Rorie rattled the gate.

"It's hard, Sire, especially with my eyes." The gatekeeper

fitted key after key into the flat lock before it finally clicked open. He gave the gate a tug.

Rorie shoved it open, the heavy gate screeching on its hinges. He shouldered his way past the gatekeeper, barking orders. "Have the guards fetch the other foreign spies from their cells – that local girl also. Have them brought to the rack room. Keep an eye open for Lord Hesselrigge – he'll be along any minute and will no take kindly to being kept waiting. And get rid of this kitchen master for me."

As everyone filed past, the gatekeeper raised his hand to catch the kitchen master's attention. "The captives ye want are that way." He pointed to a side passage. "And this time, go easy with that cleaver of yours. The moaning and groaning I have to listen to when your workers come back is something terrible."

The kitchen master grunted. Duncan's hidden dagger gently propelled him in the direction the gatekeeper indicated.

The others followed Rorie down a central passage with a heavy stench that made Alex think of open sewers. Low barred openings lined both sides. Shocked, Alex saw pale shrunken faces, eyes pleading, float up behind the bars. Behind each barred opening was a damp, dark little cell too low to stand in and no wider than outstretched arms. Inside, curled-up human forms lay under dirty rags, asleep, or too weak to raise their heads.

They came to a large, ornately carved door. On either side, lanterns flicked. They entered the dark room, and one of Rorie's guards lit the wall torches.

Chains hung from rings mounted in the wall, each ending in a manacle. In the center of the room were three wooden chairs: each straight-backed, solid, and hard-edged; each dangling leather straps. Next was an ominous, long narrow table with large straps in the middle, smaller ones at the ends. It was split in the middle and had a wheel with spokes on one side. There was only one thing it could be: a rack.

Alex thought of Annie, Katie, and Willie, and panic surged in his chest.

"Excellent!" Rorie rubbed his hands together. "Let's get things ready for Lord Hesselrigge." He adjusted the rack to a smaller setting.

It was not long before the door burst open, crashing against the wall. Two soldiers marched in and stepped to either side, each holding their swords straight up in readiness. A dark-haired man wearing a fur-trimmed blue cloak strode into the room. At his heels was the soldier Rorie had sent to get Hesselrigge, followed by a figure awkwardly springing along in a loose gray cloak.

"M'Lord Hesselrigge." Rorie made a slight bow. Rorie's soldier-henchmen stiffened to attention, as did the stable master and Don-Dun. "Ye instructed us, m'Lord, to call for ye the moment another foreign spy was apprehended."

"Indeed I did – good work." Hesselrigge spoke to Rorie, but his eyes were on Alex. "Are the others being brought?"

"Aye, m'Lord. A guard is retrieving them, except, of course, the one you sent on up ahead."

Hesselrigge paced, lost in thought. Stopping abruptly, he stared sharply at Alex. "Do ye no recognize me, Alex?"

Surprised he knew his name, Alex shook his head. As much as he had heard of Hesselrigge, he felt sure he had never met him.

"Think hard, think back – or should I say think forward – to a time on a beach not far from here, when you met an antique dealer and his son," Hesselrigge continued.

Alex was puzzled. *Think forward?*

The man in the gray cloak spoke up, jiggling his weight from one foot to another. "Think forward – that is good, Sire. That would be when one thought follows the other in a forward lineal progression. Thinking sideways – that would be good too; that would be when one thought does not pick up where another left off, but leaps to one side and picks up somewhere else instead. But how would one think backward? People often speak of others as backward thinkers, but what could it mean?"

Hesselrigge turned to the gray-cloaked man. "It means that, like ye, they are fools."

A fool! Alex looked more closely at the gray-cloaked man, who was making a great show of scratching his head, then rubbing his chin with his eyes rolled to the ceiling. Finally, he folded his hands over his head and stared at the floor.

Alex tried hard to remember the features of the professor he'd met on the airplane. It could be him, but the man on the airplane was a serious professor – *this* was a fool.

"I have it," the fool proclaimed. "Thinking backward is when one thought begins at the same place as another, but instead of progressing forward, works its way back to where the thought came from. That would be much harder than either thinking forward or sideways. Think backward long enough and ye will find where all thought springs from, which is far better than to find the conclusion of all thought, don't ye think?"

Hesselrigge laughed. "I think ye are a fool – a fool who knows naught of what he says. When I said think forward, I was referring to forward in time from whence he came."

"What is time, what is place, m'Lord, but a point of view? Perhaps we speak of the same thing, only differently."

"Ye have no idea of what I speak," Hesselrigge snapped. "I mean that this lad has traveled back in time."

"Same place, different time – same time, different place – it's all the same to me," the fool babbled. "I suppose ye, too, have come from a time that has yet to happen, m'Lord?"

"Yes, as a matter of fact."

"Who's the fool now, m'Lord – the one who thinks one can travel to the origin of all thought, or the one who thinks one can travel to the origin of all time?"

"Be careful who you call a fool, Fool!"

"No offense intended, m'Lord," the fool hastened to add. "I, too, have come from a time that has yet to happen."

"Don't ye mock me." Hesselrigge pointed at him. "And hold that tongue of yours if ye wish to see the morrow."

A loud rap sounded on the door, and a man burst into the room, clad in an elegant tunic.

"My good knight, Sir James Barr!" Hesselrigge exclaimed. "What brings ye here?"

"My apologies for troubling Your Lordship, but word is in from our spies in the countryside," Sir James announced breathlessly. "William Wallace is planning an assault on the men being sent here by King Edward to help us put down the uprising. The men are but a few hours' ride from here and are headed straight into a trap."

"So, the ones who are to help us need our help?" Hesselrigge sneered. "What help is that?"

"King Edward would be most displeased if his men did not so much as make it here, m'Lord," Sir James replied. "There is also the matter of the weaponry they bring: good quantities of bows, arrows, spears, shields, armor. . . . It would no be good for it all to fall into Wallace's hands, m'Lord."

"*Bah*, what idiots!" Hesselrigge roared. "Wallace will gain those weapons at a price. I'm sure King Edward's men will fight back long and hard."

"The ambush they ride into will leave them defenseless, m'Lord. It is the Falloch Pass in the Strathlomorand Ridge."

"Can we not ambush the ambushers?" Rorie asked suddenly.

Hesselrigge rubbed his chin. "To ambush King Edward's men at the Falloch Pass, Wallace's men would need to climb Grenochy, would they no? What if a company of our men was already there, lying in wait for them?"

Rorie smiled. "Excellent idea, m'Lord. They would be caught by surprise and would be at the disadvantage of being downhill from our men. Those who survive would be driven right into the waiting arms of King Edward's men, who would slaughter each and every one."

"William Wallace may be among the fallen!" Hesselrigge pounded his fist into his palm. "Nae, he must be among the fallen. James! Take two companies of men under Captains Killenden and Aimsworth and execute this plan."

"Two companies?" Sir James recoiled. "Should we leave the castle so poorly manned, m'Lord?"

"To withstand an attack, this castle needs no more than a handful of men," Hesselrigge replied. "Tell our spies to be on alert for an assault. Should they learn one is imminent, have your two companies surprise the attackers from the rear. Either way, we get them! Ride out quickly now, while there's still time. A promotion and a bag of silver awaits the man who brings me William Wallace's head."

Knight James Barr was not a man to waste time. He bowed quickly and strode from the room. Rorie instructed two of his three henchmen to put extra patrols on the battlements.

"Now, where were we?" Hesselrigge asked as the door closed behind the departing men. His eyes traveled slowly around the room before fixing upon Alex. "Ah, yes," he said softly. "We were about to get started."

22

INTERROGATION

"But, you were not with the antique dealer. . . ." Alex tried to make sense of it all. His head hurt. The flame of a lantern blew low, as if caught in a breeze – or starved for oxygen. Shadows flickered across the heavy oak rack.

"Think again," Hesselrigge snapped. "Who was with the antique dealer?"

"Only his son, the boy who tried to take away a board I'd found. Grant, I think his name was."

"Ah, yes, the board . . . now we're getting somewhere – the board with the carving of the bird, the instructions on how to enter the time chamber; the board ye left on the rocks pointing the way into the caves. . . ."

"How . . . how do you know all this?"

"Why would ye presume that everyone who enters the time chamber comes out at the same earlier time? What would happen if someone went slightly farther back?"

A sudden far-fetched thought reached Alex. He looked at Hesselrigge, straining to see a likeness. "Grant?" he asked uncertainly.

"The same." Hesselrigge nodded grimly. "I went through hell after ye laid that trap. My father died a slow death because of those caves. He didn't die of hunger or thirst, although we had nothing to eat or drink for days. Worst of all, he died of madness, being lost in such suffocating darkness. Let me give ye an indication of what it was like." Hesselrigge bent toward Alex, narrowing his eyes. "Our torches died after only a few hours, leaving us with just matches to see where we were going. My father had trouble breathing and started hearing people laughing – jeering and mocking him. He clutched at me and held me as a shield, but even that didn't help. He stumbled blindly into one cave after another and tried to claw his way through a wall. He even wrote pleas for help in his own blood. . . ."

Hesselrigge's eyes burned with a deep hatred. "We finally found a way out – alive, but barely so. But escaping the caves didn't help him. He kept shouting gibberish and ranting about demons and ghosts coming to get him. He died a few days later, clutching his covers and staring into nothing.

"Thirty years!" Hesselrigge shouted, his fists clenched. "Thirty years I have lived here, rising to positions of ever greater power, all the while keeping a lookout for the one responsible for destroying my past life, the one responsible for my father's death. I knew ye might head into the caves. I knew ye might find that time chamber . . . and now here ye are – barely days older than when I saw ye last. A whole life yet to live – or *not!*"

Hesselrigge leaned in close enough for Alex to feel the spray of his spit. "For what is to come," he hissed, "ye can thank yourself."

Alex shrank back. "You can't seriously be blaming me for what happened . . . I didn't leave the board as a trap! It was so we could find our way back."

"*Bah*, do ye really expect me to believe that?" Hesselrigge spat bitterly. "My father was convinced we were onto something, that the caves would contain some treasures or antiques we could sell. Ye must've known that board and those directions would lure us in . . . well, congratulate yourself: it worked! Here I am. However, I've made a new life for myself after all these years. But ye will no likely be able to say the same."

"Why didn't you go back – forward, I mean – in time? You could have gone back to find your father, to help him before it was too late –"

Hesselrigge cut Alex off. "Haven't ye figured it out yet? The time chamber goes only one way."

"There's no way forward? There's no way back to the time we came from?"

"Oh, there's a way forward alright, doing what we're doing right now, moving forward through time one second at a time. Your bones will make it back – that is, if I don't feed them to the castle dogs." Hesselrigge threw back his head and laughed. "But not making it back is the least of your worries. Ye'll be lucky to see another day. The only reason you're not dead now is because I want to savor the moment."

"What do you want from me?" Alex rasped, his throat so dry, he could barely speak.

"Want? What do ye want from *me*?" Hesselrigge mocked. "For ye not to have laid that nasty trap is what I want – but enough of that. Let's stay with the present and the matters at hand, shall we? I want ye to tell me about that scoundrel William Wallace and his band of brigands. Let's start with their numbers and arms. I may know something of his plans already, but that Wallace is a crafty villain who's won too many a battle to be underestimated. So start talking – what is Wallace up to?"

Alex sealed his lips.

"It is as I thought, and even, as I prefer. We shall do this the hard way." Hesselrigge nudged Rorie. "Who shall we strap in the rack first – him or one of his friends? Which will make him talk the fastest – his own pain or that of a friend?"

"I would say his own, m'Lord." A gleeful smile appeared on Rorie's face.

"Of course ye would," Hesselrigge said disdainfully. "That is how it would work with your own self, is it no? Not a word would pass your lips while your friends were being pulled apart on this thing, but as soon as ye were strapped down –"

"M'Lord! Ye do me an injustice!"

"Do I?" Hesselrigge stroked his chin. "*Hmm*, very well then." He pointed to Alex. "Strap him to the rack."

The stable master stepped up smartly. "Right away, Sire." He pulled Alex forward by his chain. Alex frantically pulled back.

The stable master thrust Alex's chain into the hands of one of Hesselrigge's guards. "Here, hold this while I pin him to the rack."

Hesselrigge's guard dutifully took hold of the chain. The stable master reached down, grasped the hilt of the guard's sword, and removed it in one deft motion.

"What the –" The guard's shout was cut off by a blow

from his own sword. He dropped the chain, staggered backwards, and fell to his knees. He held his throat with both hands, blood spurting between his fingers as he gasped for air.

Don-Dun instantly ran his sword through the middle of Rorie's one remaining guard, leaving the shocked man impaled and tottering. Don-Dun spun, pulled a dagger from his belt, and knocked Hesselrigge's last guard to the ground. The fallen guard flailed.

The stable master lunged with his sword for Rorie, but Rorie's sword flashed out and parried it neatly. Rorie's follow-up slice passed under the stable master's sword and would have hit the stable master had he not leapt back in time.

The stable master's sword-fighting ability, though impressive, was not up to the level of a seasoned professional like Rorie. The stable master retreated, jumping back to avoid another sweeping slice of Rorie's sword. His heel caught an uneven edge of flagstone and he fell backwards. He rolled quickly, Rorie's sword clanging hard against the stone floor right where he had been.

The next swing would have been the end of the stable master, but Alex swung the loose chain still manacled to his wrist and it wrapped over Rorie's shoulder. Momentarily unbalanced, Rorie missed. Again, his sword sparked off a flagstone.

The stable master lunged, sticking his sword directly into Rorie's gut. He gave an extrahard twist and pulled out the bloodied blade. Too late, he saw Rorie's weakened-but-still-forceful swing heading for him. The sword crashed into his upper arm, causing him to spin and fall to the ground.

Rorie staggered uncertainly, his hand over his lower abdomen. Gasping in heavy rasps, flecks of bright red blood bubbling about his lips, Rorie looked down in disbelief. His eyes turned to Alex. Grabbing the part of Alex's chain that was still wrapped around his body, he yanked, pulling Alex closer. He took a few unsteady steps forward, raising his sword. Don-Dun's sword swept up to intercept. The crashing impact jolted the sword from Rorie's grip. Rorie staggered backwards and clasped a heavy rope that hung against a wall. He clung on to the rope until his knees gave out, then fell heavily, face-first, onto the flagstones.

"No, ye do not!" roared Don-Dun. "Get over to the wall. Now, move."

Hesselrigge slowly backed away. "Ye will pay for this with your life!" he hissed.

Don-Dun slammed the butt end of his sword into Hesselrigge's belly. Hesselrigge let out an *oof* and doubled over, eyes bulging.

"Don't ye threaten me! I'm done with people threatening me!" Don-Dun roughly raised Hesselrigge's arms and shackled them to the wall.

Alex looked in horror upon the carnage all around him: Rorie, the guards, dark splotches of blood on tunics, the stone floor . . . a neck sliced open. He averted his eyes.

The stable master clutched his injured arm as the fool helped him to his feet. "It's not deep," he said, straining to see the gash in the back of his arm. "The coat of mail must've stopped most of it."

The fool ripped the sleeve off Rorie's shirt and wrapped

it around the stable master's arm, tying it tightly. Blood was already showing through the cloth.

"Good thing it's not my sword arm," the stable master said airily. He fumbled with a pouch on his belt and pulled out a key. "Here, Alex." He tossed it.

Alex caught the key and unlocked his wrist manacle. He pried the hinged irons open and the chain clattered to the ground.

A loud rap sounded on the door.

"One sound and ye're a dead man." Don-Dun growled at Hesselrigge. He joined the stable master in position, sword up and ready, on either side of the opening door.

———◆———

To Alex's shock, it was Annie and Katie who appeared first, both bound by a coarse rope about their necks. They staggered into the room, shoved roughly by a surly guard.

"It's a trap – run!" Hesselrigge roared. "Run, you fool! Go! *Helmmmmmph* –"

Hesselrigge's shouts were abruptly muffled by the fool, who struggled to stuff a dirty rag into his mouth.

The guard managed to draw and swing his sword. The stable master deflected the blow with his sword, while Don-Dun ran him through. Together, they grabbed the sagging guard and pulled him into the room. Don-Dun kicked the door shut, and they dumped him into a corner.

"They got you too," Annie said to Alex in dismay.

"Don't worry, we're with friends – we're all going to escape." Alex quickly untied the ropes from their necks. Katie was shaking badly, her eyes dull and unfocused.

"What is it, Katie?" he asked.

Katie's voice was barely above a whisper, but she managed a weak smile. "*Och*, I'm a wee bit cold, that's all. It's so great to see ye again." Shivers ran through her as she spoke.

"A blanket!" Alex called out. "Is there a blanket somewhere?"

The fool tossed over Hesselrigge's fur-trimmed blue cloak. Alex wrapped it around Katie several times.

The fool then knotted a torn cloth about Hesselrigge's head to keep him from spitting the rag from his mouth. "Who's the fool now, eh?" he said calmly.

"Damn! It's as I feared." The stable master held up the end of the rope that Rorie had clung to before falling. "A bell rope! It travels up through that small hole to the higher levels. I suspect it rings a bell in the guardroom. *That* was why Rorie hung onto it so desperately. No doubt, guards will be on their way as we speak. Let us be off!"

Don-Dun reached for the door, but before his hand touched the handle, it burst open. Everyone jumped back in panic. Don-Dun and the stable master scrambled to draw their swords. It was Duncan.

A fierce scowl spreading over his face, Don-Dun lowered his sword. "Can ye no knock and announce your presence?"

Duncan looked at Don-Dun in astonishment, his mouth open but not uttering a sound. He held out his bloodstained hands in horror.

The stable master shook him by the shoulders. "Snap out of it, man. Where's the kitchen master?"

"Dead." Duncan looked down at his hands as if wondering whose they were. "I had to . . . I had no choice . . .

he tried to take the dagger from me. . . ." Duncan paused. With a look of growing disbelief, he stared at all the dead bodies sprawled across the floor. "What on earth has happened here?"

"We killed them – that's what ye do in a battle," the stable master snapped. "So, where's your dagger?"

"I left it in him . . . oh, it was horrible. I couldn't pull it back out. . . . He kept breathing and twitching for the longest time. . . . I've never killed anyone before. . . ."

The stable master snorted. "So he *did* take your dagger?"

"Duncan?" Annie looked out from behind Don-Dun. "Is that truly you?"

"Annie!" Duncan's face broke into a big grin. "I came to find ye, lassie. I came with the professor here to bring ye back to your dad. He's beside himself with worry."

"Come, we haven't got all day." The stable master stood impatiently holding the door. "Guards will be along any minute – we must be off."

"But, we've got to find Willie, Annie's brother," Alex said. "He's still in one of the cells somewhere!"

The stable master rolled his eyes. "Not another. This is getting to be so very difficult!" He sighed. "Alright, let's go."

They hurried out of the room, leaving Hesselrigge chained to the wall. They passed row upon row of barred cells.

"Willie . . . Willie," Annie called out softly. Haggard captives stared back, looking remarkably similar with their gaunt gray faces and patchy thin hair.

Don-Dun held up a hand. "Listen."

They paused, holding their breaths. They could hear the distant screeching of the gate and the faint murmur of voices.

"That would be them!" The stable master waved for everyone to follow him. "We'll wait in here until the guards pass." He ducked into a large empty cell and promptly fell headlong over an obstacle. Landing on his injured arm, he grunted with pain.

The dark mound he had tripped over had a dagger protruding from its side and wore a leather apron. The stable master got to his feet and yanked out the dagger. He flicked both sides of its blade onto the body's tunic and held it out, handle first, to Duncan. "Ye may need this again."

Swaying unsteadily, Duncan just stared at it.

"Come on, man, the guards are on their way." Sweat shone on the stable master's face. "Would ye rather they take Annie and Alex back to the rack room?"

Duncan's hand was shaking, but he took the dagger. He clenched it tightly, as if trying to squeeze the life from it.

The stable master grabbed the kitchen master's foot and unceremoniously slid him aside. Alex felt a stickiness under his feet. Don-Dun and the stable master positioned themselves nearest the main passage, backs pressed against the wall, swords drawn. They watched for the guards.

Annie clutched the stable master's arm. "When we find Willie, can we release the other captives too?"

"Don't be ridiculous!" the stable master snapped. "We'll be lucky to find your brother."

"But we can't just leave them." Annie was in tears. "It's horrible in those cells, all cold and wet, with no room to move. . . . It's not as if they're bad people; they're just people who couldn't pay their taxes and things like that. They'll die if we don't get them out!"

The stable master raised a finger to his lips. "We'll help them, don't ye worry. But we cannae do it now. The best thing we can do for these people, indeed for everyone who lives within and without the walls of this wretched place, is to help Wallace win – any way we can. Right now that means being still, so *weesht* before we're heard."

Annie pressed against the wall and put her arm around the bundled-up Katie.

Within minutes, the echoes of clinking armor and distant voices penetrated their cell. The stable master held his free hand up behind him, cautioning everyone to be quiet. Slowly, his hands formed a tight grip on his sword. His fingers flexed and tightened, flexed and tightened. The approaching footsteps echoed louder and louder on the flagstone floor. A man flashed by, followed by five armored guards. None looked into their cell.

The sound of the receding footsteps had not yet faded when the stable master sheathed his sword and waved them out. "Quickly now, we have no time to lose. As soon as they see what awaits them in the rack room, they'll be back. Don-Dun, you and I need to act like we're guarding this lot of captives. Duncan, you announce to the gatekeeper that we're taking them up to work in the kitchens. Tell him ye're to bring the young captive named Willie with us also."

They walked purposefully to the gate, Duncan in the lead, the pretend guards ushering along the pretend captives.

Duncan stopped at the guardroom door and gave it a rap. "Gatekeeper! Come out."

There was silence within. Duncan pounded on the door once more. Furniture scraped over stone. The door creaked open the width of a head, and the gatekeeper's stubbly face poked out. "What do ye want?" he grunted.

"We want for ye to have your assistant fetch us the foreign spy named Willie and for ye to open these gates. We're to bring this lot up to the kitchens."

The gatekeeper looked them over with suspicion. "That cannae be. Lord Hesselrigge was about to question this lot – why are ye taking 'm away?"

"We just spoke with him, and those are his orders, man," Duncan said impatiently. "Give the orders that the captive Willie be brought to us and open the gate. And do it *now*."

The gatekeeper abruptly tried to shut the door, but Duncan had stuck his foot into the frame. The stable master brushed past Alex and hit the door with his shoulder. He staggered into the guardroom, with Don-Dun close behind.

There was only one other guard in the room and he was asleep on a pallet. The sound of the stable master bursting into the room woke him up, but Don-Dun's sword was on his neck before he could rise.

Annie clutched the gatekeeper's tunic and shook him. "Where's Willie?" she shouted. "What did you do with my brother?"

The gatekeeper cackled, but said nothing.

The stable master gently nudged Annie aside. He placed his hand on the gatekeeper's forehead and gave it a sharp shove. The back of the gatekeeper's head cracked against the wall with a nasty thud.

"The next one will give ye a *real* headache." The stable master kept his hand resting lightly on the gatekeeper's forehead. "Now, answer her!"

"He's . . . been taken," the gatekeeper choked.

"Where?" The stable master tensed his arm. "Quickly, man."

"It's no my fault. . . ." The gatekeeper's toothless mouth flapped. "I only take orders –"

"What's no your fault? Tell me! Where is the boy?"

"They took him to the gallows!" The gatekeeper shrieked, raising his hands to shield himself.

Blood rushing in his ears, Alex listened as the gatekeeper babbled.

"They wanted to hang one each day. It was to be a warning to all who may have thought to oppose Hesselrigge – and daily entertainment for the rest. For some, there is much merriment with a hanging. They bring out bits of rotted food to throw while they jeer and taunt the captive."

The stable master's look made the gatekeeper fall silent.

23

THE GALLOWS

"Is it dinnertime yet?" the stable master asked.

"Dinnertime?"

"Most hangings are done before dinner, when the sun's but a hand away from being down," the stable master explained. "I know this – the stable is but a stone's throw from the gallows. Most folk are done with their work then, yet have time after the hanging to go home and have dinner before the dark sets in."

"Come! There's no time to waste." It was Don-Dun. He had finished tying up the second guard. "The sun may still be up – we may be able to free this lad."

Shouts came from the distance. The guards were running back from the rack room. The stable master clenched a fistful of the gatekeeper's tunic and dragged him to the gate. The gatekeeper fumbled to find the right key. He rattled a key in the lock, cursing before trying another.

"If the guards catch us, ye will be the first to die," the stable master murmured calmly. He held his sword up to the gatekeeper's neck.

The next key was the right one; the tumblers clicked and the gatekeeper pulled the screeching gate open.

The stable master pulled the gatekeeper closer, the sword still at his neck. "Are there any more keys to this gate?"

"The captain of the guards keeps a master set in the guard-room," the gatekeeper replied, his eyes fixed on the sword.

The stable master ignored the sounds of the fast-approaching guards. "There are none others down here?"

"None – I swear it!"

The guards were almost upon them. The stable master shoved the gatekeeper back and slammed the gate shut. He reached through the bars and turned the key.

"Pro Libertate!" he shouted, jingling the keys high in the air for all the guards to see before he ran after the others.

The guards crashed against the gate, stuck their swords through the bars, cursed, and waved their fists. They created a powerful racket, shaking the bars with all their might and calling out threats of slow death.

The guards' shouts fading behind him, Alex rushed up the spiral stone steps with the others, keeping to the inside where the steps were narrow. Coming out, they ran head-long into three guards who were hurrying for the stairs, swords drawn.

"What happened down there?" demanded one of the guards, a stocky Englishman with a nose so crooked it had to have been broken more than once. "Why's the gatekeeper been ringin' nonstop?"

"Oh, it's nothing," the stable master replied casually. "He didn't look so well when we left him. Maybe he ate some of the stuff he feeds to the captives."

"Serves him right." The guard cracked a thick smile and sheathed his sword. "Need help with this lot?"

"Them?" The stable master snorted. "*Bah*, they're only bairns. I've no so much as bothered to chain them. Ye'd best go see to the gatekeeper. He's probably got his head in a bucket."

The guard chuckled and motioned for the other guards to follow. They trundled off down the stairs in no particular hurry.

The stable master blew a sigh of relief. "Thank God they were too slow-witted to notice the cloak. We can't take that chance again." He took Hesselrigge's cloak from Katie and slashed it a few times to give it the appearance of rags. He folded it so the fur trim was hidden on the inside and carefully wrapped it back around her.

———◆◆◆———

A shaft of diffused light filtered through a high window. Alex felt a surge of hope. The sun had not yet set – *Willie may still be alive!*

They could not run for fear of attracting suspicion, so they set off at a brisk walk. Alex did his best to look like a dejected captive. This effort was not required by Annie and Duncan, who supported Katie between them. Twice they had to stop for her to throw up, continuing their hurried march while she was piteously wracked with dry heaves.

When they entered the courtyard, Alex was surprised to see only about a half-dozen soldiers manning the arrow slits on the many tiers above him. Were the others patrolling the ramparts? Regardless, no doubt Hesselrigge was right – the castle was so heavily fortified that it took no more than a handful of men to repel an attack.

Moreover, what kind of attack could there be? Sir James was out there with two companies of men laying a trap for Wallace and his men, and King Edward's armed men were coming along ready to help. Even if some of Wallace's men survived all this fighting, they'd not likely be in any shape to attack a castle!

The stable master cupped his hands to his mouth. "Guards, lower the bridge! We're coming through with captives to work the stables."

A guard peered over the rail. "Who calls? Do ye not know we're on alert? The bridge is not to be lowered."

"I've orders from Sire Rorie to prepare the stables for the arrival of King Edward's men. I cannae do that if ye don't lower the bridge. Look out over the fields. Do ye see any invaders? Lower the bridge, man, or do I have to send for Rorie to have him tell ye himself?"

The guard hesitated. He disappeared into the guardroom above the gates. Moments later, there was a creaking from the heavy portcullis being raised.

"Don't expect us to lower it again, when ye want back in," the guard called down. "Once ye're out, out ye stay until we have another reason to lower it."

Alex forced himself to slump and look dejected.

The portcullis stopped rising when the spiked ends were barely waist-high. A different sound emerged: the clanging of chains and a creaking of timbers. The heavy drawbridge beyond the portcullis was coming down.

The stable master shouted for the guards to raise the bars further. As if in spite, the guards started lowering them. Cursing, the stable master bent down and rolled under the bars as quickly as his clunky armor would permit. Alex and the others scrambled after him on all fours.

The back strap of Don-Dun's breastplate caught on a spike. He twisted to free himself and bellowed for the guards to stop lowering the portcullis. The spikes pushed him flat and still they kept coming. Duncan whipped out his dagger and cut the breastplate strap. He pulled Don-Dun's arms and slid him out from under the spikes seconds before they clanged heavily into their ground receptacles.

"Curses on your graves," Don-Dun roared up to the guards. Their laughter filtered down.

The stable master did not wait for the bridge to completely lower before leading the others up the sloping first half. They reached the hinged peak, and the creaking of timbers and clanking of chains abruptly stopped. A gap remained between the end of the bridge and the elevated stone roadway. Scowling, the stable master shifted his weight on the center fold of the bridge to push it down. It did not budge.

"Lower the bridge the rest of the way," the stable master roared. He shook his fist with helpless rage. "Imbeciles!"

They shuffled down to the far end of the bridge, careful not to slip. The gap did not look too big: about six feet. But there was no way to take a run at it, and the consequences of not making it across were frightening. Below, instead of a moat, were sharp metal spikes ready to impale anyone who fell.

"We'll toss 'm across, one at a time." The stable master nudged Duncan. "You first."

"Why me?" Duncan took two quick steps back. "Try it out with the professor."

"You're lighter," the stable master replied as he and Don-Dun gripped Duncan firmly by the back of his belt and tunic. "Ready, now? One, two, three, go!"

Duncan leapt, propelled by the mighty heave. He hit the edge of the roadway with a painful thud, his long spindly legs dangling down the wall. Amid shouts of encouragement, he scrambled to keep from slipping and successfully swung first one, then the other leg up over the edge.

"Ye're next, Fool." The stable master took hold of the fool's cloak. "Duncan, get ready to catch him."

"If you do not mind, sir," the professor spluttered, "I prefer to be called Professor Macintyre. I only put on the persona of a fool to find myself in the employ of Hesselrigge."

The stable master and Don-Dun flung him out over the gap. He hit the wall lower than Duncan. Only his arms and head were above the edge. He slipped, clawing for purchase.

Duncan got him. Straining, he pulled the professor's arm, his feet slipping on the smooth cobblestones. The professor scrambled to clear the edge and fell on top of him.

Alex's and Annie's cheers were cut short as the stable master motioned for Katie. They watched breathlessly as she stepped forward and shrugged off Hesselrigge's cloak. The stable master nodded to Don-Dun. She had little opportunity to jump, but didn't need to. The heave was so powerful, she flew right into Duncan's and the professor's waiting arms.

The stable master wrapped Hesselrigge's cloak around his sword to give it weight and flung it across. Annie was next and finally Alex. Heart in his mouth, he leapt, feeling a huge thrust propel him. Wind rushed through his hair. He pumped his legs as if running. Duncan and the professor caught him, but his knees banged painfully onto the road.

The stable master stripped off his armored breastplate and leggings and flung them across. He leapt, flailing, hitting the wall far down so only his fingers gripped the edge. Duncan lunged to catch hold of his wrists. He pulled, with the professor's help, until the stable master lay safely panting on the road.

That left Don-Dun, still in full armor, the only one standing on the bridge. "I'm not going to try that," he said slowly. "Ye lot go on ahead."

There was no point arguing: no one wanted to see him leap to his death.

"Stay out of trouble," the stable master called back. "And don't ye try to take on these soldiers all by yourself – there's too many."

Don-Dun waved them away. "Go now – the hanging cannae be far off!"

They left him standing alone and forlorn, trapped on the other side. It was hard for Alex to turn away; he was sure Don-Dun was doomed. His last glimpse was of Don-Dun trudging back over the center fold of the bridge towards the blockhouse. Blinking back tears, Alex vowed to find a way back to get him . . . as soon as they saw to Willie . . . if, indeed, there was anything to see but Willie's body swinging from a rope.

———— ◆ ————

A large crowd milled about the courtyard, below. Alex shaded his eyes from the setting sun. A man stood on the gallows platform reading from a document held high before him. He lowered the document and beckoned.

"No!" Annie cried. She covered her face. Even from this distance, it was clear that the pathetic figure being dragged up the steps was Willie. A solitary man in a black robe followed behind, reading from a thick book. The man's lips were moving, but Alex could not hear him.

The stable master cursed. At full speed, he ran down the ramp to plunge into the back of the crowd. It was futile. There was no way for him to get through in time. The guards had already lifted Willie onto a stool, and the priest was making the sign of the cross.

What was needed now was a diversion. *A fire, perhaps?* But Alex had no matches. *What else is there to do? Think, think, there is no time.* . . . Alex watched in horror as the noose was slipped over Willie's head and drawn tight about his neck.

"HALT!" boomed a voice. It was Hesselrigge, his arm high, his fool standing at his side. *How is this possible?* Then Alex realized it wasn't Hesselrigge at all. It was Duncan, wrapped in the tattered remnants of Hesselrigge's fur-trimmed blue cloak.

"HALT!" Duncan boomed again. This time, he captured the attention of the men on the platform. The crowd turned to where he stood high above them.

"STAY THE EXECUTION!" Duncan shouted in a commanding voice, his arm high.

Duncan's words caused considerable confusion. The document reader was gesturing toward Duncan and arguing with the executioner, who stood motionless, arms folded. Willie was left wobbling on the stool with the noose around his neck. At any moment, he could fall and hang.

"BRING THE BOY TO ME!" Duncan folded his arms, appearing like a man who expected his commands to be carried out.

The impression did not last long. Someone in the crowd shouted: "That's not Hesselrigge!" The word "impostor" leapt from mouth to mouth.

Hesitantly, soldiers started climbing the ramp toward Duncan. They knew that if this was the true Hesselrigge, one wrong move would be the end of them.

"Go! Bring the lad to me!" Duncan commanded the advancing soldiers.

A soldier drew his sword. "That's not Hesselrigge!" he shouted. "I'm sure of it – seize him!"

Duncan bellowed threats to no effect. The soldiers came charging, swords waving and armor clanking. Duncan and the professor leapt back, looking for a means of escape.

Confident they had cornered their prey, the guards slowed their advance. They fanned out across the road to keep Duncan and the professor from slipping past.

Duncan bolted to one side, the professor sprinting right behind. Before a guard could cut them off, they leapt, screaming, over the stone barrier at the side of the road. They crashed through the roof of a market stall. The soldiers peered over the edge, watching with chagrin as Duncan and the professor emerged staggering and stumbling from amid the mounds of collapsed awnings and bundles of merchandise.

Duncan tore off Hesselrigge's cloak and flung it to the ground. He shook his fist up at the soldiers. "Come and get me, ye cowardly scum!" he shouted.

The soldiers needed no further encouragement. They

bolted down the ramp after him. One stayed behind, keeping watch over Duncan and the professor's progress through the crowd with a malevolent smile. He waved to his fellow soldiers and pointed to where Duncan and the professor jostled through the crowd without once looking back, oblivious to the soldiers closing in.

Alex caught Annie's eye. She gave him a nod and inched in next to the soldier, pretending to be interested in the goings-on below. Alex crept to the soldier's other side, trying to keep the loose stones on the roadway from crunching under his feet.

The soldier signaled for the soldiers to go left. Exasperated, he stepped right up onto the stone barrier and bellowed: "More to the left, ye idiots, that way!"

It was now or never. Alex and Annie lunged and gave the guard a hard shove.

His arms a blurry windmill, the guard teetered on the edge. His shout turned into a scream as he dropped. Alex winced as he heard the heavy thump. It was followed by silence.

The crowd was leaping with excitement. Its attention was diverted yet again by another extraordinary event: the stable master had charged up onto the gallows and was swinging his sword at the executioner. He swung again and again, forcing the executioner away from where Willie stood precariously.

The executioner grabbed the priest and used him as a shield. With each jab from the stable master, the executioner thrust the frail priest from side to side. The priest did the same, except with his Bible.

The executioner ripped the Bible from the priest's hands and flung it at Willie, hitting him on the back of the head. Willie fell, his shriek abruptly cut off when the noose clenched around his neck. His feet swung in the air and kicked frantically. The stable master leaped over and held him up by the middle to keep his weight off the rope. The executioner advanced, still using the priest as a shield.

All the while, the outraged document reader was shouting for soldiers, guards, anyone to come up onto the platform and seize the stable master. Soldiers rushing through the crowd were rapidly closing in.

The stable master abandoned his fumbling, one-handed efforts to loosen the noose. Still holding Willie with one arm, his sword with his other, he shouted to the crowd: "I am the stable master. Ye know me. I am one of ye. It's Hesselrigge and the English who are our enemies. Help me, my friends. Stop them from killing us. William Wallace is outside these walls preparing to attack. In the name of our exiled King John, I say we rise up against these tyrannical usurpers who take our lands and our lives! Who is with me?"

A deathly silence hung in the air. Suddenly, a daggered hand rose from the crowd, pointing up to the sky. "King Johhhnnn."

"We're with ye, Stable Master," shouted another. More and more daggers flashed as people held them high over their heads, chanting, "King John, King John, King John. . . ." The chant became a roar.

The soldiers in the crowd found their path blocked. They turned back, but there, too, daggers were raised against them. The crowd closed in quickly. The few flashes from the soldiers' swords disappeared as the crowd filled in over them.

Men were boosted up onto the gallows platform; others charged up the steps.

The document reader threw down his document and leapt off the rear of the platform. Still holding the priest before him, the executioner was surrounded by an angry mob. Seconds later, his black-clad body dropped lifelessly off the side of the platform onto the dirt below.

Alex struggled to find Willie in all this mayhem. He was overjoyed to see the stable master had lowered him safely, the noose no longer around his neck. The stable master stood at the front of the crowded platform, his arm around Willie and his sword raised high above the crowd. "The guards," he roared. "Take down the guards at the gate!"

The crowd surged for the gates. A cluster of guards and soldiers moved quickly into a protective semicircular formation, their backs to the gate, their sharp pikes fanning out before them. These were well trained soldiers. It would cost more than a few lives to overwhelm them. But the soldiers faced a determined and vengeful mob – one that looked as if it would stop at nothing.

When the first of the attackers fell to the pikes, those behind leapt over the impaled to battle with small daggers against the soldiers' swords. Arrows rained down from the blockhouse. Alex watched in horror as arrows stuck into one person after another. With so many in the crowd, the archers could hardly miss.

Hasty barriers were erected from materials removed from market stalls. Awnings held up by poles provided some refuge from the arrows' deadly deluge.

Alex crouched against the stone barrier of the elevated roadway with Annie and Katie. He knew they were still exposed to arrows from some of the archers, but hoped they would be overlooked. Alex shielded Katie's body with his. Annie lay beside him, her arms over her head and eyes squeezed tight.

It sounded like the end of the world. Screams, moans, and battle cries mingled; arrows clattered against the stones. Through the chaos, a soldier cried out from within one of the guard towers: "The gates! Open the gates! Sir James approaches with his men!"

"Stop them! Close those gates!" The stable master rallied another charge, but the soldiers held them off and pushed open the gates.

Beyond were armored riders, dozens of them, dirt billowing around them as they careened towards them at full gallop. The stable master was the only one to stand his ground. He cried: "Fight! Fight! Charge!" but the falling back had turned into a stampede.

All was lost.

Riders thundered through the gates, the first bearing the standard of Sir James, plumage streaming back from his helmet and visor. Ignoring the carnage about them, they charged past the soldiers, the stable master, and the crowd as if they were not even there, their horses trampling without pause over the dead sprawled in the dirt.

The riders swept up the ramp, speeding past where Alex lay huddled with Annie and Katie. They stopped, their steaming horses stomping impatiently as they waited for the drawbridge to lower. One reared and a small barrel-shaped rider with a short bow slung across his back struggled to keep it in check.

"Annie, that looks like one of Wallace's men."

Annie shielded her eyes and looked from rider to rider. "Which one?"

Alex pointed furiously. "Him – that one. Traitor! Yes, you. Traitor!"

"Quiet!" Annie hastily pulled down his arm. "Are you trying to get us killed? Look, he's seen us! Oh, you've done it now." She covered her head with her arms.

The rider was staring straight at them. There was no mistake: it was Donald. He raised a finger to his lips and winked.

Alex was shocked. *How could he change sides like that?* Perhaps he was one of Sir James's men all along and had been spying on Wallace the whole time. But Donald had fought alongside Sir Ellerslie and the others at the beach . . . could it all have been a sham?

Fists clenched, Alex fought back tears of outrage.

The horses jostled for position. One shouldered Donald's horse aside, blocking him from view. Horrified, Alex recognized first one, then several other men he was sure he had seen at Wallace's camp.

All was truly lost. Not only had Sir James successfully returned from his encounter with Wallace, it would appear that Wallace's men had deserted him or, worse, had been with Sir James all along. There was no hope for help from Wallace now.

24

A TURN OF EVENTS

Alex crouched against the stone barrier with Sir James's horsemen towering over them. These horsemen did not care about the three terrified children huddling by the roadside, but Hesselrigge did. And Hesselrigge would soon be free: Sir James's first priority would be to find him and release him.

Hesselrigge would stop at nothing to hunt them down. And once he caught them, he would not be content to merely have them hanged. No, he would more likely be in the mood for torture: torture for the men who opposed him, like Don-Dun, the stable master, Duncan, and the professor; torture for those who aided Wallace, such as Willie, Annie, and Katie; and torture for the one who, in his mind at least, tricked him and his father into the caves and caused his father's miserable death. No doubt he would save the worst for that person.

Will Hesselrigge ever tire of inflicting all this agony? Alex felt ill.

The drawbridge boomed and laid flat, a cloud of dust

rising from where it had slapped the roadway. Sir James and his men surged forward. Hooves thundered on the bridge, clattered on the stones of the blockhouse, and faded away altogether.

Annie sat up. "Where did they go?"

"I think they've gone to find Hesselrigge. They'll be back."

Shouts came from within the blockhouse.

"Don-Dun?" Alex breathed. "Oh, no. . . ." He blinked back tears.

Annie put her hand on his arm. "He might have gotten away. . . ."

Alex pulled his arm away furiously. "And how would he have done that – with the help of some fairies?" Scowling, he stood to look over the stone barrier. The arrows had stopped. Below, the stable master had rallied some men to throw cobblestones at the soldiers guarding the gates. Nowhere did he spot Willie or the professor or Duncan.

"There!" Annie pointed excitedly.

Alex squinted. In amongst the cluster of people who had taken shelter under the gallows was Willie. "Let's go," he said.

Annie was already up and running. "Willie!" she shouted. "Willie!"

Alex looked back up to the blockhouse. There was still no sign of anyone manning the arrow slits. *Where could they have gone?* He tugged on Katie's arm. Her glassy eyes looked up at him blankly.

"Leave me here." She coughed.

Alex pulled her up and supported her with his arm. He wanted to run, but the best he could do with Katie hanging from his side was a hobbling walk. Annie and Willie were with the professor and Duncan under the gallows. She rushed out to help Katie.

Ducking under the platform, Alex cuffed Willie on the shoulder. "Lucky you! How's that for the nick of time?"

Willie gave Alex a weak smile. His clothes hung in tatters. His eyes had a fearful, anxious look and his hands shook. Alex regretted having made light of the situation.

The professor clapped his hands. "Come, we'll have to make our way back to the caves now."

"But, what about Craig?" Annie cried. "We can't leave without Craig!"

"I'll stay behind to look for him," the professor replied. "But first you lot have to get out of here. It's impossible to get everyone together first."

"Hesselrigge said the time chamber takes you back in time, not forward," Alex said. "Who knows where we'll end up if we go there again!"

The professor paused. "Using the time chamber will be risky, make no mistake. But Hesselrigge has not made a study of it as I have. Where time crosses over with space and energy crosses over with matter, anything is possible. The creators of those caves knew how to bring together fundamental building blocks of this universe and, in so doing, rearrange them in ways our science is only beginning to fathom –"

"None of that matters if we cannae get out of here," Duncan cut in impatiently. "We need to wait and see if the stable master and his friends can defeat the soldiers at the gate."

"We must find our way into the caves from within the castle," the professor said. "I know there is a way in, if we just –"

"The castle! We can't go back there!" Alex was aghast. "Didn't you see Sir James go in there with his men? He will have released Hesselrigge by now. Don't you know what he will do to us?"

"Ah, but the castle is where he won't expect to find us."

Willie's head swiveled from speaker to speaker. "No!" he burst out, his voice shaky. "We can't just hide – we have to get out of here!"

"And find Craig," Annie added.

"We should go back into the castle now," the professor persisted. "I think I know where the entrance to the caves can be found."

"The gates, we've got to get out of the gates!" Duncan shouted.

Alex put his hands to his head. He felt an overwhelming sense of despair. When they were working together, he was sure, at least, that they were taking the right direction. Now, every direction seemed impossible.

Hooves thundered on the bridge.

"Oh, no! They're back already," Annie cried.

Riding fully armored, Sir James charged from the blockhouse. He held a huge sword high with one hand, skilfully controlling his spirited horse with the other.

"That rules out entering the castle," the professor said sadly.

Alex knew it also eliminated any chance of overwhelming the soldiers at the gate. Their only hope was to find a place to hide, perhaps in the stables or somewhere in the back of a market stall. Either way, he was sure it would not be long before Hesselrigge found them.

Sir James drew in his horse while still high on the ramp. The horse reared and he deftly brought it back down. Both the soldiers and the stable master's men stopped to watch as Sir James lifted his helmet off his head and threw it to the ground. There was a stunned silence. Alex moved out from under the platform to see more clearly. Confused, he saw it was not Sir James holding his sword high, it was . . . *could it be?*

"I am William Wallace!" thundered the big man on the horse. He leveled his sword at the soldiers. "My men have taken the castle. Lay down your arms now and ye will not be slain, on that ye have my word."

Alex's head spun. It was the same big commanding William Wallace he had met in the rebel camp. Suddenly, he understood. Wallace had tricked his way in, disguised as Sir James – and he'd taken the castle! No wonder he'd seen so many of Wallace's men with the man he thought was Sir James! Joy welled up in Alex – he felt like he was floating.

The effect of William Wallace's words on the soldiers was remarkable. To a man, they dropped their weapons. The townspeople surrounded them, daggers raised.

"Stop!" Wallace shouted. "I said these men would be spared, and I mean to keep my word. Open the gates."

The gates were opened. Alex's heart soared to see scores of Wallace's men waiting outside.

"Yes-yes-yes-yes!" Alex whooped, fist in the air. "They did it! The castle is ours!"

All around, people were pouring into the courtyard, emerging from market stalls and from wherever they had taken refuge. Women waved their shawls, children skipped and danced, and the elderly thrust their staffs to the skies in triumph. Cheers and shouts of "Wallace! Wallace!" and "King John! Long live King John Baliol!" filled the air.

Alex spotted Sir Ellerslie on horseback, a woman riding sidesaddle before him.

"Over here!" Alex waved.

Sir Ellerslie urged his horse forward. The crowd parted, quickly filling in behind him. At first, Alex thought she was the lady he saw with Sir Ellerslie at the rebel camp, but as they approached, he saw she was not.

Loud and exuberant people jostled them, and Sir Ellerslie pulled up in their midst.

"Hello, everyone," he called out. "I believe I have someone here whom ye may know."

He sprang from his horse and reached up to assist the woman. She climbed down awkwardly.

Annie gasped through white knuckles. "Mother?"

Mrs. McRae took hold of Sir Ellerslie's arm. "But, m'Lord," she said, looking dazed. "That child seems so very familiar – how can that be?"

"Is that perhaps your daughter?" Sir Ellerslie asked gently.

"Is she?" Mrs. McRae stepped forward and squinted. "Oh, I really wish I had my glasses; I can't see a thing without them." She paused. "Do I have children?"

Sir Ellerslie shrugged apologetically.

Tears sprang to Annie's eyes. She rushed to embrace her mother.

"Wait!" Mrs. McRae cried, regarding the girl that held her tightly. "I do have children – at least I will have them.

But that will be a long time from now. I won't be having children for hundreds of years!"

"Mother, it's us," Annie said, looking up at her tearfully. "We've gone back in time too, and now we're all together again."

"It is so nice to meet you. My, you do remind me of the daughter I will have. And look over there – that lad looks like the son I'll have one day."

"It's me, Mother. It's Willie." He held out his hand hesitantly.

"Willie. What a marvelous name." Mrs. McRae tousled his hair pleasantly. "I do believe that one day I will name my son after William Wallace."

"Some farmers had taken her in," Sir Ellerslie explained. "Apparently, she had been wandering about lost, cold, and hungry for some time and had become deathly ill. She was babbling about the horrors of hell and other such things."

"I didn't deserve to go there – really I didn't." Mrs. McRae pulled at her hair with both fists. "I was just walking my dog. It was his fault. That's right, it was the dog's fault. Maybe he was a little demon sent by the devil to trick me. He led me into that cave. . . ." She sobbed. "I got trapped in there by the rising tide. I was just trying to get out, really I was. . . ."

"It's okay, Mum," Annie said, gently pulling down her mother's hands and holding her close. "Don't worry – you're out now. We're all together again."

"We are?" Mrs. McRae's glazed eyes slipped into focus for a moment. "Is that really you, my dear, or am I going mad . . . ?"

Annie's lip quivered. "It's me, Mother, and Willie."

"Oh, good." Mrs. McRae sighed with relief. "I was so worried. But, my how you've grown. You're both so big, I can hardly believe it. Well, let's go do some chores, shall we? It must be time for milking cows."

Annie turned to where Katie lay under the platform. "Mum, that's Katie." She tugged her mother's hand. "We have to get her into a bed – she's not well."

Sir Ellerslie called two of Wallace's men. He directed them to take the McRaes to chambers within the castle's inner keep. "William Wallace will want to question them before long. Make sure they are kept comfortable until he arrives."

Alex looked hopefully past Sir Ellerslie to where the men had entered the courtyard. Could his parents be among them? A hollow sensation gripped him.

"Have you seen any others that look like they might not belong?" he asked, not knowing why he did – he already knew the answer. "You know, wearing strange clothes, speaking like me?"

Sir Ellerslie shifted uncomfortably. "No, sorry."

"Are you sure, no one?" Alex fought back tears.

Swinging back up onto his horse, Sir Ellerslie extended a hand and hoisted Alex up behind him. He gently tugged the reins and turned the horse about. "I am most impressed," he said. "Ye set out unarmed and single-handed this morning and, over the course of a day, ye raise a fighting force, put many of Hesselrigge's men behind bars, and nearly take the entire castle."

"We were done for," Alex replied. "You came in the nick of time."

"Perhaps, perhaps not. There was not much left of Hesselrigge's forces when we rode in here. Between that terror of a man fighting the soldiers in the blockhouse and the mob rioting at the gates, ye just might have won regardless."

"Is Don-Dun alright?" Alex held his breath.

"That man ye left in the blockhouse?" Sir Ellerslie laughed. "Aye, alright he is. It's a good thing he was not more successful, or there would have been no one left in the castle to fool into lowering the drawbridge for us."

Alex clung to the saddle as Sir Ellerslie maneuvered his horse around a boisterous knot of revelers. "How did you avoid Sir James's trap?" he asked.

Sir Ellerslie chuckled. "That was easy because it was our trap all along. First, we planted word with men we knew to be Hesselrigge's spies that we would attack King Edward's men. That was a ruse to draw Hesselrigge's men out of the castle. It worked brilliantly. We could scarcely believe it when Sir James rode out with *two* companies.

"We engaged them on our terms. It was a tough battle, make no mistake, but they had nary a chance. In the midst of the fight, Wallace rode right into the fray and slew Sir James with that big sword of his – took his head right off with one swing."

"One swing?" Alex echoed incredulously.

"Well, maybe it took a second to completely finish the job. Holding up the head of the enemy commander does wonders for morale. Then he took Sir James's armor and the horses of his commanders, left us to battle King Edward's most ill-prepared men, and rode out to the castle to fool his way in under the guise of being Sir James. Brilliant, isn't it? Sir James's men defeated, King Edward's men defeated, and Hesselrigge's castle taken, all in a matter of a few hours. Wallace is truly a master strategist."

As they were crossing the drawbridge, Alex asked, "Where are we going?"

"To see William Wallace."

They dismounted in the very room that the stable master and Don-Dun had killed the two soldiers. Alex followed Sir Ellerslie up long stairways. They came out on the blockhouse rooftop battlements.

From this height, the tall perimeter walls looked small and insignificant. Waves crashing against the rocks, far below, made Alex think back to the picnic they had at the ruins with Mr. McRae. Everything seemed so much simpler then.

———◦◦◦———

William Wallace stood casually among a group of men, one foot up on the crenulated wall. Upon Alex's approach, he leaned forward and rested his elbow on his knee.

"So here is our young warrior – one who comes from nowhere and sets out to take on a ruthless tyrant single-handedly." Wallace clapped his big hand on Alex's shoulder. "Truly remarkable! Ye have surprised us all . . . but tell me now, and truthfully, who is Alex Macpherson?"

Alex hesitated, feeling many eyes on him. "Can I speak with you privately, sir?"

William Wallace nodded. The men about him took their cue and left. He motioned for Sir Ellerslie to stay.

Alex wondered where to begin. He took a deep breath. Wallace and Sir Ellerslie stood impassively, their faces betraying no surprise or disbelief as he told them about the time chamber, about how he was searching for his missing parents, and how he had come from a time far in the future. Only when Alex came to the point of telling how a learned man, a professor, had also come from his time did Wallace react. He waved for one of his men, a commander waiting at a respectful distance, and directed him to have the professor found and brought to him.

Alex continued his story, telling them how Hesselrigge, too, came from the future.

Wallace squinted. "This is the strangest tale I've ever been expected to believe. Should it be true, it explains much, but leaves more that I suspect will never be explained – or if it were, I suspect we would not fathom it."

Men arrived to report to Wallace and receive instructions. Alex learned that those held in the dungeons were being released, although Wallace first wanted to know who they were, in the event there was someone of importance who either should not be released or, upon release, should be treated in some special manner. Preparations were underway in the kitchens to give them their first decent meal in a long time.

Alex also learned that, although Hesselrigge's soldiers were still locked in the dungeon where he had left them, there was no sign of Hesselrigge himself. The soldiers had freed Hesselrigge by prying loose his chains from the wall, but could not account for where he might be.

On hearing this, Wallace thumped his fist on the stone

wall. Through gritted teeth, he ordered his men to go back into the dungeons straightaway to search them thoroughly.

On the rooftop the professor appeared, accompanied by the commander who'd been sent to get him. The professor approached hesitantly.

"I-I'm pleased to meet ye, Sire." He bobbed his head awkwardly.

"I've been told ye are both Hesselrigge's loyal fool and a learned man from a far distant time." Wallace watched him warily. "Which is it?"

"Both," the professor said, "although you can leave out the part about being loyal. Hard as it might be to believe, I have, indeed, come from a future time. Thomas Macintyre is my name. My reckless foray into the past has largely come about as a result of my endeavors to find the whereabouts of some missing persons, several of whom I believe you know."

"This tale is so unbelievable, I'm still inclined to think of ye as naught but Hesselrigge's fool. Certainly, if I repeat any part of this tale to anyone, I will be taken as the fool; but, for the sake of amusement, pray tell what ye planned to do upon finding the missing persons."

"Return them, Sire." The professor spoke without hesitation. "Return them to the people they have left behind, the people who love them and miss them terribly."

"Will ye take Hesselrigge back also, back to people who love him and miss him terribly?"

"I doubt that there are any, even in our time. Also, were we to take him back, he will be a man who has committed no crime for which he could be tried. He would walk free."

"I say we try him now," Sir Ellerslie said. "I suspect we know the outcome."

"Aye, I'm with ye there." Wallace broke into a rare smile. "But we have to find him first. From last reports, he has somehow managed to elude capture in the dungeons."

"The caves!" The professor was agitated. "He might have found his way into the caves. We must stop him!"

"There is nowhere he can go that we cannae find him." Wallace's voice was calm and measured. "We control the castle and the entire countryside for more than a day's ride."

"No, the time chamber!" The professor's distress was growing. "He might escape through time. God knows what horrors he may inflict upon mankind and all our histories if he succeeds! Lend me some men, and I'll go after him. I may be able to find the way into the caves."

"I'll go," Sir Ellerslie said. "I'd be delighted to have a shot at him."

"Take a couple of men with ye, in case Hesselrigge's not alone," Wallace said. "I cannae afford to lose ye. Once we're done here, I'll need ye to run this castle and raise an army from the willing Scots living on these lands."

"I'm coming too," Alex declared.

Wallace raised his hand. "Thomas, one last question. Ye are a scholar of what is to be, a prophet of sorts, so tell me, will our flag fly o'er a free and prosperous Kingdom of Scotland in the centuries to come?"

"Aye!" the professor pounded his fist into the palm of his hand. "And before you are done, you will have driven the English from Scotland three times. Your name will always be remembered as a great hero of Scotland."

"Excellent! And do ye have any parting words of advice for me?"

The professor thought for a moment. "Beware of treachery from your own countrymen."

Wallace nodded sadly and motioned for them to make haste.

25

HESSELRIGGE'S LEGACY

The professor stepped aside to let Sir Ellerslie and Alex descend the spiral stairs to the dungeons. "I need to maintain my bearings if I'm to have any hope of finding the caves," he said. "Alex, please stop at the level that is exactly one rotation down the steps. You can use my arm as a guide." The professor awkwardly leaned over the stairs and extended his arm.

"Here," Alex called up.

The professor started down, counting steps. "They're not all the same height, but there appears to be about eleven steps to a full spiral. Wait here until I've gone down another eleven."

The professor peered up at Alex and waved for him to follow. "I believe a full spiral is eleven and a half steps. We should be able to count our way down from here."

The barred gate to the dungeons lay twisted and bent, forced open by Wallace's men. Apart from an eerie, incessant dripping, the dungeons were silent, a few torches still burning along the walls.

Sir Ellerslie disappeared into the guardroom, emerging with two men whom he introduced to Alex and the professor as Nielson and Stephan, longtime militants in Wallace's army. They nodded their greetings.

Sir Ellerslie held his lantern high. "Alex, where was Hesselrigge left? Lead the way, lad."

Alex guided them toward the rack room. They passed empty cells, each with its door hanging half-open. He paused at the cell they had hidden in to elude the guards, holding up his lantern. As he feared, the dead kitchen master was still there, lying propped against the wall, the lantern light reflecting off his dull, open eyes.

Sir Ellerslie lowered his lantern. "Nielson, when we're done here, remember to have someone haul this away. We cannae leave him here to putrefy."

"Nae, Sire." Nielson let out a ghoulish chuckle. "He'd be a right mess to clean up then, all smelly and –"

"Enough!" Sir Ellerslie saw Alex grow white. "Lead on, m'lad. Which way from here?"

Alex forced himself to look away and numbly pointed down the main corridor. He took deep breaths of the stale dungeon air in vain attempts to quell his rising nausea.

Alex showed them where Hesselrigge had been chained. There were holes in the mortar from where Hesselrigge's guards pried the chains from the wall.

"It'll be hard for him to get about with chains hanging from him," Nielson said. "He cannae have gone far."

Sir Ellerslie carefully examined the rack room, pausing over the blood on the flagstones and the bodies heaped one over the other in the corner.

Seeing the gray dead faces of Rorie and the guards in the pile made Alex feel clammy. He sat down on one of the hard chairs and slumped forward. Saliva built up in his mouth, so he spat it out. Then he retched and coughed up the few bits of food left in his stomach.

Sir Ellerslie raised an eyebrow.

"Sorry, Sire," Nielson said. "We haven't had time to clean up yet."

Sir Ellerslie cast his light along the walls and ran his hand over them as if feeling for some hidden doorway.

The professor watched impatiently, making no effort to help. "This is not the southernmost part of these dungeons," he said. "If I still have my bearings, we are at the dungeon's westerly aspect. We should examine the passages and cells to the right."

Sir Ellerslie continued his painstaking search of the room, casting his light up to the vaulted stone ceiling and down to the floor. Finally, he straightened. "Very well, let's try elsewhere."

Alex groaned. As much as he wanted to put distance between himself and the bodies in the corner – and the rotting kitchen master lurking outside – Alex didn't feel well enough to move. He held his head in his hands, wishing he hadn't come.

"Stephan, stay with the lad for a bit," Sir Ellerslie said. "If he feels better, ye can catch up with us. Otherwise, take him back to the guardroom and wait for us there."

Alex protested, rising unsteadily, but Sir Ellerslie put a hand on his shoulder and gently eased him down. "Don't worry, son. We'll take it from here. Ye've done more than enough already."

Alex was too weak to argue. He watched Sir Ellerslie leave with Nielson and the professor. Furious with himself for being so sick and weak, Alex listened to their footsteps receding outside in the corridor until all was quiet . . . deathly quiet.

Stephan whistled tunelessly and poked about with the adjustment controls of the rack table. Yawning, he climbed up onto it and stretched out. It was not long before his breathing became slow and rhythmic.

Alex wished he had thought of lying on the rack. The idea of crawling into a bed was very appealing. He ruled out lying on the floor. Remembering the stench that arose when the stable master's sword sliced into Rorie's guts, Alex felt his stomach clench up again.

He tried to think of something else. His life with Uncle Larry came to mind. While not a pleasant thought, at least it did not make him feel sick. It would be wonderful to have parents who were interested in what you did, who were always there when you needed them, ready to give you the kind of hug that said how much they loved you. Instead, he had Uncle Larry, who considered him a burden, even though Alex's expenses were paid by a trust fund set up by his parents. Then there was Aunt Fiona, who was too sick to pick him up from the airport, but never once phoned to talk to him.

Life didn't seem fair. He drew up his knees and huddled in the hard chair, blinking back tears. His thoughts strayed to the other people who might have been in this chair, people who would have been stretched out on the rack, and people who had been left to die a miserable death in one of the many tiny stinking cells. His life might not be fair, but life was clearly more unfair for some than for others.

Alex took a few sharp breaths to clear his head. He felt better. A sound in the corner of the room caught his attention. He glanced over to the pile of bodies. *Could there be a rat in there?* He thought of a rat gnawing at a corpse and felt his nausea returning.

One of the bodies moved. Even in the dim light of the two remaining torches, Alex was sure of it. Not much of a movement, but a movement it was. He saw it again – this time a whole body rolled slightly on the pile!

"Stephan!" Alex shrieked. He could not tear his eyes away. "Stephan, wake up!"

In an instant, Stephan was awake and on his feet, sword drawn. "What is it?"

"One of the bodies is still alive!"

Stephan re-sheathed his sword. "Don't fret yourself. Even if by some miracle one of them vermin is still alive, he's no going to hurt ye none."

Alex continued to stare, horrified, at the pile of bodies. For someone so mutilated, lying in a pile of corpses, to be alive, to be moving, to be trying to get up . . .

"*Och*, I'll see if there's someone to finish off, shall I?" Stephan wearily drew his sword once more, prodding about in the pile with his boot and the tip of his sword.

Suddenly two arms with a chain leapt from beneath the bodies, ensnared Stephan's neck from behind, and dragged him down – kicking and flailing – onto the grisly pile. Stephan grappled and clawed at the chain. It bit deep into his neck and cut off his breathing. There was a sharp crack. Stephan's body stiffened and shuddered. He twitched and then lay still.

Stephan's corpse rolled onto its side. Unaware of how loudly he was screaming, Alex retreated, without turning away from the apparition before him, until his back was pressed into a corner.

Rising from the mutilated pile was Hesselrigge, blood smeared over his clothes, chains dangling from his arms.

"*Ha!* We meet again! And this time, there is no one here to help you."

Stephan's sword in his hand, Hesselrigge staggered forward, the chains hampering his movement. He collapsed against the heavy rack table and strained to push it to one side, veins popping from his head. The table legs screeched over the stone. Panting, Hesselrigge jabbed the point of Stephan's sword between two flagstones. Careful to keep one of his eyes on the terrified Alex, he pushed and pried. Its end snapped. Cursing, Hesselrigge thrust the broken end between the flagstones and continued prying.

Alex took a sidestep towards the door.

"One more step and I'll hack ye down where ye stand!" Hesselrigge snarled.

Panting, he used the broken sword as a lever to lift one edge of the flagstone. He stepped on the sword handle and forced it to lie flat on the floor. Grunting and dripping sweat, he gripped the edge of the flagstone and slid it sideways, revealing a dark cavity below.

Hesselrigge held Stephan's lantern over the hole. Waving the broken sword, he ordered Alex to come forward.

Alex could not move. He could only stand frozen, staring at the blood-smeared, shackled apparition before him.

"Ye come when I tell ye, boy." Hesselrigge's chains rattled as he raised the broken sword. He gestured to the hole. "Get in."

Alex shook his head slowly, his eyes never leaving Hesselrigge. He felt about the wall behind him for a loose stone, anything he could use as a weapon. Glancing down to the hole, he was surprised to find it was a circular, stone-lined shaft.

"Well-hidden, isn't it?" Hesselrigge barked a short laugh. "No one will ever find us down there. Now, get in. And bring a lamp. We can use an extra one down in the caves."

Caves! So this is the way in!

"Go! I haven't got all day."

Alex sat on the top edge of the stone shaft and found the footholds. Remarkably, it was fairly easy to climb down. Chains rattled above him, and stone scraped against stone. Silhouetted against the light, Hesselrigge's dark form was sliding the heavy flagstone back into place.

No one would be able to find them. The professor was searching in a totally different part of the dungeons. Even when they returned to the rack room and found Stephan dead, they would be unlikely to find the hidden entrance.

Losing Hesselrigge in the caves was Alex's only hope, but he could not think of how. Hesselrigge would simply follow his light. He couldn't put it out, as he had no means to relight it later. Being trapped underground in utter blackness would be terrifying . . . and a horrible way to die.

Alex descended as quickly as he could. A narrow corridor opened into the side of the shaft. Alex scrambled into it, looking for somewhere to hide, somewhere that his light couldn't be seen. Hesselrigge was dragging heavy chains. Alex might be able to outrun him. Perhaps he could double back and escape up the shaft before Hesselrigge could catch him.

A heavy door blocked the end of the corridor. Two shriveled, mummified corpses stood propped up next to it, one on either side. For one horrific moment, it looked as if they were moving . . . but it was only shadows cast by Alex's lantern.

As he feared, the door was locked. Alex set the lantern down, placed his foot on the door frame, and pulled, but the door would not budge.

"What you need is this."

Alex spun. Hesselrigge was holding up a large key, grinning.

"I see you've met my friends, the mason and the carpenter. I had them install this door so I could be sure no one ever blundered into these caves – or came out of them, for that matter. Now no one knows about this place except you and me . . . and you will most certainly not be telling anyone."

Hesselrigge unwrapped the chain from around his wrist. Dangling from the end was the eyebolt that once fastened it to the wall. "Give me your cord."

Alex untied the short rope that held his coat about him and handed it over.

Hesselrigge tied one end to the eyebolt, the other he noosed and knotted around Alex's neck. Then he swung open the heavy door. Past it was the familiar large chamber with arching stone columns.

Hesselrigge sighed. "It's a shame. It took me years to work my way into a position of power here. Now, thanks in no small measure to you, it's over. I will have to start again in some earlier time. Still, it shouldn't take long. People are such idiots. Pretend to be their friend or their ally and the next thing ye know, they are genuinely surprised when ye stab them in the back and take over their power.

"Already, I am renowned in history. It was me who killed Wallace's wife; aye, ye didn't know that, did ye? Months ago, I had her throat cut for aiding Wallace's escape. People came from miles around to watch. I'll be known for that deed for the rest of living history. Every time someone thinks of Wallace, they'll think of the man who killed his wife – and that was me! *Ha!* What remains to be seen is in what further manner I will be known throughout history. Perhaps I will go back to the time of Jesus and become Judas. That would be a good one! I'll be Julius Caesar's Brutus and Abel's Cain. I will live . . . to destroy!"

Laughing insanely, Hesselrigge dragged Alex toward the ornately carved inner wall, with its ugly snake-haired monster-head that blocked the time chamber.

"Here's why I haven't killed ye before now." He gave the chain a sharp jerk to make Alex stumble. "Ye can climb high up on the wall and turn the controls that make the head move. Who better to bring with me for this task than the boy who's done it before, the boy who's the cause of all this. . . ."

Hesselrigge was working himself into a rage. Foaming

spittle flew from his mouth. His hands were rising up, fingers curled into claws. With effort, he regained some control and lowered his arms.

"Climb up that wall, and pull on that bird carving."

The chain was not long enough for Alex to climb that high. Hesselrigge tore strips from Alex's coat, wound them tightly into a rope, and used it to extend the rope from Alex's neck to the end of the chain. Panting from exertion, he knotted the ropes. "I'm no letting ye loose, that's certain. I didn't get to where I am today by being stupid."

Alex knew better than to say anything. He climbed, using the carvings as hand-and-foot holds.

"Higher! To your left . . . yes! That one! Pull down on that bird's head."

There it was – the bird with its piercing eye – staring back at him. Alex covered its head with his hand and tugged.

"Come on, put some muscle into it!"

Alex pulled until the bird's beak poked into the wormhole. For a few seconds, nothing happened. Then a vibration emanated from somewhere deep in the wall, a low rumbling that could hardly be heard, but was building in volume.

"Yes! Yes! Yes!" Hesselrigge laughed demonically as the great snake-haired head lowered into the ground. It came to a heavy thudding halt.

He yanked Alex onto the top of the head and up the ramp. Alex grabbed the rope, dug in his heels, and pulled back, but it was no use. Hesselrigge was far bigger and heavier. Hesselrigge unwound the chain from his other wrist. He swung it over his head, slowly at first, then faster and faster. The chain made a rhythmic whirling sound.

"Have it your way, boy!" Hesselrigge pulled Alex ever closer to the whirling chain and the heavy jagged eyebolt at its end. Alex waited until the chain was on its backswing and made a quick lunge. The sudden lack of resistance made Hesselrigge stumble.

Alex heard a light pinging sound of metal striking stone. A dagger skittered across the ramp and came to rest near the wall. Another dagger clattered against the stones, then another. Alex did not take the time to find out where they were coming from. Instead, he took advantage of Hesselrigge's momentary distraction and dove under the swinging chain. He grabbed a dagger and scrambled back.

There was a yelp of surprise. Hesselrigge stared dumbfounded at a knife that protruded from his shoulder. Then he turned and ran up the ramp, pulling Alex along behind him.

The ramp began to rise under his feet. Soon he would be trapped. Someone grabbed him from behind and pulled. There were shouts, a familiar voice. *Malcolm!* Alex frantically sawed the rope with the dagger. The last strands snapped and he was flung back down the ramp. He tumbled out above the chamber floor seconds before the huge head groaned back into its full upright position.

He felt a terrible pain at the back of his head, where it hit the floor. He knew he should get up and run, but lifting himself was such an effort. The chamber spun round and round while black spots floated past in the opposite direction. Alex felt as if he were falling backwards into a blackness that was rising up to meet him.

26

SMALL MARKERS

"Relax, take it easy."

Whoever said that sounded far away. The voice was vaguely familiar.

Alex blinked. Faces were peering down at him: Reagan and Hugh . . . and there was big George too, an anxious look on his face, and now Craig. . . . *Am I dreaming? What are they doing here?* He struggled to rise, his head throbbing. "How, how did you get here?" he stammered.

"We're to find a way into the castle," Reagan replied. "Remember? We're to open the castle gates to let Wallace in. Craig showed us a way into these caves at low tide. Now, how about you tell us how *you* got here. Is there an easier way than we came?"

"Yes, through the front gates – Wallace tricked his way in. The castle has been taken."

Reagan's jaw dropped. "You mean, we've come all this way for nothing?"

Alex gave a short chuckle before the pain in his head cut it short. He put his hand on Craig's beaming face and gave it a gentle shove. "Yes, but I'm very, very glad to see you guys," he said.

Careful not to move his head too quickly, he craned to see if the portal was still open. Dismayed, he noticed the hideous snake-haired monster-head staring back, its bottom fangs protruding up defiantly from its lower jaw. There was no sign of Hesselrigge nor of Malcolm.

"Where's Malcolm?"

Reagan shrugged.

"No!" Alex scrambled to his feet. Head pounding, he climbed the wall and pulled down on the bird's head. Nothing happened. He shouted for the others to help, to seek other carvings to twist and turn. Confused, they humored him and tried, but nothing worked.

Alex felt sure that Malcolm – the man who had befriended him, looked after him, and saved his life – was never coming back. Even were Malcolm to make it back into the caves, he did not know the combinations that made the monster-head lower. And even if he did stumble across a working combination, chances are it wouldn't be the one to bring him back to this time. No, he was gone for good. Alex covered his eyes with his arm.

Hugh shifted his weight impatiently. "So how do we get out of here?"

Alex gestured to the door. "We're locked in," he said miserably.

"Don't ye fret about no door." Reagan mustered a small smile. "We didn't come all this way to be stopped by a lock. Ye see my friend Hugh here? Well, before all this messy war business, Hugh was a player who traveled the land with his troupe. They amazed folk with their incredible shows. Ye would be correct if ye thought that Hugh's most popular stunt was dagger-throwing. He would have a pretty maiden stand tied up against a wall and throw daggers to sever her bonds. Ye never missed, did ye, Hugh?"

"Almost never." Hugh gave Alex a big wink.

"Now, Hugh had another stunt to draw *oohs* and *aahs* from the crowd," Reagan continued. "He would have himself locked up in impossible ways and have to escape before something awful happened. What's the worst one ye've been in, Hugh?"

"Oh, that would be when I was locked in some caves under a castle with a bunch of half-wits –"

"Alright, alright, enough! Now, Hugh is talented at escape. Mere locks don't stand in his way."

Hugh had the door open faster than most could have done with a key.

Climbing the shaft was no challenge for Reagan. He removed the flagstone cover and lowered a rope for the others.

The rack room was as Alex had left it. The men paused at the sight of Stephan's body, still sprawled on the pile of corpses.

"We can't leave him like this," George said – the first words Alex ever heard George speak.

Gently George lifted Stephan off the pile and laid him out on the rack table, hands folded on his chest. Reagan raised the top of Stephan's tunic to cover the purple neck wounds and closed Stephan's eyes. The men lowered their heads and had a moment of silence.

Before going in search of Sir Ellerslie, Nielson, and the professor, the men took the time to escort Alex and Craig to the stairs exiting the dungeons. Wearily, Alex led Craig over to the inner keep, where the royal chambers were housed and where he would find the McRaes and Katie. He wanted to lie down and go to sleep. It was hard to tell how late it was; the castle was ablaze with celebrations. Alex knew he could sleep through it all.

As they walked, he listened to Craig: "The tide wasnae completely out, but Reagan swam into the tunnel *underwater*. He was gone for the longest time, and I was sure he was dead – and so he would've been if he didnae find air at the other end. He kept on swimming underwater, holding his breath, right past the point of no return, all 'cause we said there was a way in. Can ye believe anyone doing that? I was sure he was dead, but then Malcolm felt these tugs on the rope. . . ."

"What rope?"

"Reagan was pulling a rope in with him, d'ye ken? He was letting it out a bit at a time while he swam. Three quick tugs meant *pull me out, I'm drowning*, but this wasnae three quick tugs; it was one tug. That meant he made it! When it was my turn, they tied a rope to one of my hands to pull me through more quickly. I was holding my breath and kicking my legs, but still I didnae think I would make it. My lungs were screaming."

"Your accent's getting stronger." Alex smiled. "You've been hanging about with these guys too long."

"So have ye," Craig retorted. "Ye're beginning t' sound a bit Sco'ish y'rself."

They climbed broad stairs into a royal paneled chamber and came to a heavy oak door. Alex raised his hand and paused. "Oh, Craig, there's something else. . . ."

"What?" Craig asked eagerly.

"It's something good, mostly," Alex began awkwardly. "But she's getting better, really, she is."

Craig looked at Alex blankly.

"You'll see."

Alex knocked. The door unlatched and opened a crack.

"Craig!" Annie shrieked. She gave the embarrassed boy a big kiss on the cheek. "At last, we're all together again. . . ."

"Annie? Who's there, dear?" came a voice from within the room.

Annie put her arm around Craig's shoulder and steered him through the door. He looked bewildered.

"MUM!" Craig ran into the room.

"Craig, oh my little boy, Craig!" Mrs. McRae wrapped her arms around him.

"See," Annie said quietly, so only Alex could hear, "Mum's much better now. She'll be back to her old self in no time."

Annie turned to Alex, her eyes glistening. "You need to come with me." She took his hand.

"What is it?"

"It's Katie." Annie's voice quavered. "Oh, Alex, she's dying! I didn't want to tell you like this, but I don't know how else to say it."

"Dying?" Alex said weakly.

"The dungeons . . . the healer said her fever came from being in the dungeons . . . he's seen it before and there's nothing he can do." Annie's voice broke.

"Katie die? That can't be. . . ."

"I'm sorry." Annie lifted her tearful face to look at him. "Come, I'll take you to her." She led him to an adjoining room. Opposite a flickering fireplace was an ornate bed-cabinet, with tall sides, a roof, and curtains. Looking lost inside was a tiny form tucked up under a mound of blankets.

"Katie?"

She stirred. Slowly, Katie opened her eyes and smiled faintly. Sweat glistened on her face; her hair was pasted flat to her head. Annie rinsed a cloth in a washbasin and tenderly wiped Katie's forehead.

Alex gently held her hand in both of his. She looked at Alex with a calm far-away look. There was simply nothing to say. Alex felt tears on his cheeks.

Katie's eyes slowly closed.

Annie rose quietly. "Let her sleep. I'll show you where there's a bed for you too."

They passed into an adjoining room complete with washbasin, commode, and large comfortable bed. Annie gave him a tight hug. "Get some sleep. You look like you need it." The door closed behind her.

Alex looked about the room. Without removing any clothes or washing his face and hands, he flopped face-first onto the bed. He clenched the pillow with fists so tight, his hands shook.

Lying fully dressed on top of the covers, he finally fell into a deep sleep. It was interrupted by a dream. A hand clamped onto his arm – a manacled hand with a chain. *Not so fast.* Hesselrigge laughed. *You're coming with me!*

Alex flailed, gradually realizing that it was but a bad dream. Then he remembered Katie, and the wrenching feeling of despair returned.

The room was lit by an eerie, silvery light from a half-moon. Nothing seemed real; everything was ghostly, hovering shadows.

Slowly, he got out of bed. He splashed cold water over his face and watched the basin return a shimmering pale reflection. He wondered if he was still dreaming, or if perhaps staring back at him from the other side of the reflection was his real, nondreaming self at the washstand at the McRae farm.

Alex crept through the passageway. Katie's door creaked as he opened it. She was awake. He sat gently on the edge of the bed. "How are you, Katie?"

"Oh, I'm fine." Katie's eyes sparkled. "I've been having such a good time playing with my wee brother, Tim, and my sisters, Agnes and Susan. My mother was there too, and she was so happy – she couldnae stop giving us hugs and kisses. My father was sitting in his favorite chair near the fire, and he was playing that game with us where we would sit on his foot and hold his hands and he would swing us up and down with his leg. Sometimes, we'd fly right into the air! He said to us, 'Och, ye're gittin' so big and heavy,' and I said, 'I'm no heavy, don't ye call me big and heavy,' and my father laughed and grabbed my leg and said, 'What's that? Where did all that come from? Is it full of oatmeal? I need to stop feedin' ye – ye're gittin' too big. Where did my wee lassie go?'"

Alex smiled and held her hand. She looked so happy. He did no more than nod and offer the odd word. He was afraid he would begin to cry and destroy this moment.

"I've had such bad dreams, Alex." She scrunched her brow. "I'm so glad they're over now." Her face brightened again as she looked at Alex. "Mind when we went crab-hunting and the hermit crab nipped your finger?"

Alex thought his heart would break. "I thought the shell was empty. How was I to know the little nipper was in there?"

"When you screamed and tried to drop the shell, it was so funny. . . ."

"Well, he wouldn't let go, would he? He hung on with those sharp little pincer claws of his . . . and it hurt!"

"Ye were jumping up and down and shaking the shell and shouting, 'Help, help, somebody help.' I laughed so hard, I fell down and scraped my knee!"

"Serves you right for laughing at me. I thought it was going to snip my finger off!"

Delighted that Katie seemed better, Alex lay beside her. They fell into a peaceful sleep, Alex still holding her hand.

———•◆•———

A cold blustery wind whipped Alex's hair as he stood, hands folded before him, high up on the cliff-tops. Around him were neat symmetrical rows of small markers that protruded from the rocky soil. Don-Dun's cart stood empty, its shrouded cargo having been lowered into the ground.

A priest called for a moment of silence, but there was none. The wind moaned and howled its way through the crags and crannies of the cliff-tops. Gulls shrieked. From below came the sound of crashing waves. And then there was the rushing noise coming from inside Alex's head.

Be quiet! Be quiet! Hands to his ears, eyes shut tight, Alex demanded a silence that was not to be.

Everyone began their walk back to the castle – everyone, that is, except two gaunt men who casually leaned on their long-handled shovels beside a mound of freshly dug earth. Alex followed the others along the cliff for several minutes before venturing a look back. The men were hard at work, swinging dirt from the mound into Katie's grave, over and over. Alex watched them, remembering how he had woken and reached over to touch Katie's cheek. It was cold. Mrs. McRae said she was gone, that she was back with her family now, that she was in a happier place. . . . No, Alex thought angrily. *Do not give me this happy place stuff. She's dead and there's nothing happy about it.*

He forced himself to turn away.

27

THE WAY BACK

Alex followed the others along the cliff toward the castle. Up ahead, Don-Dun's hefty ox, Rhua, plodded along in his usual unhurried gait, chewing nonchalantly as he pulled the empty cart. Alex skipped into a brief jog to catch up.

"There ye are, my wee friend!" Don-Dun made an attempt to be cheery when Alex fell into step beside him. He gave him Rhua's rope to lead him down the winding path.

"So where will ye be off to next? Planning to conquer any more castles?"

"We sure made short work of the last one, didn't we?"

"Aye, and ye never told me that was what we were to do. Ye tricked me, ye did."

"No, I didn't. I told you nothing but the truth."

"The truth, aye – people flying in airships, walking on the moon – ha! Ye are a fine storyteller." Don-Dun gave Alex an affectionate clap on his shoulder. "Don't ye take offense to this, Alex, but do ye remember when I told those guards that ye were struck dumb at an early age? Well, at that moment,

I meant it . . . *ow, ow,* stop!" Don-Dun laughed as Alex punched him on the arm. "Ye're gittin' Rhua all riled up!"

Rhua had come to an abrupt halt. His big eyes rolled nervously.

"C'm on, c'm on," Don-Dun coaxed him. "Alex is no hurting me – don't ye worry."

Still eyeing Alex with suspicion, Rhua took a few hesitant steps and settled back into his swaying stroll.

Random events of the past few days popped into Alex's mind. "Did anyone ever pay you for the hay and vegetables?"

"*Ha!*" Don-Dun laughed uproariously. "And who would I ask for payment, the kitchen master? Nae, m'lad, that was my contribution to the new rulers of Duncragglin. But I've got something much better. It seems Sir Ellerslie was so impressed by my soldier imitation, he's asked if I would stay on as a sergeant at arms. Called me loyal, he did; said he needs men like me to defend Duncragglin from future attacks."

"What about William Wallace? Have you thought about joining him?"

"Aye, that would be grand." Don-Dun's eyes glowed. "But those are *very* hard-riding men he's got. I'd be hard-pressed to keep up with them. Ye've got to be a younger, fitter man than me to be of any help. Thanks, but I'll do better here at Duncragglin." He paused. "But what will ye be doing, m'laddie buck?"

"I don't know."

The shadow of Duncragglin's outer wall fell over them and they passed through the open gates. Alex repeated to himself, "I don't know."

Inside, they nodded farewells and parted company. Don-Dun led Rhua over to the stables, and Alex, uncertain of what to do, remained with Sir Ellerslie and William Wallace.

William Wallace was not a man to tarry long, not even when the company was good and the surroundings comfortable. As soon as Wallace was inside the castle gates, he instructed his commanders to have the men ready to ride out at first light of the morrow. He also ordered the burying of those who'd died during the battles on Mount Grenochy and at the Falloch Pass. The digging of mass graves was to be completed by the survivors of King Edward's armed contingent and Sir James's two companies.

Stripped of armor and weapons, most of the captives turned out to be no more than frightened young men, many not yet out of their teens. They needed to be guarded by only a few of William Wallace's men. Wallace ordered that when they were done with the digging, they were to be set free to march south, with instructions not to stop until they were well past the borderlands.

There were few seriously wounded to tend to. The men either had minor wounds that could be sewn up, or they were dead.

Wallace set about the disposition of the time chamber. "We cannae have people popping in and out on us all the time," he said, ordering that a meeting be held to determine what to do.

The meeting was held later that afternoon in the castle's petition chamber. As instructed by Wallace, in attendance were Sir Ellerslie; his wife, Lady Marian; and all those who had "popped in" from another time. The petition chamber was an ornate room bedecked with tapestries with royal motifs. At one end was a thronelike chair on a raised platform, where the castle lord would sit and hear petitions. Wallace had everyone gather in the other end of the chamber, where a few benches and tables could be pulled together.

"I intend to reinforce Duncragglin's defenses by adding two turret towers to the battlements," Sir Ellerslie announced. "The earth from the turret foundations can be used to fill the shaft that leads to the caves. It would be hard for anyone in the future to find their way in, and should they discover the way, they'd have a lot of digging to do."

"Excellent idea," Wallace said. "I suggest further that some boulders be levered into place to block the seashore access, though we know that, o'er time, the sea will erode the rocks and *some* will find a way in." Wallace looked pointedly about the room.

"If I may," the professor interjected. "Before sealing the caves, we would be grateful if you would allow us to use them to access the time chamber one more time to return from whence we came."

Wallace leaned forward. "You can do that? From what I've been told, it only propels people further back in time."

"That is what Hesselrigge believed," the professor replied. "And it's likely that that's what has happened to him. Based on my reading of the settings he used to open the portal block, he indeed has gone back further in time. He may well have shown himself in history in the manner he predicted to Alex. If he went back far enough, he may even have found himself in a time that predates mankind, indeed, he may become the original man – the very missing link our scientists have so long puzzled over."

Mrs. McRae looked horrified. "Are you suggesting that all of mankind, indeed all of us, may be descendants of this evil man? And people call *me* crazy!"

"It would explain much." The professor gave a wry smile. "But this is conjecture. All we know is that whatever Hesselrigge has done in our prior history has been done. Nothing will change that any more than what we do now will change the future as we know it. What will be, will be; what has been, has been."

Fingers pressing hard against her temples, Mrs. McRae said slowly, "Professor, I am trying hard to recover from a state of great confusion. The gibberish you are speaking is not helping matters. Please tell me in plain English, can you bring us back to our own time?"

"Absolutely! I didn't come back here just to join everyone in some distant time. I came here to bring you all back to the time from whence you came. It's a bit tricky – my study of the settings is far from complete – but I believe I can do it."

Annie clasped her hands together. "We're going back to Dad!"

Willie and Craig gave each other solid high-fives.

Craig's offer of a high-five was met halfheartedly by Alex.

"What's the matter, Alex?" Willie asked. "Don't you want to go back to our farm?"

"To your farm, yes." Alex struggled to know what he wanted. "But that is not where I live. And I'm not sure I want to go back to my uncle Larry's place."

"Then don't," Craig said. "He can stay with us, right, Mum?"

"I'd love to," Alex said, part of him yearning to do just that. "But my parents are still missing. . . ."

Annie placed her hand on Alex's arm. "They may be impossible to find. They may have gone back to a completely different time. . . . Oh, come back to stay with us, Alex."

"I would love to, but my parents might be here right now, and we just don't know it. Or they might as yet show up, like Mrs. McRae did. Wouldn't that be amazing?"

"You might not recognize them," Willie said.

"Sure I will."

"But where would you stay, Alex?" the professor asked. "You do not have a home here."

Sir Ellerslie cleared his throat. "Well, ye see . . . *er*, Marian and I have discussed this," he began awkwardly. "We're getting on in years and, as you may know, we have no bairns, and . . . we thought it would be wonderful if Alex stayed here in Duncragglin with us. We would care for him as if he were our son . . . until, of course, he finds his own parents. We have no idea whether Alex likes our suggestion though."

"Like the suggestion? I love it! Thank you so much!" Much to Alex's dismay, he felt tears prick his eyes. He dropped to one knee and bowed his head. Lady Marian's hand brushed his hair.

"Rise, Alex. You are one of us now." Sir Ellerslie clasped his hand and put his arm around his shoulders.

"Thank you," Alex choked out. Apart from his brief time on the McRaes' farm, he had never felt truly wanted before, certainly not by his uncle Larry or aunt Fiona, for whom he was but a burden. At that moment, a tingling sensation flowed through his entire body, boundlessly radiating from every pore.

"Do I understand this correctly?" Mrs. McRae asked, her eyes blinking birdlike from person to person. "Alex is to stay here? Isn't this somewhat mad?"

"Alex, think of what you are suggesting," the professor said gently. "This is a dangerous time. Mr. Wallace is winning some battles, yes, but we know King Edward will be back. You will likely face great misery and hardship."

"I'm prepared to take that chance."

"And what are we to say to those back home?" Mrs. McRae said crisply. "How are we to explain Alex's disappearance?" She looked from Duncan to the professor.

"Well, er, I'm afraid the problem is bigger than that." Duncan scuffed his feet awkwardly. "You see, I, too, intend to stay . . . that is, if Sir Ellerslie and Lady Marian will permit me," he added hastily. "I am a farmer, and the kind of farming that's in me isn't done in our time. I feel like I belong here. With Sir Ellerslie and Lady Marian's permission, I would like to apply my farming methods here."

"You are most welcome," said Lady Marian.

"Thank you, m'Lady." Duncan kissed the back of Lady Marian's hand.

"But, Duncan," Mrs. McRae persisted. "How will you get the crops in on our farm?"

The professor pressed one finger against his temple. "Well, this could explain how the Macphersons came to possess Duncragglin Castle in the fourteenth century. And there was also this hitherto unexplained increase in the farming productivity in this region back then."

"Oh, you're no help at all!" Mrs. McRae stamped her foot. "Very well, if I can't dissuade you from this folly, I suppose the best I can do is wish you both well."

"Mother?" Craig nervously sought her attention.

"What is it, child?"

"I want to stay too."

"No! How can you even think such thoughts? What about me, your father, and your brother and sister? Have you no consideration for others?"

Crestfallen, Craig turned to leave, but Mrs. McRae forbade that too. He was left to slouch on the bench, with his back to everyone.

The talk turned to the logistics of returning to their time and to practical matters, such as which clothes to wear so they would not look so odd when they emerged in their own time. Alex slid over to where Craig was sitting, but Craig was in no mood to talk.

———◦•◦———

They made a solemn descent, that next morning, into the dungeons and down the shaft.

Out in the open chamber, Sir Ellerslie motioned for silence. Chalk in hand, the professor stood alone before the snake-haired monster. He was deep in thought. On the stone floor around him were his chalked scribbles: symbols, arrows, and numbers arranged in mathematical equations. The professor muttered to himself and paced from the wall to his scratches on the floor, each time adding a few more or rubbing one out.

"Yes, yes, I've got it." He waved his arm for the others to join him. "It's simple, really." He pointed a stick high up on the wall. "Craig, I need you to go up to that iguana carving and twist it. I believe you will find its head will rotate one hundred and eighty degrees. . . . Excellent, now there are a few more things we need to do."

The professor had everyone pulling and twisting carvings, some of which had to be done in unison, all of which had to be done in the right sequence and with the right timing. Alex took notes, scribbling furiously on a flagstone with chalk. Somehow, deep inside, he felt the sequence made sense. It was as if it told a story – a myth played out in symbols. But it wasn't entirely what he expected. No matter, as long as he followed the professor's sequence exactly, he would get back, perhaps with his parents at his side. He would have to persuade Sir Ellerslie not to seal off the time chamber, not yet.

A familiar deep rumbling came up through the stones, slowly building in volume as the monster-head began to lower.

Sir Ellerslie stood with his mouth agape. "Never in all my days have I seen such a sight. There truly are magical forces at work here."

"Actually, it's all physics and engineering." The professor leaped over the carved snakes onto the flat top of the lowered head. He turned and, with the portal ramp leading into the darkness behind him, he triumphantly raised his arms. "So . . . who's with me?"

Annie looked at Alex and turned away. "This is so hard," she said in a choked voice. "First I lose Katie, now you."

"But, Annie, I'm not lost, I'll still be here."

"Don't you understand, Alex? The moment I'm back in my own time, you'll be dead, long dead."

Alex had not thought of it that way. It troubled him. It seemed wrong somehow. "I think it makes more sense to think of us living in parallel separate worlds," he said, taking her hand.

She held him out at arm's length. "Every year, if you can, at noon on the day of the summer solstice, go to our hideout on the point. That's the longest day of the year. Bring a picnic and sit on the boulder next to the fire pit. I will be there too. If you're right and we're in parallel worlds, we'll be together then . . . okay?"

Alex nodded. "Bring something to eat," he said. "Surprise me with something and I'll bring you a surprise too."

"Deal." Annie gave him one last hug – a big tight hug that almost squeezed the air out of him. Then she was gone up the ramp with her mother.

Willie slapped Alex's hand awkwardly. "Take care of yourself. I'll think of you often."

Alex clapped him on the back. "Be good."

"I doubt that." Willie gave Alex a broad grin. "But I'll try."

Craig was hanging back. Alex suddenly noticed he was crying and trying to hide it.

"Craig, old buddy, you'll always be my pal. We've been through some crazy times together, haven't we?"

Craig turned his tearstained face towards Alex and grabbed fistfuls of Alex's shirt. He jerked Alex forward. "I'm

coming back. Remember that. I'm not done here yet." Then
Craig, too, was gone.

Alex watched the McRaes walk arm in arm, up the ramp
into the portal, together with the professor. A hollow, yearning welled up inside him. His throat clenched. He watched
Annie, then Willie, briefly turn and wave as they walked
away. Part of Alex wanted to go running after them. They
were the best friends he ever had, and now he was going to
lose them. But he knew he had to stay. They might meet
again, it might even be soon. . . . The professor had left
instructions on how to use the portal controls to return to his
time, should he find his parents. He also had his own notes,
scribbled in chalk. He might see them again.

He repeated this over and over to himself as he stood
watching his friends ascend the far reaches of the portal
block. Tears streamed down his face as the rumbling started
once more and the snake-haired portal block began to rise.
"Good luck!" he shouted after them, waving frantically.

A few muffled shouts, distant waves, and they were
gone. The portal closed and Alex was left staring into the
snake-haired monster's eyes, furiously wiping his face and
feeling alone.

"Your time will come, Alex." Sir Ellerslie placed his arm
about his shoulders. "Your time will come . . . but for now,
let's go. There's much to be done."

So much to be done indeed, and he, Alex Macpherson,
would do it, in his own time!